Jodie Wise Nails It!

A coming of age story

DOROTHY TOPFER

Jodie Wise Nails It!
First published in Australia by Dorothy Topfer 2026
www.dorothy.topfer.com

 A catalogue record for this
book is available from the
National Library of Australia

ISBN: 978-0-6451559-8-3 (pbk)
ISBN: 978-0-6451559-9-0 (ebk)

Front cover image: Olena Rudo (shutterstock) © 2023
Cover background image: Andrew Fletcher (shutterstock) © 2022

Typesetting and design by Publicious Book Publishing
Published in collaboration with Publicious Book Publishing
www.publicious.com.au

Dedicated to the people of Tasmania who
make this such a special island.

Other titles by this author:

The Legacy

Sabine

Perfect Breaks

Past Presence

Also available on Kindle:

The Lost Spirit

Unravelling

Remembrance

The Life and Death of Gypsy Carmichael

Before

Would life always be like this? Totally boring. Everything so predictable – living with her crazy mum and suffering through the interminable time spent at school. Her only friend Pepper, the dog – and maybe Will. Yes, definitely Will. He and the athletics competitions were all that made school tolerable.

Each day wondering if there would be anything in the house for dinner.

After

The shocking image of her mother's face lingered and refused to be banished no matter how hard she tried. A bruised and bloody mess – one hand reaching out as she pleaded with her daughter to run – and run she did.

Before - 1975

Chapter One

Jodie surveyed the plate that had been thumped down in front of her on the chipped Laminex table. At least there was something to eat tonight. And for once it wasn't too bad. Reheated rissoles and gravy with mashed potato - leftovers from the pub. The overcooked vegetables – carrots and peas she would overlook. But she was finding it harder to ignore the lecture from her mother that was the accompaniment to their meal.

She focussed on carefully cutting the rissoles into bite sized pieces, head down staring intently on the job at hand and willing her mother's voice to fade into some sort of background noise. Her mother was in fine form. *Harangue* was the word that sprang to mind. Yes. She liked that word. Maybe it was something she could use in her creative writing class at school this week. Jodie sounded it out in her mind. *Haranguing* sounded better and had a rhythmic flow. Yes, that would be her word of the week.

'Listen to me when I'm speaking to you, dammit. And look up!'

Jodie reluctantly raised her head and gazed at her mother across the table. Why was she so angry? What had she done wrong this time?

'It's bad enough that I have to slave away, day and night at that dive of a pub to keep a roof over our head. You should be grateful for all I do and not run wild around the village.'

Run wild?

Jodie's forehead wrinkled in puzzlement. When had she ever run wild? Her days followed one after the other in monotonous regularity. Walk to school, walk home afterwards, walk to Nanna and Pop's house for cake and walk the dog. In fact, lots of walking but no running wild.

She frowned and shook her head.

'No need to go acting all innocent on me, young miss. We live in a small town. Don't you know everyone watches you and tells me what you are up to. Just because I'm stuck at the pub being nice to losers doesn't mean I don't hear what you get up to with that young Will McBride. He's trouble do you hear me? Take my word for it the whole family are no good. You're to leave him alone, do ya hear?' said Jodie's mum with a spray of spittle that landed on her own uneaten dinner.

It was clear to Jodie that this was no idle command. Not that she intended to take it seriously, but at least she should argue the point. Never would she, Jodie Wise, be seen as a pushover.

'But mum, Will is in my class at school and it's not like I can avoid him in a village this size …. And anyway, we both walk the same way home. What do you want me to do? Ignore him or walk ten steps behind? Come on – you can't be serious. And anyway, he's my friend.' Jodie tried her best pleading expression but to no avail. Her mother's face was stern as she glared back at her.

'You're too young to understand. Only 12 years old so you don't get it. That family has caused more grief in this district than you would ever know. And their reputation will rub off on you if you aren't careful.'

'Well mum, if you're so sure we should have nothing to do with them, then why do you work in their pub and why do we rent this house from Will's dad?'

Seeing her mother lost for words she pressed on: 'Well? And why is it that Nanna and Pop are happy to have Will visit them?'

'Hmmph!' Her mother shook her head and said in disgust. 'Maybe you are as bad as them. I give up but don't blame me if you come to no good.'

With red varnished talons Donna reached for her cigarettes and pushed away from the table as she snorted her anger.

'I'm outa here. Tidy up and go to bed. I won't be home until late.'

And with that Jodie's mum left the table and the room, the sound of slamming of the front screen door terminating her presence in the house.

Jodie slumped over her plate, her hand reaching for the comfort of her dog who throughout had been pressed tightly to her leg. Pepper hated the sound of angry voices and would do his best at such times to make himself invisible.

'Never mind Pepps. You can relax. She's gone now. Here, you have my dinner. I don't want it after all.'

The plate with the remaining meat, gravy and overcooked vegetables was placed before him and without hesitation Pepper ate furiously as if the food could be removed at any moment. An occasional wiggle of his tail expressed gratitude for such a thoughtful treat. Too soon the plate was licked clean and removed by his owner, who he could sense still needed comfort. He leaned back against her leg and once more the hand reached down and rubbed his ears. If Pepper had been a cat he would have purred but all he could do was lean in a bit closer while giving a gentle burp.

'Pepps, I don't get it. Why is she so cranky all the time and what has she got against Will and his family? If she hates them so much why do we live in this dump they own and why work at the pub? I'm sure there are lots of other places to work at if she wanted. Why?'

Pepper, as if sensing a response was required, gave a gentle lick to Jodie's hand. It wasn't much but somehow it was enough. Giving a deep sigh Jodie gathered the plates and cutlery and headed to the sink. It was time to wash up – not only the dinner plates but also the dirty dishes from breakfast. First though she needed to boil some hot water to use for washing up.

Jodie had not exaggerated when she described their home as a dump. It was either that or a 'renovator's delight'. Whatever the description it wasn't a very comfortable place in which to live.

Originally a farm worker's cottage built of weatherboards sometime in the 19th century it was dark, cold and damp. For a long time the cottage had stood vacant and neglected until Donna and baby Jodie had moved in. At that time the bare minimum had been done to make it liveable. A simple kitchen installed in an alcove off a sitting room and a bathroom and laundry built in a lean-to off the back door. The pipes for the kitchen and bathroom ran along the outer walls so that in the depths of winter the pipes would freeze - meaning no morning shower nor cup of tea first thing. Winter was always a challenge. The only heating was the original fuel stove in the sitting room and an open fire in the front room. On a cold night going to bed early was the best option. Those were the nights when Jodie was grateful for the furnace-like warmth of her little dog who liked nothing better than to snuggle up beside her.

Washing up done and her homework completed there was nothing further to do but go to bed. As she lay in bed with her furry friend beside her Jodie repeated her now favourite word over and over until it became a form of hypnotic chant – harangue, haranguing, harangue, haranguing and so on until she fell into a deep, dreamless sleep.

It was very late when her mother returned. Jodie was sound asleep and didn't hear the giggles as two people stumbled along the front path, tripped onto the veranda and fell into the house. Pepper stirred, opened one eye but didn't bark. He knew the sounds of the mistress returning home.

Chapter Two

Another day at school. Now over. Nothing memorable and too hot to spend time outside at lunchtime. Creative writing held in the afternoon, which was an ideal opportunity to find a use for Jodie's new word. A word she was discovering wasn't that easy to place in flowing prose. Maybe it would become a word for private use only; to call to mind next time her mother had a rant.

She hadn't seen her mother that morning. Her bedroom door had remained firmly closed. Jodie left for school early so she could detour via her grandparents' house and leave Pepper there for the day.

School finished for the day and now she and Will were heading for home but first they ambled towards the river which they crossed every day. The river crossing was via a weir wall built many years ago as a way to dam the river water for the villagers' use. Too hot to do more than slouch along the footpath, trying as much as possible to stay within the patches of shade. Too hot to do more than exchange intermittent conversation. Until they reached the river where in the shade of a venerable elm tree they settled on the riverbank, removed shoes and socks and relaxed up to knee height in the river. The river flowing sluggishly was summer warm but still cool enough to be refreshing.

They sat side by side, idly staring across the river, from time to time throwing whatever was at hand into the slow flowing stream – a stick, a pebble or a leaf.

Now was the time.

'Will? Can I ask you something?'

Will turned and considered Jodie, staring at her from under his thatch of wheat coloured hair. This polite hesitancy was not the Jodie he knew. Something must be up.

'Sure. Fire ahead.'

'It was something mum said last night. How your family are trouble and I'm not to mix with you anymore.'

Seeing his frown she rushed on as if seeking to reassure him.

'Don't worry. I don't believe her and of course I still want us to be friends … that is, if you want to? But I don't get it. Why is she so against your family? Did something happen?'

'Beats me,' shrugged Will. 'No offence Jodie but your mum has always been a bit – well a bit full on – if that's the right word. She's had a few run ins with various people in the village. You know how it is. These things blow up and then blow over. Don't worry about it. Maybe she'd had a bad day at work or something. Anyway it's not like we can avoid each other. We're in the same class at school and how are we going to avoid walking home together from school? Am I meant to leave at a different time to you? Like a spy stalking you!' He smiled at his own joke.

'Yeah that's exactly what I said to her. Or something similar,' she corrected.

'So let's pretend you never heard her speak and maybe she will forget soon enough.'

Will stood and reached down to pull Jodie up.

'Come on. Are you cool enough? Do you reckon your Nanna might have some cake for us?'

'Reckon so. Nanna is forever baking and she never minds if we have seconds.'

Together they headed across the weir and along the dirt track towards the cluster of houses on the other side. Jodie knew her home wasn't far away to the left up a little rise and hidden by the overgrown windbreak planted long ago by the original owner, a farm worker. Today, though, she headed straight ahead towards a place at the end of the road out of which a small, ragged terrier appeared and raced towards them, barking a greeting as he ran.

'Pepps, I missed you too,' Jodie said as she crouched down to be licked in greeting.

'Yuk, Jodie. Germs!' protested Will who by now was also fending off an enthusiastic greeting.

'Pepper, that's enough. Come on. It's too hot for this. Let's go find Nanna. Where is she and where's the cake?'

In Pepper's small terrier mind all things revolved around food. His vocabulary might be limited, but he knew what the word *cake* signified. With a bark he wheeled around and scampered up the drive towards the house and around the side path towards the back door.

Everything about this house spoke of loving care – from its well-tended front garden full of fragrant late summer blooms to its pristine painted weatherboard façade and neat front porch complete with a *Welcome* mat placed just so before the front door.

The garden along the side path was likewise a thing of beauty but not for these two whose rumbling stomachs demanded to be filled. Preferably by home-baked cake.

They had barely reached the back screen door when it was opened.

'Come in. I was expecting you two,' said a smiling woman - who must be the one referred to as Nanna, or Carol Daley by her friends. She had that warm and welcoming manner that all grandmothers are expected to have. With grey curly hair scraped back into a messy bun, wearing a grubby - but nicely grubby apron and smelling deliciously of baking.

'I've just this moment finished icing an orange cake. So, make yourselves comfortable and sit down at the table. I'll cut you a piece, but only one piece each mind.'

Seeing disappointed faces she smiled. 'One piece for now. Just enough to give you energy to go find Pop and bring him in for afternoon tea. He's out the back somewhere – probably with his beloved goats.' The smile she gave as she said this took the sting out of her words.

Not only was there cake but there was also lime cordial – a full jug of lime cordial, deliciously chilled with clinking ice blocks. The children ate and slurped giving blissful attention to the task at hand. Once their slices had been eaten and the remaining crumbs on their plates carefully scavenged with questing fingers they pushed out their chairs and went to the back door, Pepper following.

'Don't be long now,' Nanna called after them. 'Tell your grandpa I've made a pot of tea and he won't want it to stew.'

The path from out the back door led past the usual back yard infrastructure. Raised vegetable garden beds – full of flourishing plantings – of course. And to the other side a clothesline – not one of those fancy Hills Hoist clothes lines but one of the old-fashioned kind – with two lengths of wire running between two posts – the sort that needed to be propped up with a long pole. Not a thing of beauty and usually something most people were happy to replace when finances permitted. At the end of the path a wooden fence. Opening a solid timber gate they stepped into another world. A world of farm sheds, chickens scratching underfoot and, in the distance, an elderly man heading away towards an outer paddock with a bucket in each hand. Behind him trotted four goats clearly fixated on the contents of those buckets.

'He's putting the milking goats away. Come on, let's catch up.' With that Jodie grabbed Will by the arm and they chased after Pop with a barking dog close behind. The noise was enough for Jodie's Grandpa to stop, turn towards the approaching children and wait for them to catch up. The goats also stopped and nuzzled at the buckets.

'Well look who's here. And just in time to feed the girls. Now then young ladies – no jostling.' He looked down at the four goats nudging him and gently pushed them away.

If Nanna was exactly how one would expect a grandmother to be then Pop was a bit of a surprise. Joe Daley had been a gun shearer in his younger years. That and an active retirement outdoors had honed his body to a wiry muscular strength. The tattoos that ran along his forearms spoke of a wicked youth and provided a source of much fascination to Jodie and Will. No one else they knew had such arm decoration.

'Hello, Mr Daley,' greeted Will as they drew close.

'How many times do I have to remind you. No Mr Daley young lad. Call me Joe and we'll get on just fine.'

He turned to Jodie and smiled a greeting. 'Hello, lass. Give me a hand with the gate and then Will and I will give these girls their dinner.' He smiled as the goats pushed against him trying to get their heads into the buckets of food: 'They seem a bit peckish!'

Goats fed they turned and headed across the paddock for home. Jo paused and smelled the air.

'I can smell rain, so I suppose you young ones shouldn't linger.'

As if on cue the massed clouds behind them were darkening and a growl of thunder could be heard in the distance.

'But not before we have more cake Pop. But we will leave some for you. And Nanna said she had made a pot of tea for you and you were to hurry – oops, I forgot to tell you that!'

'Never mind that'll be our secret.'

Joe Daley, aka Pop or sometimes Grandpa, smiled at his granddaughter – a strange little person to be sure but one close to his heart.

The children made quick work of their second sitting of afternoon tea. By now they were both conscious of the brewing storm and were anxious to get home.

'Sorry but we have to go,' said Jodie as she reached for her school bag and hat. 'I don't want to get wet but maybe Peps and I will pop in tomorrow if that's alright with you?'

'Anytime. You know that. Would you like to stay tomorrow night?'

'Yes please!' Jodie, anticipating a decent meal, tried not to sound too enthusiastic, but she sensed she hadn't fooled her grandparents. She was aware of a brief exchange of a loaded glance between them that spoke volumes.

'It's Saturday tomorrow so I could come here after breakfast? Or maybe before!'

'That would be lovely, my dear. Now off you both go. I hope you get home before the storm hits. Bye, Will. Do pop in any time.'

'Bye Mrs Daley' said Will as he left by the back door. He was yet to be on first name terms with Jodie's grandma and he wasn't sure he could come to referring to Mr Daley as Joe. But somehow he felt that Mr Daley – or Joe would expect him to.

The rain was starting to spit and the thunder was growling much closer as they ran as fast as they could. Pepper scampered behind, not concerned about the imminent rain but enjoying this new game. At the corner Jodie waved goodbye and headed up the rise to her home. Will still had a way to run but she knew with his turn of speed he would make fast work of it. Will was fast but not as fast as her. That's why she nearly always beat him in the sprint races at school. Not that they were competitive. Which is what Jodie explained each time she beat him in a race. As if he believed her.

Fast she may have been but not as fast as the storm which had arrived with full ferocity by the time she clambered up the front step. The noise of raindrops thundering on the front porch roof almost drowned out the noise of the yelling coming from inside. But not quite.

Chapter Three

Jodie cautiously opened the front screen door and froze. Pepper, in mid-shake also paused and with pricked ears and tail between legs listened. He knew an angry voice when he heard it.

'What do you mean I owe you? How dare you? After all I've done for you.'

Her mother must be on the phone. But who was she talking to? Whoever it was they had got her riled and when her mother was like this, she was best to be avoided. Carefully she tiptoed across the room to her bedroom and silently shut the door. Both she and Pepper were drenched and needed attending to. Being mindful of her responsibilities as a diligent pet owner Jodie first looked after her dog – gently towel drying Pepper with her own bath towel and then quickly changing out of her wet school clothes and using the same towel on herself. There wasn't then much else to do but lie on her bed and try not to listen to the continuing angry conversation. It being Friday there was no homework that needed urgent attention so all that remained to do was to snuggle up with Pepper and start on the book that she had borrowed from the school library – a book by someone called Roald Dahl. Something about a giant peach. Maybe it would provide a distraction – although the thought of a peach made her stomach rumble. The orange cake, while it had been delicious, was not enough to fill her up. She so hoped her mother had made something for dinner and wasn't going out again.

A knock on her door sometime later signalled her mother was finished with whoever she had spoken to and was now ready to speak to her daughter. The door opened and her mother sidled in with a suspiciously sweet smile on her face.

'Ah there you are. I didn't hear you come in. It must have been while I was on the phone.'

Jodie glanced up and with her finger marking her place in the book prepared to hear whatever it was her mother needed to tell her for clearly her mother has something to share. Jodie was suspicious. This sweetly smiling mother who was now asking how her day had been was a marked contrast to the haranguing mother of the night before.

Donna leant on the doorjamb. 'I'm not sure if you were here when I was on the phone?'

Jodie nodded.

'That was my cousin Ken. I don't think you've met him? He lives up the top end of the island – up near Devonport. Ken rang 'cause he had a favour to ask. Not that I owe him anything, but he got me at a weak moment. Sometimes I'm amazed at how kind I am.' Donna smiled complacently as if in awe of her generosity.

Again Jodie nodded. There was nothing she could say in response. This person before her must have hijacked her mother as she didn't recognise these words coming out of her mouth.

'So there's nothing for it. I've agreed out of the kindness of my heart to take in his daughter for a week or two or longer to give him a respite. Ken says Bonnie has been running off the rails and he thinks I have the experience to manage out of control children.'

Donna paused as if she was now becoming aware of the significance of these words. She gave a little shake of her head and continued: 'As if I know what that means. Anyway, I've agreed and he is bringing Bonnie over to us on Sunday. You'll need to tidy your room as you and Bonnie will be sharing. I'm pretty sure I can borrow a mattress from mum and dad and you can sleep on that and let Bonnie have your bed.'

The sheer horror of what her mother was saying was starting to dawn on Jodie. Not only was she being asked to share her precious room with some sort of distant relative that she had never met -and until now didn't even know existed - no, not being asked at all. She was being told to share – but her room was so tiny they would barely fit in.

'But mum my room is too small – how can we fit a mattress in? And anyway it's my room. Can't she go to Nanna and Grandpa's? Or on second thoughts can't I go there?' she asked hopefully.

'That's not happening. Forget it, Jodie. Ken says Bonnie needs a calming and stable family influence and he feels we can provide that.'

Again Jodie shook her head. This time in disbelief. Who did her mother think she was kidding?

'Anyway, that's my decision – well, mine and Ken's and you just have to make it work. I'm sure you will enjoy having another young person stay. Bonnie is much your own age. I seem to recall she's about three years older than you. Like a big sister. I feel almost envious of you imagining the happy times you're going to have here in this bedroom sharing secrets and bonding. Ah you'll have such fun.'

This said with a saccharine sweet smile that made Jodie shudder. Would someone please return her mother. She had no idea how to manage this version. Then as if to make her experience even more surreal her mother suggested Jodie join her in the kitchen and help her with dinner. Her mother – cooking dinner? No way!

Chapter Four

'Nan. It's SO not fair,' moaned Jodie next morning as she sat at the kitchen table watching her Nanna dish up her breakfast. Pancakes as requested by Jodie. As far as Jodie was concerned her Nanna was the best. She would always ask her granddaughter what she wanted to eat and then would immediately oblige. And even as she was undoing the maple syrup bottle in anticipation of her treat, Jodie was still stewing about the indignity of having to share her bedroom with a total stranger.

'Not only do I have to share my bedroom with some so called relative I've never met but I have to give up my bed and sleep on the floor. Mum says she is family but how do I know that for sure? Her father says she has *run off the rails*, whatever that means. There's every chance she could be an axe murderer and I could be bumped off in my sleep!' Jodie's voice rose hysterically as she contemplated her gruesome fate – murdered by a distant relative long before she had achieved her dreams – if only she understood what they were.

Nanna was having none of this and knew the best way to calm down her wild grandchild was to feed her and this she did by placing a plate of just-cooked pancakes in front of her.

'There you go. See what you can do with that. Are you alright with maple syrup or would you rather lemon juice and brown sugar, dear?'

'Mmmm both,' mumbled Jodie, her mouth already full of pancake. Then remembering her manners added an indistinct, 'please.'

The sound of a screen door clattering and Pop appeared.

'Do I smell pancakes? Are there any for me? And Pepper?'

'Of course. They'll be ready in a tick. There's time while you wait to pour yourself and Jodie a cuppa. I've just filled the teapot.'

Joe Daley eyed the pancakes being dished up for him and smiled his approval.

'Well, miss, you should visit for breakfast more often. This makes a great change from my usual tea and toast. I could get used to this.' He smiled at his wife who just rolled her eyes at him.

Jodie giggled. Her plate was now empty and as she slurped her tea – with lots of milk and sugar sweetened just as she liked it – she remembered how unfair life presently was. If only she could live with Nanna and Pop. Her life would be perfect.

'Why can't I stay here with you and let this so-called cousin stay with mum?'

Joe looked across at his wife with raised questioning eyebrows. He had been outside doing chores when Jodie had arrived and described the tragic events she was about to endure. Nanna brought him up to date.

'Joe, a bit of a change for Jodie. Her distant cousin Bonnie, Ken's girl is coming to stay for a little while and Jodie would rather not share her room.'

'Ahh,' exhaled Joe staring significantly at his wife and then looked at his granddaughter. Her feelings were made obvious by her body language – tightly crossed arms, pouting lips and head down. He smiled. This little one often reminded him of the drama queen that had been her mother when she was growing up.

'Sooner or later we all have to share our rooms. Look at your poor long-suffering Nanna. She has the joy of putting up with my snoring every night. But she doesn't ask to move.'

'Well, Joe Daley I might one day! Don't push your luck!' smiled Nanna who then continued. 'Seriously Jodie. I think this news has come as a bit of a shock to you. But promise me you will give Bonnie a chance. You may end up liking her and anyway think of it from her point of view. She may also not like being uprooted from her home and being sent to live with strangers.'

Jodie with head to one side considered what her Nanna had just said and concluded she just might be correct. Although come to think of it if she had been told she was moving to somewhere else that could very well be a move for the better. She smiled – poor Bonnie. Wait 'til she saw the dump she was moving to!

'Okay then. I suppose I should try to be welcoming but please if it doesn't work out can I come and stay with you two?' Jodie's expression was so plaintive that her grandparents laughed, which set the dog barking.

Somehow this lightened the atmosphere and conversation was then able to move to more pleasant subject matters, such as how to spend the Saturday and what to cook for dinner. Nanna with an eye on Jodie's attire which not only was faded and worn but also outgrown suggested a shopping trip to Hobart.

'I'm thinking some new shorts and t-shirts and maybe something for when the weather cools down.' Glancing at the shabby sandals on her granddaughter's feet she added 'Maybe some new shoes too. We'll be back by lunchtime and I'm sure your Pop will need a hand with something in the afternoon. Is that alright with you Jodie dear?'

Jodie, her mouth full of pancake and unable to speak, indicated her agreement by nodding her head vigorously. A trip to Hobart always entailed a visit to the bookshop and most likely ice cream or a milkshake at the café nearby – or possibly both. With new clothes – and even new shoes she would be able to show off to this Bonnie person tomorrow. Maybe that might make up for the dismal surroundings that would soon be greeting this unknown cousin.

***

The rest of the day passed happily. As expected shopping in Hobart with Nanna was a fun filled experience. The anticipated ice cream and milkshake were both consumed at different times. Somehow Nanna managed to sneak in the opportunity for a haircut and

Jodie's straggly hair was shaped into a smart bob. All afternoon Jodie kept tossing her head as she admired the way her hair flicked from side to side in a silky swirl. The hairdresser had commented admiringly on the blonde highlights in her hair and gave her a few tips on how to maintain the style. Jodie felt rather grown up as she tentatively ran her hand across her locks. She now felt rather special in her cut off jean shorts and checked button up shirt - a bit like a country girl. Nanna had bought her some new sandals which actually fitted her and they both laughed as Jodie threw the old pair into the bin outside the shop.

'Pop! Where are you? Look what we bought. And I've had my hair cut – or styled as the lady hairdresser said,' Jodie called as she ran in via the back door, the screen door crashing closed behind her and setting off Pepper in a cascade of barks. Then all momentum halted as Jodie saw who was sitting at the kitchen table across from her grandfather. Her mother. Not only was that strange - her mother rarely visited but the sombre expressions indicated that whatever was being discussed was serious. Her mother was speaking when she glanced up and saw her daughter entering the room. Then her expression changed to one that Jodie was familiar with. Her mother was not pleased with what she saw.

'And what is this? Where have you been and where did you get the money to buy those new clothes and your hair? What are you - a thief? If you've been taking my cash just you wait Miss. Wait til we get home and you'll get yours!'

'But, but ...' stammered Jodie, all the pleasure at her afternoon of treats quickly evaporating before Donna's glare.

'Never you mind Donna,' interjected Nanna as she entered the room manoeuvring her body and arms laden with shopping through the screen door then handing the bags to Joe who had leapt up to help her. Slumping into the nearest chair she reached for the teapot and commenced to pour tea into what had been her husband's cup. Both husband and daughter watched her as she drank deeply then with a sigh she turned to her daughter.

17

'Ah, I needed that. It's been a long thirsty afternoon and now before we continue Donna, my child I think you need to take back what you've just said and apologise to your daughter. You see Jodie and I have just had a lovely afternoon shopping in Hobart and I've treated her to some much needed new clothes.' She held up her hand as if to ensure she wasn't interrupted. 'I'm sure you had intended to do the same and I regret I may have deprived you of a little treat with your daughter but if that is so there are still more clothes to get for winter. Young Jodie is growing like a beanstalk. It's a wonder any of her old clothes fit.'

Trying not to smirk, Jodie exchanged a glance with her grandfather, who winked back at her. Clearly Donna was no match for her mother.

Donna held her hands up in surrender. 'OK I get it. I jumped to conclusions, and I was wrong. Sorry Jodes. I got it wrong. Lucky you to be so spoilt. And yeah, I quite like the new hairdo. Actually, it makes you look so much older than 12. But nice.'

Donna pushed back her chair and made to get up. 'I have to work tonight. Mum and Dad, are you alright if Jodie stays again?'

'Of course, dear, You know she can stay with us anytime,' said Joe smiling across at his granddaughter.

'When does your visitor arrive? Tomorrow?'

'Yeah. Mid-morning, I think. Make sure you have Jodie back by then. Or better still, earlier as you have still to tidy and set up your room Jodie.'

'Don't you worry,' said Joe. 'We'll all be there to tidy and to greet young Bonnie. I haven't seen her since she was a baby and that was years ago. And I'm sure you Ma here will bake a cake. Won't you Ma?'

'Certainly will, Joe. And Jodie can help me. Although maybe you should get out of your new clothes into something older. Bye Donna.'

It was clear Donna was being dismissed as her daughter and mother busied themselves with the next task and her father started to clear the table. Giving a shrug Donna left the room. Her departure unnoticed as the three left behind were chattering about plans for the evening and happy in their own little world.

Chapter Five

Next morning Jodie woke early. In time to catch the first rays of the rising sun flickering on the bedroom walls and to hear the chirping of sparrows outside her bedroom window. And she wasn't the only one awake. She could also hear the murmured conversation of her grandparents coming from the kitchen down the corridor. The to and fro of their discussion reminded her of other times in her childhood when such a sound brought her comfort. For this had been Jodie's bedroom in her earlier years. The place of retreat after her mother's marriage had ended when Jodie was almost three years old. She had no memory of her father and she was instinctively reluctant to trust her mother's description of that 'sad loser'. When asked, her Grandpa merely smiled and said words like 'some people are just not meant to be together pet.' With a young child's focus on the here and now, over time any thoughts of her father faded into the background and it was only when strangers asked about her father that the thought of him came to mind.

This morning as she stretched out those rested muscles and reached to pat the sleeping dog beside her Jodie's thoughts were on the day ahead. Would this Bonnie person be a new friend or would she be like so many others she had met at school and be a know-it-all bully sent to make her life a misery? Being constantly reminded that she was different to the others – a child of a divorced mother, dressed in mismatched grubby clothes and made to feel like she was an outcast. Luckily Will spoke to her although usually after school and the head teacher Mr Webster encouraged her with her running. 'As fast as my greyhounds,' he would say when praising her for winning again at sports day. But it was hard feeling so like an outsider and being constantly judged. Maybe this Bonnie cousin would be different and become a friend? She hoped so. Otherwise, it could be a total disaster.

'Well there's nothing for it Peps. We might as well get up and face what is about to happen. Maybe one of my new outfits might help? The denim flares perhaps?'

Jodie took Pepper's yawn as a yes. In no time she was dressed and heading for the kitchen. The kitchen was already warm and smelling of baking. Her Nanna attired in an apron - as always - was fussing over the stove. Opening the oven door a fraction and peering anxiously inside. Her grandfather seated at the Formica kitchen table, cup of tea before him and busying himself buttering a slice of toast.

They both looked up as she entered the room.

'Good morning, Jodie dear,' smiled Nanna. 'And don't you look lovely. I just knew that green shirt would go nicely with those jeans and reflect the green of your eyes. Go join Grandpa. If you're lucky he might share some of his toast with you. I'll join you in a moment. I was just checking to see if the quiche I'm making for our lunch is almost done.'

The breakfast ritual passed quickly – as it often did. Grandpa and Jodie both eating heartily as they competed for each slice of toast as it popped out of the toaster at the end of the table. Nanna sipped her tea and waved away the offer of toast.

'No. I don't think so. It will be a bit of an eating day. I want to make sure our visitors have lots to eat so I was busy yesterday making cake and biscuits as well as what I have been baking this morning. Joe, once we are done here would you mind putting the foodstuffs in the car? I think we need to get up to Jodie's home and check everything is ready for our visitors.'

Jodie, remembering the mess that was her bedroom, grimaced. Seeing her expression her Grandpa patted her arm: 'Never you mind love. We'll have it sorted out in a flash. I've already taken a single mattress up there and some bedding. It's stacked in your front room, but we'll sort it out in no time. You'll see.'

Between the three of them the loading of the battered Ford Falcon station wagon took no time at all. The foodstuffs were carefully spread along the back seat. A cardboard box containing bottled milk, butter and cream was placed in the luggage compartment along with an assortment of plates, cups and saucers and cutlery – all swaddled in assorted tea towels that bore images of various holidays interstate or of assorted Australian wildflowers or wildlife.

Nanna opened the passenger side door and ushered Jodie and Pepper in. 'Here, you hop in first and hold onto your dog. I don't want him jumping into the back and getting into the food.'

She turned and called to her husband. 'Joe, I've forgotten the tea caddy and the tea pot. Would you mind?'

'Tea? Who needs more tea,' grumbled Joe, a twinkle in his eye negating the impact of his words. 'Sure I'll get the tea but I might also grab a bottle of beer or two from the fridge for us blokes.'

'Whatever. Just get cracking. We don't want to be late.'

With a mumbled 'Women!' Joe turned and as directed soon returned loaded up with the aluminium teapot, a tea caddy and two bottles of beer, their outsides already bejewelled with beads of condensation.

The drive to Jodie's home only took a few minutes. A few anxious minutes for her Nanna who was mindful of the precious cargo on the back seat. But somehow, they made it without any mishaps. Once stopped in the driveway she shooed her husband and Jodie out of the car and inside.

'Go sort out things and I will take my time getting this stuff inside. I suspect I have to first tidy the kitchen.'

Jodie laughed at this. Of course, her Nanna would have to tidy the kitchen. When had it ever been tidy?

'Oh and Joe. Please wake Donna. She's sure to still be asleep.'

Up the front stairs, across the rickety front veranda and into the front room where a single bed mattress was leaning against the wall and draped with spare bedding. It was clear from the silence in the house that Jodie's mother was not there. Joe after checking Donna's bedroom and finding it empty, merely shrugged. He was used to his daughter's behaviour. She would turn up when she was ready and hopefully before the visitors arrived. In the meantime his granddaughter needed his assistance. First thing to do was to strip Jodie's bed and make it up with clean linen. This they did as a team all the while Joe telling jokes and singing silly songs thus reducing his granddaughter to fits of giggles. Then they turned to the assorted debris that clutters any child's room - old, battered toys, books and clothes all collected and packaged away in boxes or drawers. Tidying done Jo stood back and surveyed the room. It grieved him that his granddaughter lived in such an inadequate room when there was a perfectly good bedroom for a little girl back at his place. But what was he do to? Jodie was the responsibility of her mother and all he could do was be there to pick up the pieces, which was what he was literally doing now. He considered the worn wooden floor underfoot. Nice boards – blackwood he thought but the considerable gaps between the boards ensured the room was much better ventilated than it need to be. Fortunately he had had the foresight to bring a rug with him that would do the trick.

'Just you wait a tick Jodie. I've got something in the car that will go nicely in your room. He soon returned carrying a patterned carpet square that he carefully unrolled and placed it in position between the open space from the bed to the far wall.

'There you go. A perfect fit! We'll put the mattress over here in the corner and you ladies will have a lovely bit of carpet underfoot to keep your feet warm......and stop the drafts I hope,' he muttered under his breath. 'Now off you go and give your Nanna a hand while I sort out this mattress.'

Out in the kitchen Nanna had been busy washing dishes and wiping the stove and the miniscule kitchen bench. She greeted her granddaughter by handing her a tea towel – a clean one Jodie noticed.

'Here. Take this dear and wipe up these dishes. Mind you, make sure you put them away so we have some space. I'll start to bring in the food – and keep that dog away from under my feet. I so don't want to trip over him.'

There was an old bone in the fridge that Jodie used to entice a very eager Pepper into the backyard and then Jodie set to with the tea towel. She had never seen the kitchen look so neat. If only Nanna could visit every day.

It wasn't until everything was in order and the house deemed suitable for visitors that they heard the sound of a car turning into the driveway. But it was a false alarm. Not their visitors after all. Merely Donna being returned from wherever she had been the night before. Donna greeted them all with a cheerful wave as she turned for her bedroom.

'Hi everyone. Great to see you but I'm beat. I think I'll have a little nap. Make yourself at home won't you.'

Donna's mother surveyed her daughter. Clearly dressed for wherever she had been last night after she had finished work – in a short multicoloured halter dress and platform shoes. Her hair tied up in a messy bun. Mascara weeping below her eyes, much like panda eyes. She had the look of someone who had partied hard.

'Not so quick, Donna. No sleeping for you. Have you forgotten Bonnie and her father are arriving shortly. Bonnie who will be living with you. Her father is expecting you to be a calming and positive influence on her. Looking at you now I think that might be most unlikely.'

Donna sniffed. 'Can't a girl have a bit of fun? Alright don't glower at me. Give me five minutes and a shower and I will be a new woman. Just you wait and see.' She turned to go to the bathroom then turned back again. 'A mug of coffee wouldn't go astray ... Please.'

Donna was almost as good as her word. Not quite five minutes but say ten minutes later she re-appeared freshly washed, wet hair combed back and makeup repaired. Dressed in jeans and a t-shirt she was a different Donna to party Donna from a little while back.

'Happy now, Ma' said as she twirled before her mother who said nothing, just handed her a mug of milky coffee. Donna took a long slurp then considered her parents and her daughter who all stood before her. She was not one to be cowed and after another slow mouthful she spoke.

'Alright I get it you are all cross with me but hey – I'm here now. I can see you've been frantic tidying my hovel. Thanks, by the way. It looks great and after all, we are all family to this Bonnie girl so I guess we'll all have to do our best to be a calming and positive influence.'

Donna's face broke into a wicked grin and she raised one eyebrow, 'Or if that doesn't work we can all make it so awful she will plead to go home and never stray again!'

Chapter Six

Despite her spoken antagonism to sharing her room Jodie couldn't help but feel curious about this so-called cousin who was to visit. Apart from her mother, Nanna and Pop and a missing father whom she had never met, there was no other family - until now.

How this cousin and her father fitted into the family tree was a mystery to her. Her questions had gone unanswered or were only ever responded to in a vague manner.

'Oh, she's a sort of distant cousin – a few times removed,' her mother would say and then would abruptly change the subject matter by ordering her to bring in extra firewood or to do some other chore. Jodie sensed there was more to it but realised no-one was prepared to share it with her. Maybe this mysterious cousin would explain.

When the car finally pulled up she hung back on the front porch as her mother and grandparents walked down to welcome them. Bonnie's father was first out of the car – bouncing over to Carol and Joe and enveloping them in hugs. His enthusiastic greeting reminded Jodie of the advances of a golden retriever – all bounce and hair.

'Joe, Carol – it's been ages.' He smiled and hugged her, beaming with enthusiasm. Jodie thought if he had been possessed of a tail it would have been furiously wagging. He turned to Donna and again bounced towards her, arms open wide, to demonstrate his intention to hug. Jodie smiled as she saw her mother tense – not welcoming the overt affection but realising it was unavoidable.

'Ken. Hello there,' Donna said as she offered a cheek for a sloppy kiss. 'So glad you could make it. Now, where's your daughter?'

Ken turned towards the car and waved at the shadowy figure in the front seat, indicating she should get out.

'Ah, the little minx. There she is. Awfully shy you know and not sure about meeting all these relatives. I've told her all about youse, but girls – you know.' He raised his voice 'Come on, Bonnie. Shift your arse and get out.' His arm waving became more agitated and he took a step towards the car.

Maybe this overt threat encouraged Bonnie but next thing the door slowly opened and a foot then a leg appeared. Jodie watched intently. The leg appeared bare as did the foot then a body slid out – clad in the shortest skirt Jodie had ever seen. Even shorter than that worn by her mother. Platform shoes held in one hand and a black jumper completed the outfit. The jumper clinging tightly to her body and creeping up to expose her stomach. Jodie was impressed. This cousin was clearly a trend setter as was also demonstrated by the darkly outlined eyes, flicked back hair do and the glossy lips. Maybe this cousin wouldn't be too boring after all. Despite herself she crept down the stairs and moved closer.

Ken reached for his daughter and pulled her across.

'Here she is. My little girl! Bonnie these are your relatives. Donna here I suppose you should call Aunty Donna. Carol and Joe – what does she call you?'

'Same as Jodie does I suppose,' said Joe. 'Nanna and Pop will do us just fine, or you can always call us by our first names if you want.'

Bonnie stared at them all, gave a nod then turned back to the car to reach in for a small hold all and started to walk up the front path towards Jodie.

Ken shrugged, all his bounce now gone and in a dejected tone he continued: 'she doesn't say much and to be honest she really didn't want to come to stay but I gave her no choice. Maybe some time away will knock some sense into that head.'

He smiled at them all. 'I really don't know what else to do so am hoping being with you all will make a difference. But if it doesn't, well just send her back.'

They all turned and looked up the path to observe Bonnie as she drew close to her sort of cousin. The contrast between the two was marked. One a gawky child all legs and angles – yet clad in her new jeans which were still stiff with cardboard-like newness. The other, only three years older but streets ahead in sophistication. It was clear they were from different worlds. Neither spoke as they took a moment to take in each other's appearance. In the distance the murmuring of adults talking of this and that as the two young women considered each other. Then a decision reached, and Bonnie reached out and touched Jodie on the shoulder.

'Come on. Show me around and take me to my room.'

Jodie grimaced 'There's not much to show and sorry, but we have to share. You'll get the bed though.'

With an eyeroll Bonnie said, 'And I thought things couldn't get much worse.'

***

And these words were repeated by the end of the day when they were laying in their beds – Bonnie in the bed, Jodie and Pepper snuggled on the mattress. Ken had stayed all afternoon with a quick trip down to Carol and Joe's place – all the while chatting and laughing. By the time he left, after calling out instructions to his daughter *to behave* the welcoming silence that descended following his departure was appreciated by all.

Dinner was a basic meal – comprised of leftovers from the lunch so lovingly prepared by Jodie's Nanna. Much to Bonnie's disgust there was no tv and nothing to do but to go to bed and read. Bonnie making it very clear she considered reading a waste of time, unless it involved reading a fashion magazine of which she had brought quite a few.

They lay in their beds pretending to read but in reality both mentally processing the day's events. The question that had been nagging at Jodie had to be asked.

'Bonnie, tell me. What happened that they sent you here to us?'

'It was so overreacting by my dad and the headmistress. Just a bit of smoking and snogging behind the sheds at school. It was nothing really, but little miss goody two shoes teacher's pet Avril Carmody had to go and blab. And apparently they had to make an example of me. You know saying such behaviour cannot be tolerated, bad example for the juniors – blah, blah blah.'

'Still,' there was a complacent tone in Bonnie's voice. 'The snogging was awfully good. And I now have a boyfriend. Dave said he couldn't let me take all the blame. So he said it was his fault. Not that they believed him. They said I was a troublemaker and a bad influence. And Dave says he likes me just this way. He's suspended too. But tomorrow I'll ring him. You can talk to him too if you like.'

Despite herself Jodie felt impressed. She would never have dared to misbehave in such a way – assuming that is that there might be anyone that would possibly want to snog her. Perhaps she needed to be as grown up as Bonnie for such things to take place. Just as she was starting to drift off to sleep Bonnie let out a screech.

'What's that noise? There in the roof?'

'Noise? What noise?' Jodie mumbled as she felt herself being pulled back into consciousness by her cousin's cries.

Above them in the ceiling cavity they could both hear the pitter patter of tiny feet as they crossed the ceiling.

'Oh that. That's mice. They live in the ceiling, and you'll hear them most nights.'

'No way!' Bonnie's voice raised an octave in alarm. 'They'll be in our room next. What sort of dump is this?'

'It's alright. If they come into the house – which is unlikely as we have a cat – and also Pepper is a great mouse catcher – they won't come in here. They're more likely to go into the kitchen looking for food.'

'Good luck if they can find any,' Jodie added muttering under her breath.

The sounds of nighttime scampering had always been part of the background noise of Jodie's childhood and she found it hard to understand why it should so upset her cousin. Didn't everyone have vermin in their home or shed? And the possums had yet to make their regular nighttime appearance. Some nights she was convinced they held the possum Olympics on the veranda roof with many heats of the veranda 50 metre dash. Now that should definitely excite Bonnie!

Bonnie was still muttering, but at least the shrieking was no longer. The day ended with Jodie dozing off in her surprisingly comfortable bed lulled to sleep by the sounds of her cousin bemoaning her fate and the dump in which she had been imprisoned.

And next morning Jodie woke to similar words.

'What a dump!' said Bonnie as she returned from the lean-to bathroom out the back. 'How can you live this way?' she demanded as she kicked at Jodie in passing.

Struggling to consciousness Jodie opened a bleary eye and tried to focus on the indignant person, who was now hopping around on one foot as she struggled to put on a pair of what looked like too tight jeans.

'Dump? Yep it is a dump. But do you think I have any choice? If I had my way I'd live with Nanna and Pop, but mum insists we live here. I suppose she has her reasons but ...' Jodie felt tears well up as she contemplated her life. No friends apart from Pepper and maybe Will. A home no-one wanted to visit and while she could try to ignore the dump-like nature of her residence it now felt like her cousin thought it was her fault. If Jodie could change her life she would. But what could she do? She was only 12 after all.

A quick breakfast of tea and toast eaten while seated on the front steps in the morning sunshine and then Bonnie was demanding to be entertained.

'Well then. What do we do now?' asked Bonnie after taking a final slurp from her mug.

Jodie stared thoughtfully at this relative of hers. What to do? The answer was obvious. Nothing! She suspected that answer would not satisfy Bonnie. She thought hard.

'I suppose we could walk down to see Nanna and Pop and take Pepper with us. He always likes a walk. Mum has already left for work, so we don't need to worry about her. And I can show you Pop's animals – or Pop can,' Jodie corrected herself. 'And there's always cake. And then I can show you the sights around the village – not that there are many...'

'Is that it?' Bonnie's tone of voice indicated her displeasure. 'How about going into Hobart? Can we do that? Go to the movies or something?'

'Sure. Maybe Nanna or Pop might drive us in, or we can catch the bus.' Jodie faltered. How could she explain that a trip to Hobart was dependant on funds and she had none. Perhaps best to come out with it. 'Trouble is I have no money.'

Dismissed with the wave of her hand. 'Nah. Not a problem. Dad left me with heaps. He said I should treat you. So maybe a bit of shopping, hey?'

'Alright then. Sounds good. Let me rinse these and you go, get ready and we can then see if Nanna and Pop are at home. You'll really like the animals. The goats have just had babies – kids they're called. You're going to love them.'

'Really? I doubt it. Smelly and pooey. Can't imagine that.' Bonnie's nose wrinkled in disgust as she frowned at her cousin. Even pulling a face she looked cute. It's so not fair thought Jodie. Why couldn't she look like that?

As they wandered down the hill and towards Nanna and Pop's house Bonnie's moaning trailed away as she gazed around her and commented on their surroundings.

'It's a kinda cute place. I like those little cottages – similar to yours but they're not falling down and that stone two storey place is lovely. I'd much rather we were staying there. I bet I'd have my own bedroom there instead of being stuck with you in that dumpy mouse ridden bedroom.'

By now Jodie was getting sick of all this moaning. Would she ever stop? Didn't she realise she wasn't wanted here and Jodie was just putting up with her.

Before she could help herself she blurted out: 'Quit your moaning, will ya? Do you think I want to share my room or give up my bed to someone like you who just bitches all the time. I know I'm stuck with you – hopefully for not too long but can you just keep quiet? Please.'

Jodie ended her outburst with her voice all a wobble and her eyes awash with tears. She didn't ask for this person to be foisted on her. It was all so unfair and why did she feel Bonnie was blaming her for being banished. If she had her way she would send her straight back where she came from.

Yet her words had an effect. As she spoke Bonnie halted, turned and stared at Jodie in astonishment. Maybe she hadn't realised the effect of her complaining. And as Jodie came to understand in the days that followed, Bonnie's personality was flamboyant, prone to run off at the mouth and speak before thinking. Now she was thinking and realising that her words had caused obvious distress to her cousin.

'Oh come on. Don't take it to heart. It's nothing personal. I'm still mad with dad for sending me here to outer Siberia and I suppose I was taking it out on you. Sorry. It's not your fault and I shouldn't have been so mean. But hey, if you were sent away wouldn't you be cross?'

Jodie, with her head to one side, considered the possibility and smiled.

'Well. Actually, I wouldn't mind being sent away. Maybe to some posh boarding school where they had lots of animals and Pepper could come to.'

'You poor thing.' Bonnie shook her head and reaching out to give her cousin a cuddle she continued, 'You know what. When my banishment ends how about you come back home with me and I can show you what living really is about.' She added as a further enticement 'You can have your own bedroom and no mice – guaranteed.'

'I'd like that.'

The two children arm in arm continued their perambulations towards Nanna and Pop's house – all animosity forgotten as they chatted and laughed and discovered they had so much in common. Nanna who was out in the front yard picking flowers paused as she saw them come into sight and smiled. Maybe having young Bonnie come to stay would be a good thing after all. A friend for Jodie was just what she needed. It was a pity the judgemental families in this village and the many vindicative women ostracised her granddaughter, who for no fault of her own, was the child of a single parent.

Of course, there was cake – plenty of it – and biscuits and sausage rolls. The baby goats were inspected and cuddled and found to be very cute as promised.

'And not too stinky after all,' Bonnie conceded.

To Jodie's surprise she came to enjoy the weeks that followed as she and her sort of cousin explored the village and spent time in Hobart whenever they could persuade Nanna to take them. Occasionally they caught the bus and sat up the very back ignoring the glares from the other passengers as they laughed and joked about nothing in particular.

Sure, Bonnie still continued to pronounce how boring everything was on a daily basis. Although this was more often than not, said with a twinkle in her eye and an attitude of defiance as if to provoke a response from Jodie. Initially Jodie felt defensive when Bonnie proclaimed how bored she was. Now she laughed and poked her cousin in the ribs while telling her to get over it.

It being the end of term break there was no school to distract them, so they were free to make their own fun. Occasionally they would see Will in the distance as he rushed to the shop on some errand. Apart from a casual wave in their direction they had no contact. Until one day when all three ran into each other at the local grocery store at the same time. The shop was on the main street and housed in what had once been the blacksmith's shop. Crammed with goods and with narrow aisles it wasn't until Jodie turned one corner and literally ran into Will that they saw each other.

'Will! I didn't see you there. Oops. Here let me help you pick that up.'

They both bent and collected the scattered cans and a loaf of bread that had fallen when they collided.

'It's all fine,' Will smiled. 'See even the bread isn't too squashed. Typical of you though – eh? Always running somewhere.'

'And who's this?' came a voice from behind Jodie as Bonnie appeared peering over her shoulder.

Introductions made and to Jodie's surprise Bonnie became almost gushing in her conversation with Will. Was she flirting? To her surprise Jodie felt unimpressed. Will was her friend and she didn't want to share him.

They parted ways outside the shop with promises from Will to catch up when he had a chance. 'Not sure when. Lots to do on the farm at the moment to help dad. Working with the sheep, you know.'

Once they were a safe distance away Bonnie commenced her interrogation.

'He's gorgeous you know. That surfie hair- so divine - and so tall. You said he's in your year at school but really, he could pass for 15 just like me. If only he was a bit older I'd be seriously tempted.'

'Will? Gorgeous? Give over. He's just Will. My mate.'

'Lucky you. Now I'm starting to see at least one thing I like about this place – oh and you of course, and your Pepper. I'll be sad to go home next week. It's been much more fun than I expected. Even staying in your dump of a home and putting up with your very strange mother had been – well – has been a bit of an adventure. You can never tell what she will say next! I'll miss it and you. Promise me you'll come and stay next holidays? With Pepper of course.'

Hearing Bonnie's words Jodie stopped in the middle of the pavement oblivious to the elderly couple trying to pass her. Bonnie leave? She'd known that would happen at some stage but had hoped it would be some time away. Some of her daydreams had included speculation of Bonnie declaring she wanted to stay with them forever. It was so much fun having someone to share with. To share a room, adventures, confidences and laughter. She sighed and felt an arm sneak around her shoulder.

'Cheer up, buddy. We have a week and then we can plan what you want to do when you visit my place. You will love it. Your own room. The food's awful. Dad can't cook but then neither can your mum! I will write – promise. Although maybe not often as I hate writing. Maybe I'll send you a card. And I'll certainly ring you. Say why don't we agree to talk every Sunday night? I'm sure to be home then. We can pretend you're my little sister and I'm away at boarding school. Just like in a story.'

'Can't I be the one at boarding school? I so wish to be away from here.'

'Careful what you wish for. Or at least that is what my dad says. I have no idea what he means.'

Chapter Seven - 1978

The Trauma

What Jodie came to describe as *the trauma* took place when she was 15 and without warning her entire world upended itself. In the days and weeks that followed she craved the once so boring life that she had previously despised. She would have given anything – sell her soul even – to still be able to grump at her mother or roll her eyes in disdain at any of those requests to tidy her room or wash the dishes. Anything.

Those moments were gone – all gone. All that lingered were the images of her mother's agonised face seared into her brain that played behind closed eyes each night, those blood smeared hands pushing Jodie away as her mother pleaded with her to run. Her mother's words also played themselves out in her brain over and over again.

'Run. For god's sake run before they come back. Get help. Quickly there's no time to waste '…'

Many months later when she was able to sort of calmly review the events of that time Jodie came to realise that life leading up to *the trauma* had changed. In particular her mother's behaviour had become markedly different. More often than not she had been calmer with less irrational angry outbursts and had seemed to be almost happy. On occasion humming and even singing around the house as she readied herself to go to work. There had even been times when she hinted at changes in their future – how their finances and life would improve. Perhaps they might even move house. Jodie who could see no reason why they would ever have the funds to move had dismissed such talk as mere fantasy.

Yet something was different. No longer was there a procession of different men being brought home. In fact Jodie wasn't sure who her mother was now seeing – except she was sure there was a mysterious someone as she regularly spent nights away from home or didn't return home at night after work until the next morning. And when Jodie, feeling like she was the mother, asked where Donna had been her questions were dismissed with a wave and a 'never you mind, young stickybeak. You'll find out in time.' And with a wink Donna quickly changed the topic of conversation to something more mundane – like was there anything in the fridge to cook for dinner or should they go down to Nanna and Pop's. As far as Jodie was concerned the answer to that question was obvious. Dinner at Nanna and Pop's house won out every time.

The night Donna died was like any other night. Donna was at work at the pub until 10pm. Jodie had found something to eat for dinner – cheese and biscuits for both her and Pepper. It had been a long day at school with the afternoon spent on the oval training for the upcoming regional athletics competition. She was entered in the 100 and 200 metre races and was determined to place if not win. By evening she was worn out. Homework was abandoned as a waste of time when she kept nodding off over her books. Early to bed and straight to the deep sleep of the exhausted. It felt like she had been asleep for ages but at some stage, maybe midnight, Jodie's dreams were disturbed by screams. She struggled to wake, feeling like she was swimming to the surface of a dream that wanted to pull her down. But the screams were agonised and sent a tremor of alarm through her body. And also through Pepper. With a ferocious snarl he leapt off the bed and raced out the bedroom door barking hysterically as he went. The screaming and barking merged in a cacophony that lingered with Jodie long after.

Another voice – an unidentifiable voice merged with the sounds – screaming something like: 'Get off me you mongrel!' Then a sickening thud and a whimper. And then silence. The silence struck fear into Jodie's heart. By now she was creeping out of her room to the front door uncertain what she would find. And what she found was far beyond her worst imaginings. Her mother slumped in the shattered doorway, in a pool of rapidly expanding blood and moaning faintly. And her little dog lying motionless beside her with his neck at an unnatural angle. Jodie's focus was immediately on Pepper who she scooped up and held tightly. Maybe if she could hold him close then whatever damage had been inflicted would knit. But instinctively she already knew that would not work and his little spirit had already left his damaged body. Beyond words all she could do was shed tears onto Pepper's lifeless form.

Jodie was not able to recall how long she stood there in an agony of grief. It may have been only a few minutes, or it could have been longer but eventually she registered the faint moans coming from her mother.

Still holding Pepper she crouched down and touched that part of her mother's battered face that wasn't covered in blood.

'Ma? What happened? What do you want me to do? Ring the ambulance? Get Pop?'

'No. Don't ring,' she whispered. 'They could come back and get to you. Just run and get Pop. He'll know what to do. Go – and run as fast as you can.'

And run she did. Avoiding her mother's body which was blocking the smashed front door she raced back to her bedroom and dived through the bedroom window. This was a tight squeeze, especially as she was still clutching little Pepper, but somehow the adrenalin coursing through her veins gave her superhero strength.

Little did she know that the last agonised look back towards her bloody and battered mother slumped on the floor with hand pressing on a blood-soaked abdomen would be her last glimpse of a living mother. She shuddered as she gazed down on the lifeless and misshapen body of her little dog clutched tightly in her arms. He was beyond saving. Her heart was breaking and all she wanted to do was to collapse on the floor with Pepper and hold him close. It was only instinct and her mother's whispered words that commanded her body to leave the house and run.

But run she did – down the hill around the corner to Nanna and Pop's house. It was late and the darkened house made it obvious they were in already in bed and asleep. This being a small community and in the 1970's the house was, as always left unlocked. In rural Tasmania in those days it would not have occurred to anyone to lock a house or a car for that matter. A crashing as the front door was hurled open was sure to have roused her grandparents even if Jodie's screaming had not.

***

Later on – much later on when the police were interviewing Jodie in the presence of her grandparents, she was asked why she didn't call 000. Jodie was at a loss to answer this question.

'I don't know. It all happened so quickly that maybe I couldn't think logically. One moment I was asleep then my dog started barking furiously and woke me up. I could hear my mother's voice screaming at someone to go away. Pepper, that's my dog. Well, he charged off my bed and rushed out to where mum was – by the front door. I heard him snarl and then a massive thud which I think was him being hurled away and then another thud and mum's screaming stopped. I ran out and well you know what I found.'

'And – answer the question please.'

Jodie could feel the tears welling. Why was this officer being so mean? Was she under suspicion of being the murderer? He stared at her as he waited for a response. Jodie struggled to answer.

'It was all so surreal. Like my worst nightmare. I had no idea what had happened. And mum whispered what I had to do – she told me not to phone 'cause I think she was worried the person might return. She told me to run and get Nanna and Pop. I couldn't think – just obey I guess. Is that shock do you think?

When you can't think independently? Do you reckon it would it have saved her if I had called 000?'

'Officer,' Pop interjected. 'Is this really necessary? You can see young Jodie here is already traumatised and I'm not sure if this line of questioning is getting us anywhere.'

'I apologise, Mr Daley. You see we are trying to get an idea of the timeline of events. It is unlikely that the outcome would have changed if Miss Wise had called 000 instead of running to your home. According to the Coroner, the victim,' the officer tilted his head down as he referred to some printed matter on the desk then turned back towards Jodie, 'your mother's injuries were so severe that there was little that could have been done to save her. Perhaps that's enough for today. We have already explored with you all whether you knew of anyone who might have a motive for harming Ms Wise. But if you think of anything further please make contact. Thank you to all of you for your time. And especially to you, Miss Wise. I'm sorry to once more have to drag you over the events of that terrible night.'

The Police Station was in a side street off the main road near the park. As they walked back to Nanna and Pa's home very little was said. Jodie in the middle flanked by both grandparents who held each of her hands and from time to time gave a little squeeze. All were lost in their own thoughts and they walked in silence. Nanna thinking of practical stuff – how they needed to make a loving home for their granddaughter, how they needed to pack up what should be kept from Donna and Jodie's old home – not that there was much worth keeping she thought and how to put a stop to the scurrilous gossip that was circulating around the village. In the absence of an arrest, speculation was swirling about who could have done it. Some even suggesting it was Jodie. If her granddaughter heard that Nanna didn't know if Jodie would react with fury or would such talk inflict even further heartbreak.

Pa's thoughts were focussed on getting even with the bullies that were inventing the gossip. If he found out who they were he would not be accountable for his actions.

And Jodie. Well, her thoughts were more often than not with Pepper. If only she had held on to him that night and not let him run out to protect her mum. Better still if only the bedroom door had been shut. Pop had told her she should be proud of what a hero her dog had been, but as far as she was concerned that was no consolation for the loss of her best friend. She missed him so much her very being ached. Her dear friend and constant companion.

Everyone seemed to think she was devastated over the loss of her mother and maybe one day she might be. Her mother had been such a complicated person Jodie wondered why anyone thought she should now miss the strife and conflict that accompanied her mother. That loss didn't create a vacuum. It created peace.

The loss of her dog, however, felt like losing a limb, a part of herself. She couldn't help but keep checking if Pepper was following or at night curl up to create a nest for her dog. Then she would remember Pepper no longer needed her warmth or companionship but was buried cold and alone in Nanna and Pa's garden, soon to be sheltered by a tree which they would plant this weekend.

It wasn't the loss of her mother that haunted her. No. It was the image of her mother's battered and bloody face as she begged her to run. Should she have declined and said: 'No mum, it is better if I ring 000.' To be honest with herself that would be the last thing she would have done. All she had wanted to do was get away. And even now all she wanted to do was never go near that house again. If someone took a match to it tomorrow she would cheer.

There didn't seem much point holding a public funeral – Donna had so few friends and with so much speculation swirling around in the village Carol and Joe saw no need to expose Jodie to the public. Once Donna's body was released by the Coroner they arranged for a private funeral and cremation attended only by Carol, Joe and Jodie. Even Bonnie and her father as the only other relatives were excluded as a way of keeping arrangements low key. In time her ashes would be scattered somewhere that they thought might be significant to Donna. At this stage they had no idea where such a place might be – 'the backseat of a car' muttered Joe in the disapproving presence of his wife. But for now her ashes were kept in a not so tasteful urn and hidden out of sight in the laundry. Carol didn't think Jodie needed to be reminded of her mother's remains.

Jodie stayed at her grandparent's house. She had no interest in ever returning to the cottage she shared with her mother and Pepper. Joe had been dispatched to clear out her room and bring back her belongings. The police tape still secured the front porch and the front gate had been locked. But Jo was able to enter via the back door and take away what he needed. The rest could stay there and be taken away with the house when it was demolished, for the owner had decided that because of recent events the house should not be preserved. And as the owner explained to Joe: 'It was falling down anyway. I had always intended to rebuild there and only delayed things because I was trying to help out Donna and her lass. And anyway no one else will want to live there after what has happened. It has to go.'

Spending every day with her grandparents and helping with the farm animals was all Jodie wanted to do. She refused to return to school. Even the upcoming athletics carnival did not tempt her. To be the object of attention and speculation was more than she could contemplate. It may have been different if her school environment had been full of supportive fellow students. But the reality was that her only support was Will who was as grief struck about the loss of Pepper as she was. Most afternoons he would pop in on his way home after school and they would walk down to the river and spend some time in silence, sitting on the bank and watching the ducks and other wildlife. His solid presence was a comfort. On weekends he would come around, ostensibly for cake and often bringing his sheepdog to play with Joe's working dog. The sheepdog, a Smithfield terrier named Missy was no Pepper substitute but to some extent she was a grey, black and white fluffy comfort – full of energy and excitement.

One afternoon while Jodie was lying on the bed in her room, pretending to read, but in reality reliving the events of that terrible evening, a bit like the images were on a continual loop, her attention was distracted by the sound of voices. Her grandparents' voices she could identify but there was another deeper and slower voice. In recent weeks there had been very few visitors, apart from Will. Clearly the village had determined that they all were pariahs – even her grandparents who until now had been universally admired as village elders.

So, who could it be?

Eventually curiosity got the better of her and cautiously Jodie crept down the corridor to the kitchen doorway. There by the kitchen table she saw her grandparents seated with a stranger. A man not as old as her grandparents but to Jodie's 15-year-old eyes, still an old man. Tall, muscular with the tanned strength of an outdoor worker he had receding blonde hair which may have been curly but was now flattened as a result of wearing the sweat-stained battered hat that was resting on the table.

Carol looked up as she saw Jodie lingering by the doorway and spoke, 'Ah, Jodie. Come in and meet Charlie Wise. Charlie this is Jodie.'

Charlie stood up as Carol made the introductions and smiled at Jodie. Meanwhile Jodie's brain was on fire as she stared at this man. Charlie Wise? Why, he had the same surname as her. Who could he be?

As if reading her thoughts Charlie nodded 'Yes Jodie. I'm your father. I'm sorry I haven't been able to get to you until now. When your mother was alive it wasn't possible – for reasons I won't go into. But I'm here now and I want to help out however I can.'

Jodie stared at this man. Now this wasn't what she was expecting. The absent father had never figured in her thoughts. Her mother, if she ever spoke of him was critically dismissive. Her impression was that the marriage had been a short-lived disaster and that Donna had fallen pregnant on their honeymoon in the days after the wedding. There had been no photos of Charlie in the house and for that matter no photos of him in Nanna and Pop's house.

Jodie studied him intently. If he really was her father, and she supposed she must believe him for now, then it must be his height and fair colouring that had been passed on to her.

She wasn't the only one staring. Charlie was also examining his daughter and exclaiming to Carol and Jo how grown she was and how much she resembled his younger sister.

Carol nodded. 'Yes, that could be so. Jodie didn't take after her mother, so I guess she's more like your side of the family.' She picked up the teapot. 'More tea Charlie?'

'Thanks. Wouldn't mind if I do.'

The pleasantries continued while Charlie affably drank his tea and munched on the freshly baked ANZAC biscuits.

Meanwhile Jodie, feeling suspicious, glared at her grandfather as she mouthed 'What the?'

Her grandfather shook his head and pointed to the vacant chair at the table. Clearly she was in for a serious discussion. Carefully she sat down then looked at each of the adults in turn.

'Why do I feel like you are plotting about me? Out with it!'

Carol was first to speak.

'Yes dear we have been discussing you. As you know things are pretty uncomfortable here. The village has worked itself into a tizz about your mother's death. It doesn't help that the police are still no closer to working out what happened or who could be the murderer. So in the absence of any motive or a suspect I suppose it is only natural that they start to suspect us – her family. The villagers that is – not the police. They've pretty much cleared us but as we've been told they're stumped. We worry how you are going to get on if life here continues to be unpleasant. Joe and I are tough. We will see this out. But you are so young and are already carrying a terrible burden and we've been trying to find a way to give you space so you can put this behind you.'

Jodie shook her head. As if this was a simple process of putting the recent events behind her. Couldn't her grandparents understand she would be forever scarred?

Joe, who had much sympathy for his granddaughter, spoke as if he could almost read her thoughts.

'Maybe not put it behind you. Like us you will be forever altered but a change of scene and some distance from these disgusting people in this village will not only help you but may even give them time to change their attitude. We can but hope. We've been wracking our brains trying to sort out a solution and then Charlie appeared with a proposal.'

'Yes, I did.' Charlie smiled across the table at her and with arms out wide as if offering a vista of hitherto unimaginable delights he continued. 'I know it must be a shock to you to discover I exist - your father and all. Carol and Joe here can vouch that I really am your father.' He paused and looked, first at Carol then Joe who both smiled and nodded.

'So what I propose is that you come and live with me for some time. Time enough to put some space between you and recent events and time to settle into a different environment. As far as environments go it isn't too shabby. I manage a large property up Cressy way. Nice old house where the owner lives surrounded by a fancy garden and I have a comfortable manager's cottage. You can live there with me – go to school if you wish or help on the property. Extra hands are always needed. And maybe we can get to know each other better and trust me Jodie I will do my best to help you get through this.'

Jodie could see from his sincere expression that Charlie was well intentioned. But really! This was all too much.

She shook her head. 'No. I don't know you and I don't know this place you're talking about. It could be Buckingham Palace for all I know, but it's not my home. No way! Why can't I stay here? Or go to Bonnie?'

Her grandfather spoke: 'Maybe in time there might be room for you to stay with Bonnie but trust me things are a bit shaky up there at the moment. We've talked this through and really believe you leaving the district could be an effective short circuit to all the angst that is brewing.'

'Why should I have to run away? I've done nothing wrong.' Jodie could hear her voice rise in tone as tears and hysteria were developing.

'Oh Jodie dear.' Her grandmother was beside her and enveloped Jodie in one of her speciality hugs. 'Trust us. It's for the best I promise. Please give it a go and if it doesn't work then of course you can come back. But I would be asking you to commit to staying up on the property for some time – some years I expect until life calms down and hopefully they will find who killed your mum. Things can take a long while to change in this neck of the woods.'

'No!' Jodie screamed in despair and bolted from the room.

After

Chapter Eight

The Back of Beyond
Sometime in March
(no idea of the date – every day is the same)

Dear Nanna and Pop

I nearly cried when you rang tonight when I heard your voices. It was so lovely to speak to you both. I miss you so and I hate it here. I don't understand why I have to stay away as if I'm being punished for something I didn't do.

It's so unfair and I'm not sure who I should blame – you two, Charlie or all of you?

I really, really hate it here. Our house is ok I guess but there's nothing here but sheep paddocks, countless sheds and sheep as far as the eye can see. There is a big old house where the owner lives – 'the Boss Lady' Charlie calls her. And maybe one day I'll meet her, but I don't care and I don't want to be here.

Please, please come and take me home. Tomorrow would be best. If not sooner.

From a Tasmanian Hell Hole
Some day in March

Dear Bonnie

I don't understand why I can't come and live with you. Nanna said things are a bit grim up your way. What's happening? And anyway it can't be as grim as here. Everyone tells me that this is for the best, but I can't see why I have to be stuck in this sheep prison.

Charlie, who says he is my dad, seems ok I guess. But really how do I know if he is my dad? I asked him to show me some photos to prove it and he says he will when he gets a chance but for now he is busy with the revolting sheep. Something about getting the ewes ready and healthy to meet the rams, Gross. It's all so basic here. And I'm meant to help once 'I've settled in'. As if!

You should see this place. It's set in some big valley – broad, windy and cold and all belongs to the one farm. Owned by the same family since forever. I haven't met them yet – and I don't want to.

Please, please can I come and live with you?

Lots of love from Little Orphan Jodie (as far as I'm concerned I'm now an orphan as how do I know Charlie is really my father?)

Still living in Outer Siberia
Still March

Dear Nanna

Thanks for the jumper and the warm socks Nanna. You've no idea how cold it is! That man called Charlie – no I won't call him dad 'cause he has never been part of my life - anyway he tells me that even though we've had our first frost, it is only early autumn, and it will get much colder. Great! No really – not great.

I feel for the sheep who have just been shorn and unlike me have no woolly jumper. But Charlie tells me the ewes don't need heavy coats as that would just make for trouble in lambing when they would have trouble getting up. I wonder if anyone has asked them?

Anyway, the jumper is very soft and pretty. I like the flecked blue colour and will take good care of it. When I wear it I will think of you knitting it for me. Probably sitting by the fire and watching tele while you knit. I can hold that thought in my mind and it makes me feel a little bit happy.

Any other warm clothes you can send my way would be welcome.

Don't think I have settled in. It's still awful. Cold, smelly and awful.

I get it that I should stay away but does it have to be for so long?

It's my birthday soon – as I'm sure you know. My birthday wish is for you and Pop to come and visit and bring birthday cake.

Please, please, pretty please.

xxxxxxxxxxxxxxxxx

From the banished Birthday Girl
Still March (but only just)

Dear Bonnie

Thank you for the birthday card. I like a joke card. Yeah turning 16 is meant to be pretty special but here it was just another day. In fact Charlie didn't even know it was my birthday. Another reason that he cannot be my father. Surely he was there at my birth as he was still married to mum at the time. I suppose he might have forgotten … I guess.

Anyway, he didn't know until Nanna and Pop turned up the next day with — you guessed it — the best birthday cake ever! Chocolate of course. With chocolate buttercream in the middle and all around. And flakes of real chocolate on the top. Yum! More sugary goodness than I've eaten for ages.

You see the food here is pretty ordinary. It's ok if you want to eat lamb. 'Cause that's all there is. Yuk! Charlie tells me they kill a sheep every week for us, the Big House and the stockman and his family. All we seem to get is chops. So every night for dinner it is grilled lamb chops, potatoes and what other stuff Charlie can scavenge.

But Nanna — one of my favourite people even if she has sent me away — has come to the rescue. Not only did she arrive with cake, and enough food to last for the week but she also brought me a cookbook. The Australian Womens Weekly Cookbook. Do you know it? I've marked the easy recipes and have told Charlie he needs to take me to the shop so I can buy something other than lamb. If I'm going to live here I think I need to eat something else other than lamb. Or I could turn into a sheep!

Must run. I can hear Charlie returning. His old truck can never sneak up on anyone. It's way too noisy.

Lotsa love
xxxxxxx

Still March (I think)
although it could be April

Dear Nanna

That cookbook is amazing! Thank you so much. I've already baked a cake – not as good as yours but Charlie seemed to like it. As did his dog Buster.

And I also made roast chicken and another meal of meatballs and pasta from the recipes in the cookbook. I plan to work my way through this cookbook – so long as I can find the ingredients at the local shop. We go there once a week and to be honest it's pretty ordinary. But Charlie tells me I can ask them to get stuff in.

Even the lamb recipes look interesting. And at least I know I'm sure to be able to source lamb in this hell hole.

Nothing much else to say – except that I hate this place – but you probably already know that.

Charlie says he is taking me over to the Big House tomorrow to meet the Boss Lady. Everyone refers to the house and the boss like they are up there with God and they should start with capitals. Sounds like I'm to be inspected to see if I'm satisfactory. Maybe she'll send me away? I wish.

Have you thought about boarding school?

Whatever. I still love you and Pop.

From your sad granddaughter who is now about to try to make lamb casserole. Maybe it will make the lamb taste nice.

Xxxxxxxx and hugs- lots of hugs – even for the goats.

Chapter Nine

Even to Jodie's unobservant eyes she could see that Charlie, usually so laid back, was rather tense that morning. As they sat on the front veranda eating toast and Vegemite and sipping tea she could see his foot tap, tap, tapping on the floorboards.

'Hey. What's up? What's with the foot?'

'Hmm?' Charlie looked down at his foot and immediately it was stilled.

'Well?'

'It's nothing. I was just thinking.'

'With your foot? That explains a lot!' Jodie grinned as if to take the edge off her comment.

Charlie smiled back.

'I was thinking about how I need to take you over to meet the Boss Lady this morning and how long that will take. There's lots of chores to get done today.'

'Well, a good visit is a quick visit. So I'm happy to say hello, smile sweetly and then bolt.'

'You don't know the Boss. She will want to know everything about you.'

'Doesn't she already? I feel like most of Tasmania knows my sad story and has formed an opinion about me. Generally it's an unfavourable opinion, like they think I did it.' Jodie frowned and pouted as she said this. Her expression vanishing when she saw the compassionate expression on her father's face.

'It's alright. I'm tough and I can cope and I can deal with this so-called Boss Lady. By the way, what's her name?'

'Her name is Joan Fraser. And she really is a decent person. I wouldn't still be here after all these years if she wasn't. Joan knows we call her the Boss Lady and I think it amuses her. She can be a bit intimidating but at heart she is very kind. You see she has had a tough time of it.'

In response to Jodie's questioning look Charlie put down his now empty mug as he settled into his story.

'I gather she was a city girl, raised in Hobart. Met young Alastair Fraser, fell in love and moved back here to the family property which had been held by his family for generations. *Gourock* it is called, named by an early Fraser after some place in Scotland.

Alastair died young leaving her with two young lads – twins who were then primary school age. I'd recently taken up this job after I split with your mum. Both Joan and I were new to the responsibilities of farming without Alastair's oversight. It was tough at the start but somehow, we managed and as we became more experienced – well it got better – never easier. Because farming is never easy. The local community were great during those early days – happy to lend a hand or give advice. Now things are ticking over quite nicely. I have some decent station hands. We've worked on the sheep genetic mix. The wool they produce is second to none. So we now need to maintain the quality herd and hope for good seasons.'

He reached down and grabbed the mug, then stood up and stretched.

'Come on. We should get this over and done with. Bring a hat. We might go up to the stockyards afterwards. There is a ewe with a dodgy foot that I brought in last night. I need to check in on her. Maybe spray the foot again.'

They drove across to the big house in Charlie's battered truck with Buster, the black and tan working dog in the back. It wasn't far and they could have walked. Jodie in her explorations had already identified the well-worn track which led to the big house.

It traversed a small paddock that Charlie referred to as *the House Paddock* and then ended at a small gate in the middle of a row of ancient pine trees that she assumed marked the start of the yard.

Today though they drove further along a dirt track that took them to the back of the big house. If they were to continue, they would end up at the shearing shed, sheep yards and other assorted unidentifiable farm buildings.

Again, another gate which they pushed through and entered the most amazing garden Jodie had ever seen. Apart from the one line of conifers to one side, the other boundaries were marked by lines of beautifully pruned hedges. Sheltered by these living barriers from the ever-present wind that gusted down the valley, the garden inside was its own protected microclimate. Another world, in which plants, birds and insects and even humans could flourish.

Jodie could hear the hum of bees and the call of birds. The gurgling jubilation of magpies, the chatter of parrots as they dined on the gum blossom nectar, and the screech of cockatoos somewhere in the distance. Over in a corner she could see several bee hives. She pointed them out to Charlie.

'Yes, they're Roman's bees. The honey you sometimes have on your toast is from those bees.'

'Roman?'

'He's the gardener here. Most likely Joan is out in the garden with him somewhere. She's not much of an inside person. Let's wander around and see if we can find them.'

Jodie followed Charlie – slowing down every so often as she peered up paths that led beside overgrown flower beds or through plantings of ancient trees. There in the distance was a gravel tennis court – looking like it needed a bit of care. And nearby a rustic painted timber summer house. She could imagine the ladies from times long past dressed in white lacy dresses watching games of tennis while they drank cooling punch – no doubt being waited on by convict servants who were possibly her ancestors.

Charlie calling out to her. 'Hurry up and come here' broke Jodie out of her daydreaming, and she rushed to catch up with him.

She found Charlie standing near two people beside a flower bed next to the house. Seeing the house for the first time she now understood why it was called the Big House. for it was enormously elegant – stone, double storied with possibly attics and stretching out some distance with a range of outbuildings snuggling in behind. And that was only the side view. If the side view was so grand she wondered what the front might be like?

But for now her attention was attracted by Charlie waving her on.

'Joan, let me introduce you to my daughter Jodie. Jodie this is Mrs Fraser who owns this beautiful place, and this is Roman who keeps the garden under control.'

Jodie, being mindful of her manners and aware of Charlie's keen gaze, smiled politely then shook hands, first with this woman called Joan Fraser and then Roman the gardener.

'Pleased to meet you Mrs Fraser and you, too, Roman.'

'No Mrs Fraser please. Joan will do just fine.' She twinkled. 'Or you can call me Boss Lady like everyone else.'

This smiling woman was not quite what Jodie had expected. Her expression was sympathetic and understanding. Her smile authentic and welcoming. This evoked in Jodie an unexpected feeling of coming home. Like this was a person she could trust and, given the events of recent months, that was an unexpected feeling.

Joan's appearance was also unexpected. She didn't look like a grand lady. Dressed in a shabby checked cotton shirt and grubby jeans there was nothing of the landed gentry about her. Grey-streaked hair pulled up into a messy ponytail completed the underwhelming presentation. Yet none of this was noticed when she considered the twinkling electric blue eyes and the friendly smile. She found herself smiling back and muttering various inanities which Joan promptly dismissed.

'Enough of that. We're just glad you are here with us and I for one hope this is a place you will come to love – just like we all do. I know your dad has plans to train you up as a farmer.'

Joan noticed Jodie's grimace, misinterpreting it as a reaction to farm work not understanding it could be a reaction to Charlie being referred to as her father.

She continued: 'But of course I'm really keen for you to give Roman a hand, that is if you want to learn more about plants. Poor Roman could do with some help if you can spare the time?'

How could she refuse?

'Of course. I'd be happy to help.' And as she said this Jodie realised that being in this magical place would be no hardship. She was used to pretty gardens. Her grandparents' garden had been well tended and full of beauty. But this was on another level. Here in the flower bed beside them she could recognise some of the daisies much loved by her Nanna, but by and large the other plants and the towering trees, many starting to show their autumnal colours were a mystery to her.

Roman had been standing quietly, leaning on a shovel and observing the others while the conversation flowed around him. He had taken the time to consider this young woman about whom he had heard so much.

He was not fooled by the effort she was making to be polite. The impact of her mother's death was obviously percolating just under the surface. Roman was no stranger to trauma, and he could sense the effort Jodie was making to seem like she was coping. He suspected it wouldn't take much for Jodie's world to come crashing down. This was a vulnerable and traumatised person and if he could do something to help, he would.

'I would appreciate any help you can give me Miss Jodie,' he said in a soft accent that she later learned gave clue to his Polish origins. 'I am weeding today but tomorrow I have to finish planting the spring bulbs. It's slow and tedious work but a helper makes it so much easier.'

Jodie studied Roman as he was speaking. He wasn't a very tall person. Maybe not even her height. Stocky and muscular with the strength of someone used to outdoor physical work. Like Joan his eyes were his best feature. Eyes of a warm dark chocolate that glowed with sincerity. How could she refuse?

'Of course I will help.'

'Excellent. Well, that's all sorted then. Come around tomorrow morning and bring a hat. What time Roman? Nine?'

At his nod Joan continued: 'Nine in the morning it is. Now I'm off to sort out what has gone wrong with the pool filter. Charlie, you said something about an off-colour ewe? Is that where you are headed? Alright then and while you are up at the yards you might want to introduce Jodie to old Copper.'

Joan glanced at Jodie who was looking puzzled. 'Copper is my son Euan's old horse. Euan is off on the mainland studying, so poor old Copper is turned out to pasture. Old but can still be ridden and has perfect manners. Seems to me you will need a horse to ride if you are helping your father with the sheep. He will be perfect for you. Now I must rush. Nice to meet you Jodie. I'm sure you will soon settle in and become part of our family. Too many men here so it will be lovely to have another female. A female human that is. All those ewes don't count!'

And with a wave she was gone leaving a very puzzled Jodie staring at Charlie.

Chapter Ten

A s soon as they were through the gate and back at the truck than Jodie turned to Charlie.

'What was all that about? Now I suppose I'm happy to help in the garden, but what's this with the horse? I've never ridden in my life and I don't think I've even patted a horse. Why should I now?'

Charlie nodded. 'Yes, it came out of left field that one. Typical Joan, she is always one step ahead. Of course, it makes sense that you would need a horse and Copper is perfect. Wait 'til you meet him. You'll fall in love with him like everyone else does. Euan is away on the mainland studying agricultural science and no one else rides poor old Copper. But neither Euan nor his mother would dream of selling him. Copper is family. You'll see. But let's sort out the ewe first.'

The sheep yards were a short distance away further along the dirt track they'd previously travelled. Far enough away to be out of smelling distance from the house. Next to the yards was an enormous wooden shearing shed, raised off the ground so sheep could be penned underneath if the weather was bad before shearing. The last thing you would want before shearing were wet sheep Charlie explained.

And in the adjoining yard they found a miserable ewe.

'Poor dear,' sympathised Charlie. 'Not only does her foot hurt but she is missing the flock.' He climbed the wooden rails then strode over and grabbed the unhappy ewe who was by now even unhappier as Charlie flipped her over and examined the problem foot.

'That's a relief. It now looks much better, and I can see that she can now weight bear. But I think, just to be safe I will give it another spray, leave her in today then we'll turn her out tomorrow.'

He reached into his pocket, removed a small aerosol can and with the ease of long experience, deftly squirted the offending hoof and upended the ewe before she even knew what had happened.

'There you go old girl. You're so much better. So I think a little treat is in store. Some grain perhaps? Hang in there. I'll go get you some.'

Grain dispensed, water trough checked and, after pausing to be sure the ewe was happily munching, they then walked past the woolshed towards another group of buildings.

By now Buster had joined them, having decided there was nothing to be gained by guarding the truck and that all the action was to be had with his master. He trotted beside Charlie, every so often looking up to see if there was something his master wanted him to do. But for now Charlie was focussed on the other human.

'So we're heading to the stables and horse yards. They're not used much these days. But we still have horses turned out in the paddocks behind. There's Copper of course. Also my mare Misty and a child's pony that gets occasional use.'

'Hah! Maybe I should ride that?'

Charlie just snorted. No reply was necessary.

He opened a gate into a yard and ushered Jodie in. To her left she could see a row of stables – three in all that opened into individual yards which then opened into the yard they were in. At the end of the stables was a closed door which Charlie told her held saddles and the accoutrements necessary for horses – brushes, rugs and the like. A large paddock opened up off the yards. And there, up a slight rise stood three horses at ease in the shade of a group of gum trees. Heads down and tails flicking they were totally relaxed.

'There they are. I won't catch them now but I did remember to bring a pocket full of treats, so we'll just say hello and I'll introduce you to Copper.'

'But they're resting. Why should they come near us?'

'You'll see,' Charlie smiled complacently, sure of his powers. It only took one yell and the three heads swung up and around. The grey horse, which Jodie assumed must be the one called Misty, whinnied then started to walk down the hill towards them. She was clearly the boss as the other two fell into line and followed.

Misty was a pretty dapple grey with dark flowing mane and tail. She held her head high, ears pricked as she focussed on the people standing by the yard. Pretty though she was Jodie's eyes were immediately drawn to the horse following close behind. So this was the famous Copper. Looking at him it was clear why he had been given that name. His coat glowed and sparkled with a coppery fire. A white blaze ran down his nose lending distinction to his features and like Misty he also had a darker shade of mane and tail. The shaggy white pony bringing up the rear didn't even rate a glance.

'What do you think?' Charlie glanced across at his open-mouthed daughter.

'Well Misty is beautiful of course. But I've never seen a horse like Copper before. That coat. How does it get to be so iridescent?'

'All his own work I'm afraid. No secret potions. It's just how he's made. And that is him in paddock condition. I'm sometimes tempted to rug him to see if it would get even brighter. But I'm not sure he would appreciate being rugged.'

By now the horses had drawn near and were sniffing both humans.

Charlie put a gentling arm on Jodie.

'Just let them sniff and get to know you. They know me but you are new to them. Hold out your hand and let them sniff you. We'll give them some carrots once they've identified you. That's it. Alright now I'll show you how to give them a carrot and then you can have a go.'

Charlie reached into another of his many pockets and pulled out a handful of carrots which had been chopped into halves. The horses knew carrots when they saw them and all three whickered in anticipation.

'Steady on you guys. You must take turns. No pushing please.'

The horses clearly knew the routine and with precision each gently mouthed a cut carrot from Charlie's flattened palm.

'See that's how it's done. I'll give some to Misty and the pony and you can treat Copper. That way he'll be keen to be caught by you tomorrow.'

'Tomorrow?'

'Yep. We'll use the horses to return the ewe to the flock once you are finished with Roman.'

'But ...but I've never ridden before and he's so tall.'

'Well, you have to start somewhere. Trust me Copper is the best. A prince of horses and once you ride him all other horses will feel inadequate. Look at him snuffling you. I think he has been lonely and misses being useful. He needs to be with a human again. I'd ride him but I often don't have time to ride Misty as it is and she even gets neglected. Don't you miss?' He rubbed under Misty's chin as she leaned into her master.

Jodie tentatively reached out and stroked the satin-like neck of this amazing horse. And to her surprise this giant of a horse not only stood still and let her pat him but turned his head towards her and gently grabbed her hat and dropped it at her feet in the dirt.

'There. I knew he would like you! He wants to play,' laughed Charlie. 'He's a bit of a card. Likes water too. He can turn on the tap in the yard and play with the hose if we're not looking. I totally understand why Euan and his mother cannot bear to part with Copper, but it is such a waste to keep him twiddling his hooves out in the paddock. You being here will be really good for him. I hope you're prepared to give it a go?'

Jodie reached down to retrieve her hat which she promptly placed on her head and stepped away from Copper's questing lips.

'No. Copper that will do. Manners please.' She turned to Charlie and with a smile said 'Arright I'll give it a go. But only to help out Copper mind you. I'd hate to see him lonely.'

With another nudge she could feel her hat being dislodged and once more landing in the dust. If a horse could grin Jodie was sure that was exactly what Copper was now doing!

'Just you wait 'til tomorrow you coppery horse you. Tomorrow there will be no slacking around. You will need to teach me to ride.'

Jodie was feeling so charitable with the world that she didn't object to her father linking his arm with hers as they headed back to the truck. In fact, it may be that she didn't even notice as her thoughts were filled with the joy of bonding with another animal.

***

Dinner that evening was roast lamb – lamb again. But this time flavoured with rosemary and garlic and served with gravy made from the pan drippings. In Jodie's opinion it was a marked improvement on grilled chops. After it had been devoured, the scraps shared with Buster, and the plates washed and cleared away Charlie disappeared to his study. It was sometime before he returned with a large cardboard box which he carefully placed on the coffee table in front of the lounge. Patting the space next to him on the lounge he called Jodie over. She eyed him apprehensively. Sitting next to him was a bit too close for her taste.

'Come on over please. There's something I want to show you. It took me a while to find this box as I'd tucked it away behind a lot of other stuff. Painful memories I suppose.'

Taking a handkerchief out of his pocket, he carefully wiped the dust off the box lid, then gently eased the lid away to reveal a box full of photo albums. Intrigued, as Charlie knew she would be, Jodie drew closer and finally tentatively sat on the lounge next to her father. Charlie reached in to retrieve the first album from the box.

'I'm not sure what order they may be in but here we go.'

He opened the first album, shook his head and put it to one side.

'No. Not that one. That's much later on. Let's try this one. Ah yes,' he smiled. 'This brings back memories. We were so young. Look Jodie. There's your mum. She was such a stunner. This was taken first time I met her at a B&S ball. You know, a Bachelors and Spinsters Ball is the proper name. We were all so drunk that night. Just like at any other B&S. But even so I fell hard for your mum that night and knew I had to find out where she lived. Took a while, but eventually I tracked her down.'

He took one more smiling glance at the photo in his hand and then passed it across to Jodie. Jodie stared down at this photo of two laughing young people with arms entwined grinning at the camera. Their joy with each other clearly obvious. Her mother, so young and almost unrecognisable from the woman she had grown up with. Her young skin unlined, hair glossy with healthy living and a smile bright with happiness. No sign of the bitter woman she had become and the changeable mother Jodie had grown up with.

The young man could be none other than Charlie – much more blonde hair of course, eyes and smile bright with the ecstasy of standing close to this young woman.

More photos were handed over. Photos that tracked the progress of their romance and reflected the fashions of the day, culminating with a stiff wedding photo.

'We were so young. Definitely too young to take on matrimony,' Charlie shook his head as he contemplated the photo of the young couple holding hands and standing in front of a stone church that Jodie identified as being in their village.

'When was this?'

'Let me think. You were born in '63 I think. March? Yes?' He glanced at Jodie who nodded. So he did have an idea of her birthday!

'So I suppose that means we were married in '62. There is a marriage certificate somewhere in my papers if you want to see it. You were what they call a 'honeymoon baby'! Look at us. Not only awfully young, but both of us so uncomfortable. I'd never worn a suit before. It was a hire suit and I was glad to give it back. And your mum- well she looks a bit like a plastic doll – all hairspray and wearing a stiff satin wedding dress inspired by some celebrity wedding no doubt. It was a happy day – I think, but all I remember was the stress and worry of saying the right thing and not embarrassing anyone. Terrified of having to give a speech. Out of my comfort zone, I guess. And then you came along. There must be some photos of baby you here somewhere,' said as he dug further into the box.

'Ah, here is your mum – almost at term. Those tent maternity dresses were an eyesore. Not flattering at all. You were a dainty baby – 7 pound or thereabouts if I recall. But looking at this photo with your mother wearing that hideous tentlike dress you'd be forgiven for thinking she was about to give birth to an elephant.'

And certainly it wasn't a flattering photo. Donna was wearing an elaborately flowing navy spotted dress, the many metres of fabric flowing from a yoke just below a pointed white collar. No wonder her mother looked unhappy in that photo. Imagine having to be seen like that in public. She handed the photo back to Charlie who promptly returned it to the box.

'Let's never look at that one again. I imagine your mother would want us to burn it but it's history which for good or bad – or bad fashion taste – we should not forget.' He ferreted further and pulled out a pink album entitled *Baby's First Album*.

'Ah, here it is. Your first few months of life. Let's see,' and he started to turn the pages.

The first page displayed a birth notice that must have been cut from the local paper announcing the birth of a baby daughter to Donna and Charlie Wise of Bronte Rivulet. And granddaughter of Carol and Joe Daley of the same village. The next page was the handwritten notes of baby Wise's first days of life in the hospital when every feed, wee and bowel movement were closely monitored. Charlie turned another page.

'Ah here are the photos – look at you! Just born. I wasn't meant to be there but somehow the staff took pity on me and let me sneak in. So that's why there are lots of photos.'

The pages were turned slowly, as the two of them with heads close together exclaimed at the images of the baby and her young parents.

'Looking at you now and I can see hints in those photos of the woman you've become. Born with very little hair it soon shone gold and you've kept that fairness. Your eyes were blue in those early days, but they quickly changed. You were an easy baby which was just as well as your mum couldn't settle to motherhood. Luckily by then we had moved back in with Joe and Carol and they really stepped up and took over night feeds.'

He sighed deeply and shook his head. 'Maybe if I had been older I would have hung around. But we - Joe, Carol and I - thought my presence was just making things worse with Donna and that it would be for your own good if you had a more settled mother. Maybe that was the wrong call. Maybe I should have insisted on taking you with me. But people seem to think a child is always better with their mother. Even one like Donna. And I couldn't take you away from Carol and Joe.'

'So, I left and got as far away as I could – although I couldn't leave Tasmania. It was the hardest thing I have ever done but I thought it was the best for you. And your mum too I suppose. But by then our relationship was pretty much over. Carol and Joe would keep in touch. They'd tell me what you were up to and send photos. See, here are some of your school photos. First day of school. What a cutey you were. And I was so proud of you growing up and succeeding with your running and your schoolwork. You don't know how many times I was tempted to sneak in and take you away from that dump you were living in and bring you up here. But Joe said you were happy. Were you?'

'Was I happy? Probably not. At school it was hard – so many bullies but I managed to survive and keep them in check. I had Will you see and he would protect me if people got too mean. One kind friend. And I had Pepper.'

At this Jodie's voice choked and tears fell.

'If not for Pepper life would have been totally dire. I owe him so much and look what happened. I let him down.'

The sobs, for so long held tightly under the surface now erupted and there was nothing for it but to ride the flow of grief to its conclusion.

Charlie reached an arm and pulled her close.

'I'm sorry I didn't meet Pepper. But Joe has told me how much that little dog loved you. How he looked out for you every afternoon and didn't let you out of his sight except when you were at school. It's a wonder he didn't try to sneak into the school grounds.'

A watery chuckle greeted this comment.

'Well he did in the early days but Pop put a lot of work into getting him to understand that he had to stay with them during school hours. To start with they used to walk me to school and be there at the 3 o'clock bell and somehow Pepper came to understand he couldn't come in with me. He was very smart you see.'

'Yes, and smart enough to know he had to protect his family.'

Sometime later after emotions had settled and as Jodie once more flipped through the photo albums, she paused, as a question formed in her mind.

'What I don't understand is why you have all these albums here and not with us back at Nanna and Pop's place?'

'Well, you see. I needed something to remember you by. And even to remind me of the good times there were with Donna. Trust me there were good times – especially in the early days and then later …lots of bad times. So I stole the albums. Maybe Carol and Joe guessed where they had gone but they never said anything. When I left I took nothing but these albums and my clothes, hopped in the car and drove as far as I could that night. I stayed at a pub at Campbelltown and got talking to some people in the bar. One of them, a farm manager of another property near here in Cressy, said he thought the Frasers were looking for someone to help the current manager who was close to retiring. Next day I drove to this property and the rest is history. I knew a little bit about farming having done some shearing contracting but there was so much to learn. Luckily the Frasers were very generous and cut me a lot of slack. And that's why when Alastair died I had to step up. I owed the family so much.'

Charlie yawned and stretched.

'All this talk about the past is so exhausting. I think I'm for bed.'

He gestured at the box and the albums, some of which were still scattered on the coffee table.

'They're all yours. After all this is your history. Your story and they deserve to be with you. Goodnight Jodie. Sweet dreams.'

'Goodnight Cha…..Dad.'

Somehow that term Dad rolled easily off her tongue. The look of delight on her father's face when he heard her speak made saying that word all worthwhile. Why, she wondered, had she stubbornly refused to acknowledge Charlie as her father? Was it because she felt so hurt that he didn't try to fight harder for his daughter or was it all those years of conditioning by her mother to regard her father as a loser? She suspected she would never know, but for now it felt good to put all that hurt behind her and focus on calling this man the name he clearly yearned for – Dad.

Thoughtfully she gathered the remaining albums and placed them in the box. There would be time to study them later when she wasn't so tired. Her father was right. All this discussion had been so exhausting. Yet somehow life changing. Understanding her past had given her a new perspective on herself and the people around her. Teeth cleaned and pyjamas on she then scrambled into bed and reached across to the bedside table to turn out the reading light.

But before she did so a thought occurred to her. Jodie gazed around the room as if seeing it with fresh eyes. This wasn't a spare room prepared for the occasional visitor. She realised that this must be a room prepared for a daughter in the hope that one day that daughter might come to visit – or stay. Such a girly room with a brass bed, multiple cushions, a quilt in matching fabric, a pink light shade and pink, mauve and blue floral curtains. A younger Jodie would have been delighted to sleep here. The 16-year-old Jodie, whilst appreciating the thought that had gone into the décor, found it a bit too young for her taste. Yet she knew she would never say so to a father who must have long dreamed of having a little girl staying with him. Thinking of those lost years hurt her to the quick – when he could only follow his daughter's progress through instalments of photos received periodically in the mail. But that was the past and as Jodie again reached for the light and this time turned it out she made a promise to herself that she would find space in her life for her father. Maybe not a big space but somehow, she suspected he would be happy if she just shared anything with him.

Chapter Eleven

The next morning Jodie woke to what had become the usual morning sounds: the chirp of the sparrows under the eaves accompanied by her father's tuneless whistle as he clattered kibble into Buster's metal feed bowl. Then the call for Buster which really was not necessary as Jodie could hear him scratching at the back door and whining with anticipation for his breakfast treat.

She knew that the next sound would be a soft call to her to see if she was awake and ready for a cup of tea. At this time of day a grunt was all that Jodie was capable of yet it seemed to be enough. Shortly after there was a quiet tap on her door and her father appeared with a steaming mug of tea – flavoured with milk and sugar just as she liked it.

'Here you go miss. It's still early so you have plenty of time to get ready. Don't forget that Roman is expecting you this morning. I've got to rush now – some issue with the tractor. But I'll come and find you about midday and we can sort out that ewe and you can have your first riding lesson.'

With that he quietly left the room leaving Jodie to stretch and roll over to reach the mug of tea. That first mouthful was bliss. The perfect wake-up treat. The second was even better.

She could hear her father now on the porch talking to the dog as he prepared to leave. The stomp as he settled his work boots on his feet. The flap as he shook out his Driza Bone coat and the whistle as he called Buster to follow. As if Charlie ever needed to whistle Buster to follow. He was as good a shadow as Pepper had ever been.

The thought of Pepper once again filled Jodie with an immense feeling of loss and sadness. And thoughts of how she had been responsible for his death. Why had she not shut the bedroom door like she had always done. If only... If only...

But there was no escaping it. That had been a bad night and she did play a part in Pepper's death. Yet that little dog was only doing what he had always done. Guarding his family and now there was nothing she could do to bring him back except preserve his memory and remember him with love. It struck her then that there were very few thoughts about her mother. In fact she felt quite relaxed not thinking of her at all. Jodie wondered if this was a sign that she, Jodie, was somehow lacking. Shouldn't any reasonable person mourn a parent?

Nope, she decided. Not that mother! Instantly energised she jumped out of bed and dressed for the day. Dressed appropriately for outdoor work – old jeans, checked shirt and windcheater. The day promised to be warm and sunny, but she could tell it was still autumn cool.

A further cup of tea drunk and several slices of toast hastily consumed and she was then ready to trek along the track that traversed the House Paddock. A slight delay as she raced back to locate a hat and feeling rather pleased with herself Jodie arrived at the side gate just on 9am.

This side gate, which once must have been a thing of beauty with ornate metal work in a lacy pattern was now mottled with rust and down on its luck – literally down as it had fallen off its bottom hinge and rested on the earth. It took a big shove to make it move sufficiently for Jodie to squeeze through. But once through all was forgotten as Jodie breathed in the clean air redolent of the fragrance of flowers and heard the chiming sounds of small birds fluttering in the bushes. Her feelings sorrow and tension immediately evaporated and her shoulders relaxed as she felt the garden infuse her with its magic.

How to find Roman in this overgrown and tangled space that seemed to go forever? Using the house as her point of reference Jodie tried to remember where they had wandered yesterday. It was confusing as they had entered by another gate. She remembered there had been bee hives somewhere. If she could find them then it might be possible to trace her path. She paused and listened intently. Yes, there underneath the sounds of chirping was another sound. A constant hum which must be the bees. She set off in the general direction of the hum following a path edged with rose bushes and to her satisfaction came across a clearing in which three bee hives were installed. Beyond the clearing she could see glimpses of the house and set off determinedly in that direction.

And then the sound of whistling and Roman appeared steering a wheelbarrow along a gravel path. He spotted her, stopped and waved.

'Good morning, Miss Jodie. Just in time. I'm heading out the front to plant tulips there. I was hoping you would be here to help me. As you can see I have an awful lot of bulbs to plant.'

He gestured towards the contents of the wheelbarrow which seemed to be crammed with netting bags each containing about six or so shiny brown bulbs. Tulips, Jodie guessed.

'Happy to help. I've never grown tulips before, but I suppose they're like other bulbs. Pretty much look after themselves.'

'Well, they like this cold climate and so long as they get the right soil and sun they seem to cope with most things. The Boss likes me to lift them at the start of summer. Me, I'd leave them in the ground. But she is in charge, so I do as I'm told.'

Roman twinkled and smiled as he said this – his brown eyes shining as if he was sharing a major confidence with a co-conspirator. By now they had emerged onto a driveway that ran along the side of the house. Close up the house – even the side of the house was impressive – built of honey coloured stone it extended for quite a way until the two storeys ended and a smaller outbuilding connected behind.

Jodie's attention however was focussed ahead and as they turned the corner she gave a gasp as the considered the front of the house now on display. She had never seen such a place before. The houses in Bronte Rivulet, although often built of stone were small with no pretentions of grandeur. This building, especially when seen from the front, appeared to be proclaiming to the world that it was important and worthy of respect.

Her gasp of amazement attracted Roman's attention and they both paused. He watched Jodie as she gazed upwards, taking in the ornate portico, the many twelve paned glass windows and the attic windows protruding from the third storey.

'It's really something, isn't it?' he said smiling at Jodie.

'I've never seen anything like it. And people live here? It's not a museum or a palace?'

Roman chuckled. 'It's just a very grand family home. Built by some Scotsman years ago who wanted to make a statement about how important he and his family were. Built by convicts most likely so he didn't have to spend a lot of money making this statement to the world.'

Maybe built by my ancestors, Jodie thought but she didn't say anything. Speaking about one's convict ancestors was still something rarely mentioned in public although she suspected many in Tasmania shared such ancestry. Being descended from free settlers was considered a thing of pride. Being descended from convicts was apparently a shameful matter. Yet as far as Jodie was concerned the fact of surviving those early days should be celebrated regardless of the person's origin.

Roman moved on and pointed to a freshly prepared garden bed in the middle of a circular drive at the front of the house.

'Here. This is where we are to plant the tulips. It will take a little while as we have so many bulbs. I prepared the soil the other day, but there is a system we have to follow. I will drag channels in the soil and then we will stand the tulips pointy end up at a space this distant.' Here he held out his hands a certain distance as if to demonstrate the gap.

'There is a colour scheme to follow – of course.' Roman smiled. 'Don't worry. It will all become clear. I will finish the prep if you would please put the different colours into separate piles on the ground over there. You will see that the labels describe which colour is what and then we will start once I've prepared the channels starting from the middle. Maybe I will plant and you can hand me the right coloured bulbs.'

Jodie had never expected something so repetitive would end up being strangely satisfying. Yet it was. Sorting out the tulips gave her an opportunity to consider the colours – orange, red and purple. She commented to Roman that it all sounded rather bright.

'I thought tulips would be pink or white. Yet these are going to be rather vivid.'

'Yes, that is so. Last year we did pink and white. You and I will plant last year's bulbs out the back in big pots in the courtyard. But this year The Boss wants colour – lots of colour. I hope it isn't too much. But we will soften it with some ground covers which I'm bringing on in the greenhouse. A bit of white in the ground cover – violas and Sweet Alice. You can also help me with that if you want?'

The planting process passed fairly efficiently. Starting in the centre of the bed Roman planted the first colour – red. Each bulb was passed across by Jodie who now stood carefully on the churned soil. Then Roman marked a number of spoke-like rows from centre to edge.

'Just like the spokes of a wheel' he said.' We will plant lines of red along these spokes and then we are going to infill the orange or purple between the spokes. It will be interesting to see. Maybe too interesting! And maybe next year we will be back to pink and white! I certainly hope so as I suspect this colour scheme will only produce headaches and not applause.' Roman smiled at his humour.

At 11o'clock Roman paused and stretched, his arms pressing into his back at waist height.

'Aah that feels better. Time for a break. Come on this way. There's a nice spot over near the tennis court. I brought a thermos of tea and some cake and two mugs. Time for morning tea.'

Jodie hadn't thought to bring anything and immediately apologised. Roman striding ahead gave a funny noise and shrugged.

'No need to apologise. I've already allowed for you. Two pieces of cake and two mugs. It's a treat to have someone to share the workload with.'

Once settled on the bench and basking in the warmth of the sunshine Roman focussed on pouring the tea and opening the container that held the cake.

'Black tea I'm afraid. But the cake is good. Cooked by The Boss yesterday. She often shares with us.'

The cake was indeed good. Fudgy and covered with a thick chocolate buttercream. Just how Jodie liked it. She licked her fingers and thoughtfully considered her tea. No milk and no sugar. Not how she liked it. Yet to refuse would be rude and she was thirsty. So maybe she could distract herself by asking questions and drink the tea quickly – a bit like taking medicine.

'Roman?'

'Mmmm?' said Roman indistinctly. His mouth was full of cake.

'Would you please tell me a bit about yourself. I'm curious as to why you ended up here on this farm? I can tell you've come from somewhere overseas and Tassie is so isolated. What made you think of this place? And this farm come to that?'

'Ah Miss Jodie. It's a long story but maybe it's something I can start on today – Chapter One so to speak and we can add to it each morning tea. Would you like that?'

Jodie nodded. Another way to take her mind of her gloomy thoughts that morning. And if Roman told her a bit every day, then that would give her something other than Pepper to think about and something to look forward to each day.

Roman swallowed the last of his cake, took a slurp of his tea and looking across at his young companion smiled.

'Now let me see. Where should I start?'

'At the beginning?'

'Let's see then. I was born many decades ago. No point saying the exact year as it will make me feel way too old. But let's say before the Second World War. I was still a young lad when Poland was invaded by the Nazis and at first because I was so young I didn't realise the significance of what was happening. I suppose I assumed life would continue the way it had always been. We lived in a small village – my mother, father and older sister, Anna. My father taught at the village school and my mother looked after all of us. It was a good life. Lots of freedom to race around the countryside with my friends – doing all the usual things. You know climbing trees, building forts and fishing with mixed success. Of course, like everyone in the village my parents were avid gardeners and maybe that's where I inherited my love of growing things. My father would focus on growing vegetables, and my mother would be passionate about ensuring the front garden was awash with flowers except of course in winter when it was bitterly cold and snow or slush was everywhere. We weren't wealthy but what with father's teaching salary and the food he grew we got by. It was all I knew and I was happy...' his voice trailed off as Roman looked down at his dirt-stained hands.

'And then?'

Roman looked up and gazed at his companion, so unaffected by war, yet in her own way already affected by a deep trauma.

'It all changed and in a terrible way. You will forgive me if I skip recalling those terrible years that followed. These days I've found it best to focus on the good times and push the worst away. Suffice it to say that what you see before you is the last surviving member of my family. You see, my mother was Jewish and in those times that meant a death sentence for us all. Somehow my father managed to smuggle me away and I eventually ended up in a refugee camp in England. That's all I want to say about those years. When I recall my family I try to remember the good times – my mother's cooking, my father's baritone voice as he sang with my sister as she played the piano after dinner. Those are the memories I treasure, and no-one can ever take them away from me. I held onto those memories during the dark days and then once I arrived in Tasmania to start a new life. I knew I owed it to them to make the best life I could and not to be weighed down by sorrow.'

Roman glanced sideways at Jodie. Did she understand what he was trying to say. That sorrow must not be allowed to overwhelm her life. To create a future it was necessary to first heal and accept the past.

'And then?'

'And then we will move onto Chapter Two some other time. How I moved from England to this place on the other side of the world.' He laughed at Jodie's impatient expression. 'Patience Miss Jodie. We have work to do. Those tulips won't plant themselves!'

The next task was to plant last season's tulips in the pots located in the courtyard – wherever that was. Jodie pushed the wheelbarrow and followed Roman back along the gravel driveway along the side of the house, past the outbuildings until they reached a U-shaped courtyard on the other side of the house. Paved with stone and sheltered from the prevailing winds by the house and its extending wings this clearly was a popular space as was indicated by the many chairs and dog beds grouped around a large outdoor table.

'Here are the pots,' said Roman as he pointed to two half wine barrels on either side of a double door.

'Pots. You're kidding me! They're enormous', laughed Jodie. Never having seen wine barrels before she was amazed that something so large could accommodate small bulbs.'

'Pots they are and today we are going to cram so many tulips into them that they will look spectacular come spring. Come, there's lots to do and your father will soon be here.'

With a sinking feeling Jodie realised that this morning's interlude had just been that. An interlude and the reality of being with her father would soon resume. Although her attitude towards her father was changing it was still early days and she felt reluctant to spend too much time with him. Much better he was away doing farm chores all day.

'I can come back and help you again tomorrow?' she asked anxiously as they both randomly pressed tulip bulbs into the prepared soil.

'Of course. I would be grateful if you had time to help me every morning. Mind you, some chores are just that – chores and are not too exciting. Such as pruning, mulching and burning off all those trimmings.'

'A bonfire! Ooh I'd like that,' said Jodie, her voice rising an octave.

Roman smiled. It was easy to forget how young Jodie was as her demeanour could often be so solemn and self-contained. But then, in an instant her age would be revealed with her comments like just now and her enthusiasm for playing with fire – like all young children.

A cough alerted them to the approach of someone. Then the sound of a match being struck and the aroma of tobacco wafted towards them.

'What a co-incidence. We speak of fire and here's the smell of something burning,' joked Roman. 'Good day to you Charlie,' said Roman as Charlie strolled into the courtyard.

Charlie drew on his cigarette and took his time to exhale a long stream of smoke before speaking.

'G'day Roman. I hope my girl has been a help this morning. Will we make a gardener of her?' asked Charlie with a smile.

'Absolutely. I have got so much done with Jodie's help. I might even be able to take the afternoon off as I've pretty much caught up with the backlog.'

At Jodie's anxious look he continued. 'But I will still need Jodie to lend a hand tomorrow if you can spare her. We need to start the mulching and that is a two-person job.'

Charlie considered Jodie who eagerly nodded her consent. Whatever magic Roman had worked it appeared to have been successful as was evidenced by the enthusiastic recounting of her morning's experiences during the walk back to Charlie's utility.

'Well there.' Said Charlie, 'I've learnt a lot from you just now. I never knew anything about tulips but now I feel like I've had a crash course. And it sounds like I will be learning all about mulching tomorrow. And look at your hands! Proper farmer hands now.'

Jodie glanced down at her grimy hands and considered the dirt ingrained under her nails. Not that it mattered. Everyone on the farm – even The Boss had equally disgusting nails and hands. She considered her father's hands resting carelessly on the steering wheel.

Ingrained with dirt they were also cracked and calloused. Maybe that future waited her. She gave a mental shrug. She really didn't care, although she suspected Cousin Bonnie would be horrified.

'Where are we off to now dad?' asked Jodie. She was finding with practice that calling Charlie dad was getting easier. Although she was still not sure she thought of him as her father.

'Off to check the ewe and if she is well enough you and I can escort her back to her mob. Maybe you might like to ride Copper as we take her back to the others.'

Jodie's eyes flared in alarm, and she took a deep breath. Yesterday the thought of a riding lesson sometime in the future had not seemed so daunting. But now she was not so sure. How could she explain the terror that engulfed her at the thought of trying to learn a new skill even if it involved a horse who she had been assured was a gentle giant. Couldn't she just walk the ewe back or even better run behind her. Even though she knew it wasn't in the ewe's best interests she half hoped they would arrive to find the ewe at death's door.

But it wasn't to be. When they arrived at the sheep yards it was apparent that the ewe was in excellent health and baaing frantically when she recognised the provider of sheep grain.

'Hey, old girl,' greeted Charlie as he hoisted himself over the rails and in one smooth movement once again tipped the ewe over before she knew what was happening.

'Mmmm. Not quite sorted but pretty close. Another day and then you will be good to go.' With a glance at Jodie he continued. 'Sorry Jodie. No riding lesson today. Maybe tomorrow, but for now you can help me feed the horses and maybe give them a brush.'

Charlie was no fool and he could see by Jodie's sudden relaxed posture that his suspicions were correct. Maybe, in his enthusiasm to include his daughter in his life he had rushed things. So many missed years to make up for. It was possible he had failed to recognise how much the sudden changes in Jodie's new environment had impacted on her. He should not forget how those recent traumatic events still resonated.

It was time to slow down. Clearly time spent with Roman was a good thing. Maybe time caring for the horses might be enough? But what else? Going to school was not an option. Jodie had already made it clear that her school days were never to be repeated. That she was not open to even trying out a new school. Maybe he would discuss this with The Boss? After all she must have encountered similar issues when her husband died and she had the twins to raise. Yes. That was a good idea. Although Jodie could do with a friend. A pity the farm hand's children were so young. What about Bonnie? Now there's a thought! Perhaps he could convince Jodie to invite her for a visit?

He turned and glanced at Jodie who was looking steadfastly ahead and lost in her thoughts.

'Hey. I've been thinking. Do you reckon Bonnie might like to visit? Not much to do here I suppose but it's a change from Devonport and she might like to see the lambs which will be born shortly.'

'You mean it?' Jodie swivelled around to gaze at her father. Her excitement palpable.

'Of course. That is if you want to. You'll have to entertain her. I'm way too busy.'

'I'll ring her tonight. Thanks dad. What a great idea.'

'Yes, it was,' said her father full of satisfaction as to his genius.

Chapter Twelve

From Sheep Heaven
Baaaa

Hey Bonnie

It was so good to talk to you tonight. It feels like ages since we had a decent chat and I can't wait for you to visit. Do you reckon you can get her soon? Very soon would be great – as soon as possible would be even better but I guess I will fit in with your other social commitments?

I can't believe you dumped that guy. He sounded so amazing. Did you dump him for someone else? And what else are you doing? Are you still planning on moving to Hobart? And what does your dad think about that?

I have so many questions but I guess they will have to keep 'til you turn up here. And good news you will have your own bedroom! But if you want to relive old times I can always drag my mattress into your room.

There's so much to tell you about life here. It's pretty ordinary but heaps better than I expected. I really thought my banishment to sheep Siberia would do my head in but so far it's turned out to be good/ average. I'm learning lots from Roman the gardener, and he's quite funny. It's good to be outside in the big garden. Wait 'til you see it. You could get lost in it and they would have to send out a search party – or follow a trail of breadcrumbs as is done in the best fairy tales.

Dad is ok, I guess. See, I call him dad now. He has presented me with incontrovertible evidence that he really is my dad in the form of photo albums. I'll show them to you. OMG the fashions in those photos! They're appalling. And the hair styles. Gross. But the photo albums do prove he was once part of my life and really is my dad. So I'm working hard on calling him dad and trying to think of him that way.

Great news about getting your licence. Will you be driving yourself here? I hope so. Maybe we can then go exploring and possibly find some decent clothes for me? I'm getting a bit sick of wearing the same checked shirts and grotty jeans every day. Ring me once you work out when you will be here and I'll make sure I'm on the front porch waiting for you and not doing farm chores out in the wilds.

I can't wait to see you. So much to talk about and with a bit of luck you will be here when the lambs arrive. Then it's all hands on deck to feed the orphans. But it's worth it. They're so cute. Pity they grow up to be boring smelly sheep.

Lots of love
Your Farmgirl Cousin Jodie xxxx

***

'Come in off the veranda Jodie. It's getting dark and way too cold to linger. I'm sure we'll see Bonnie's car lights when she turns off the road. You'll catch your death. Anyway, Buster will bark as soon as she gets close. You know what he's like.'

'Alright then. Don't fret,' Jodie grumbled as she reluctantly came through the door, banging it hard behind her. All this waiting was getting to her, as was her father. She just hoped Bonnie was still going to turn up and not leave her to spend another evening watching mindless current affairs shows or even worse Aussie Rules on the tv. She needed some likeminded company – and she needed it now!

As if on cue she heard the faint sound of a car engine and then the dog started to sound off with excitement as a visitor pulled up at the front gate. Buster so loved a visitor.

'She's here! Finally!' Jodie's excitement even transmitted to her father as they both raced outside. Bonnie's reception couldn't have been any more welcoming. An overexcited black and tan working dog practically jumping over the gate as Charlie raced to restrain him and Jodie waving frantically at Bonnie indicating where to park. Then the process of unloading her small red car, hugs, kisses and exclamations. All talking at once.

'Yay, Bonnie. You made it at last. I feel like I've been waiting for hours. Here, let me carry that bag.'

'Nice car Bonnie,' said Charlie. 'They're a good make. How was the trip?'

'A car. Hurrah,' interrupted Jodie. 'Now you can take me somewhere else. An adventure!'

With a laugh Bonnie grabbed both Charlie and Jodie into a group hug and pecked both on the cheek.

'Hey you guys. Calm down. You'd think I was royalty the fuss you're making. Not that I'm complaining. And hello to you too, Buster,' she said looking down at the dog who was squeezing in between them. 'It's great to be here. Not that I can see much. It being a bit too dark already. Gotta love Tassie winters – dark early and dark late. I can't wait to see the place in the morning.'

'There's really not much to see' grumbled Jodie. 'It's just one big windy plain full of fluffy balls of wool.'

'Don't listen to her Bonnie,' said Charlie as he hoisted up her two suitcases and pointed the way up the path to the front door. 'It's actually rather beautiful.' At Jodie's scoffing sound he added: 'alright then. Bleakly beautiful in winter. But soon, very soon when spring peeps through, the pasture is emerald green, dotted with tiny white fluff ball lambs. Really pretty. Come inside. The fire's lit and dinner is almost ready. Jodie has cooked a lamb roast. One of her specialities.'

'Funny that,' scoffed Jodie. 'Imagine me getting to specialise in lamb roasts at this place of all places. What a surprise. But this way. Your bedroom is up this corridor next to my bedroom. Or we can share just like the old days.'

The two bedrooms were up a corridor near the main bathroom and some distance from Charlie's room. After depositing Bonnie's luggage in the spare bedroom Charlie left them to it. Not that they noticed him slipping out of the room as the two girls were fixated on each other. Already Bonnie had bounced on the bed and pronounced it *adequate*. Jodie pulled the small corner chair closer and regarded her cousin.

Bonnie had always seemed so much more sophisticated to Jodie. But now she seemed even more so. The black clothes – velvet jeans and ruffled top, the pierced ears, the heavy make-up with her hair cascading in elegant ringlets down her back made Jodie conscious of her own inadequacies.

'Hey. I love your hair. And the red colour. Is that permanent?'

'This?' Bonnie with careless fingers caressed a ringlet that fell across her shoulder. 'Everyone is getting a perm these days and I thought I should try one. And the colour is meant to make my eyes *pop*. What do you think?'

What did Jodie think? She had no idea. As far as she was concerned Bonnie inhabited a different world. It had always been like this since the first time they had met. Sophisticated and confident. Words that Jodie knew so didn't apply to her. But maybe, one day with lots of exposure to her glamorous cousin, some of it might rub off. She wasn't too fussy – even a little bit would do.

'Well, I think you look amazing and I would love hair like yours.'

Bonnie critically assessed her cousin. At least her hair was long. Tied back in one thick plait it owed nothing to the latest fashion. But it was thick and healthy and still remained blonde with caramel depths. Maybe she could suggest a new style. But her clothes! Pure country hick. Reaching out she clasped Jodie's hands, turned them over and closely inspected them.

'I can see I am here not a moment too soon. You poor dear. How did it get so bad? I suppose these hands are the result of hard labour. Our ancestors would be proud of you, but as far as I'm concerned this has to change. Starting tomorrow we will work to revive these poor hands, soak and scrub off the dirt. A bit like that detergent commercial where they soak the hands in dishwashing detergent. Maybe we should try that first? What fun. I can be your very own beautician!'

What a difference a visitor can make thought Charlie as he watched his daughter relax into giggles over dinner. Bonnie was in fine form teasing her cousin and challenging Charlie.

'I suppose you might be a sort of uncle, but I think I will call you Charlie. Alright?'

'Of course. Whatever you like Bonnie. Just so long as the two of you stop ganging up on me and show me some respect as the elder of this household,' laughed Charlie.

'No way,' said Bonnie, as Jodie almost choked with laughter.

The laughter continued throughout dinner. Charlie and Bonnie vied with each other to see who could tell the best jokes. Some were funny and some, mostly told by Charlie were so awful they were almost funny. All agreed the roast lamb was delicious. Even Jodie conceded it was alright for lamb.

After dinner they clustered around the fire and played board games – starting with Scrabble and ending with Monopoly. The rules were rather fluid, the choice of words used in Scrabble creative, the allegations of cheating constant and the laughter non-stop. So much so the Jodie's cheeks felt sore from laughter. The evening ended when Charlie after giving a massive yawn decreed it to be bedtime.

'You young ones can continue to party but that's it for me. I need to hit the sack. We have to move the ewes that are close to lambing to another more sheltered paddock. So I'll be up early. What do you two plan to do?'

Jodie gazed across at Bonnie, who raised questioning eyebrows.

'Well dad I'm not sure. I was going to pop over to see if Roman needed a hand so long as Bonnie can cope with a bit of time in the garden. I hope you can? It's the most amazing garden I've ever seen. What do you reckon Bonnie?'

'Sure. And maybe you can give me a bit of a guided tour after that Jodie?'

'Of course. Not that there's much to see. Just paddocks. But I could take you to the horses. They like a carrot and a bit of a brush.'

'Deal. So long as we can sleep in!'

'Silly. You're on a farm now. There's no such thing as sleeping in!'

***

As predicted the girls stirred early although not as early as Charlie. The sounds of his departure, the barking of Buster and the distant crows of the rooster all combined to be a better alarm than any clock.

Jodie who as promised had moved her mattress into Bonnie's room woke first. She stretched and yawned then reached for her discarded rolled up socks and threw them at Bonnie, accurately landing them on Bonnie's face.

'Eeew. What was that!' Bonnie's hand reached out from under the covers and grabbed the sock bundle. 'Really? Is that the way to wake your beloved cousin? A gentle tap on the cheek or a whispered hello would be more than enough. Is this the way to treat a visitor?'

A pillow was hurled in response and then the situation descended into chaos. Pillows, clothing and even the odd soft toy were hurled in abandon until both girls collapsed in laughter.

'Oh, I so missed you,' said Jodie as she wiped tears of laughter from her eyes. 'It's all so serious here. Everyone's nice of course and polite – a bit like they don't want to upset me. But there's no one to laugh with.'

'Then I got here in the nick of time before you descended into total seriousness. After all the one thing I specialise in is frivolity. Or so my father says. So I will do my absolute best to make every day as silly as possible. But first I need something to eat. What have you got?'

Jodie put her finger under her chin as if to mime thinking. Breakfast was generally rather basic but maybe with the assistance of her growing cookbook library (thanks Nanna), she could think of something.

'On today's menu I can offer you toast, tea and toast, tea or maybe pancakes? I've never made pancakes before, but I have a recipe. We could give it a go I suppose.'

'You're on!'

By the time they had finished the meal the kitchen was a total disaster. The girls surveyed the mess in wonderment.

'How could we have made such a mess for only one meal?' said Bonnie.

'No idea. Just being creative I guess. Still it was worth it,' said Jodie. 'I never realised pancakes were so easy. I think I might make them every day. We haven't got long 'til we have to meet Roman. I'm dressed – or near as – so I'll do a quick wash up and that will give you time to get ready.'

Soon after the girls left the house most of the dishes washed and left to dry and they headed out the gate across the House Paddock towards the Big House. Bonnie, who had arrived in the dark looked around taking in the view.

'It's not as bad as I imagined from your description. Sure it's a big wide plain – but it's a grassy plain and the hills on either side are rather pretty with the gum trees. And I can hear lots of birds. Look! Those cockatoos are heading our way.'

They paused and considered the flock of white cockatoos who were rising with a screech from the hillside.

'So many. Maybe fifty and so noisy. Where are they off to?'

The noise as they flew overhead was overwhelming. Almost ear splitting. It was as if they were calling to each other and urging themselves along. The birds wheeled around and headed up the valley.

'It's possible they're heading to the where the sheep are. If dad has put some grain out for the ewes the cockatoos will be after it. I guess they get hungry too.'

They soon reached the side gate and after a bit of a struggle they managed to open the gate sufficiently wide to squeeze through.

'Oh my,' said Bonnie panting with exertion and as she wiped the rust from her hands onto her jeans. 'Is this gate historic? A family treasure perhaps? Is that why it is still here? Has anyone thought of a new gate?' she smiled at her own humour.

'Hah! It's a farm. There's always something else more important that needs mending. And I suspect I'm the only one that uses this gate these days. Dad usually drives to the back gate.'

'Listen to you! You've turned into a proper farm girl, dirty nails and all! I can see I need to rescue you before you are totally lost to farm life. It will be a challenge but I'm up to it! No time to lose.'

Then, having entered through the gate and after catching her first glimpse of the garden Bonnie paused and continued: 'Then again. No rush. Maybe I should just do some research.'

She turned to Jodie: 'Seriously Jodie, this is gorgeous. What a place! Is this garden for real. I can see a tennis court and the cutest little summer house. And are those bee hives over there? And what is that big building I can see hiding behind all those bushes?'

'That's the Big House.'

'Well, I can see why it has that name. Such an original name I don't think!'

Bonnie grabbed her cousin's hand.

'Come on. I want to see the rest. What else is there in this place?'

'There's a pool over that way and more garden than I've ever seen. But we really need to find Roman. He's expecting us. Maybe he's out the front. You can explore later while I help Roman.'

'Oh no. I'm here to help.'

By now they were on the side driveway and heading towards the front. Bonnie, eyes wide in amazement, had been reduced to silence. A welcome silence as far as Jodie was concerned. In her opinion the magic of the garden revealed itself when she was quiet and allowed the space for the birds and wildlife to be heard. The wrens that flittered in the bushes and trilled their hearts out, the rabbits that hid in the shadows and the occasional wallaby that would dash from out of the garden all combined to cast a spell unlike any Jodie had ever seen.

In the silence she could hear the sound of tuneless whistling that she identified as a distinctive sound that only Roman could make.

'Come on. This way,' she said grabbing Bonnie by the elbow.

They eventually tracked Roman down by the front of the house where he was busy trimming the edges. Bonnie's eyes were saucer wide as she took in the impressive portico that framed the front entrance and her silence continued as she was seemingly lost for words.

Introductions made; polite conversation exchanged, then tasks were allocated. Roman was not one to waste time when so much needed to be done and he had helpers on hand. He needed to get maximum effort from them before they disappeared. He knew young ones didn't like to linger.

'I will continue to cut back this edging and if you two could make a start on the roses that would be a great help. Jodie knows already how to do it so perhaps you can show Bonnie here what to do. The necessary equipment is in the garden shed out the back. And please put the prunings in the wheelbarrow. I will come and join you once I'm finished here. Got it?' he said in a tone that indicated he assumed they had.

'No worries Roman,' smiled Jodie. 'Come on Bonnie. To work! And you'll be pleased to know there are gardening gloves you can use.'

Whilst Jodie had already received a lesson in rose pruning it was soon clear that Bonnie had no idea nor indeed any interest in learning. This Jodie accepted with a shrug and set her to pulling out the weeds in the garden. Not that she did much. Bonnie was too busy talking.

'Did you see the entrance to the house? Like something out of a fancy historic movie. Do you reckon we can see inside? I bet it's really fancy inside.'

'I don't know. I've only seen it from the outside.'

'Yeah. I suppose that would be right. You being part of the servant class and all that? Not fit to mix with them that live in the Big House.'

This comment made Jodie feel defensive. She hadn't felt like she had been treated as a lesser person by Joan Fraser. In fact Jodie had felt that Joan and Roman had both welcomed her. It's just they all worked so hard and maybe there was no time to invite anyone inside the Big House. But how could she explain those vague feelings to her cousin. So she just contented herself with a grunt, safe in the knowledge that Bonnie would soon move onto some other topic. And sure enough she did.

'And there's twin sons your father said. One at uni and one somewhere else. Where?'

Jodie shrugged. She had no idea and no interest in the sons or their whereabouts. How could she be concerned about total strangers who she may or may not meet one day. She hoped Bonnie would move onto some other topic – hopefully one less challenging. It was with a sigh of relief that she saw Roman approaching. And even better still he was approaching carrying his thermos and three mugs.

'Time for morning tea. No cake this time I'm afraid but at least we can have a little rest on that bench over there and enjoy the sunshine and the wintersweet.'

'Winter what?' asked Jodie.

'The flowers on those bare stems near the bench. They're called wintersweet. A name that describes them perfectly. Funny little flowers but so fragrant. Do lean in and have a smell but watch out for bees. They like them too. I can't blame them. There's not much in bloom this time of year. And funnily enough those plants that are in bloom are the most fragrant of all. It's almost as if they have to shout loudly to attract the bees. I'll point them out to you sometime when we are walking around the garden - the wallflowers in the courtyard, the osmanthus that I have pruned into round balls around the side, the almost overpowering laburnum hedge that screens the clothesline area and of course who can forget the daphne?'

Jodie smiled at Roman's enthusiasm. How could she forget the daphne when she had no idea what he was talking about?

Tea poured into three chunky mugs and as Jodie was taking a tentative sip she remembered Roman's story of the other day.

'How about Chapter Two of your tale Roman?'

'Of course, Miss Jodie, so long as your cousin doesn't mind missing out on Chapter One?'

'Don't mind me,' Bonnie dismissed his concerns with a casual wave. She was enjoying the experience of seeing Jodie interact with this interesting foreign gentleman. And lingering in this lightly scented environment was also rather pleasant.

'Now where were we?'

'In England. You'd escaped Poland.'

'Oh yes. I'd reached England and we were in a displaced persons camp. I suppose while they worked out what to do with us. I was there for some time and to be honest it was a sad time. Displaced was truly an accurate description. I was displaced from my family, my home country and all that was familiar to me. Even exiled from my language. I had very little English but during those years I worked hard to learn the language and the customs too. It was all so strange. Yet I knew it was not the country for me. I knew there was no going back to Poland but equally I could not stay in this cold country that was reeling from the effects of the war. When the opportunity came and I was given the choice of where to relocate I chose Australia. Not because I knew anything about this country but because it was as far away from Europe as I could get. I suppose if I had known about New Zealand I might have moved there but that country was unknown to me. So eventually I ended up in another displaced persons' camp but this time in Australia. On what you call The Mainland. But even this Mainland wasn't far enough away from Europe. There was Tasmania. Now that seemed like a safe place to me. So far away. Next stop Antarctica. And it was an island. Harder to invade than just driving across a border like had happened in Poland. When I arrived in Hobart I couldn't believe how tiny it was and how everyone seemed to know each other – just like in my village back home. All of a sudden I felt safe and I knew I could make a future if only I could find work. But what could I do? I had no trade. Just my muscles.'

'So what happened then?'

'I had made contact with a priest in Hobart. He and his congregation had welcomed me and other new arrivals and helped us in many small ways. It was through that priest I met Mr Fraser when he was making one of his periodical visits to Hobart. Probably about the time he was courting Joan, The Boss Lady, although I didn't meet her until much later. Now

Mr Fraser was a true gentleman. A good man and one day he offered me the opportunity to come here and work on the farm. He was a bit vague as to what I should do. If I recall he said something along the lines of we'd work something out. There was always something to do. Even from the outset I trusted him and I accepted. I caught the bus up from Hobart and he collected me and brought me here. When we arrived – at dusk as I recall. A summer dusk, so it would have been about nine-ish. He stopped at one of the cottages not far from where you are now and said: 'Welcome to your new home.' The lights were on and the people that worked on this farm in those days – and there were a lot of them then – spilled out with many cheers and welcomed me in. Even now speaking about it I become a bit emotional. So please excuse me. It was a tremendous feeling of being greeted by total strangers and to feel safe at last. They had stocked the kitchen, made the bed and did all to make me feel at home. I could relax.'

There was silence as the girls digested what they had heard. Then Bonnie, ever the restless one spoke up.

'But did you ever want to leave? You must have still been awfully young after all.'

'No. I had found my safe spot. And as the seasons passed and my contacts in the community deepened, I came to appreciate the beauty that surrounded me and the friendships that I have developed. Sometimes I wonder how after such tragedy I could end up with such a contented life, but maybe having been through bad times it makes me appreciate the good times.'

Roman drew a deep breath and exhaled. 'So that is my story. Not so different from that being experienced by so many others in those days. I like to think that if my parents could see me now they would be happy with where I have ended up.'

He stood up, gathered the now empty mugs and thermos, and said 'Enough chatting. We have roses to prune. And trust me, there's an awful lot of them.'

***

'Well, he didn't exaggerate about the number of roses,' grumbled Bonnie as she inspected her arms for scratches from the rose bushes. 'How could such beautiful flowers come from such vicious plants?'

'You did great and I really appreciate your help given you don't even like gardening.'

'Maybe I could learn to like it if I was lady of a manor such as that.'

Later that evening over dinner of lamb chops (again) the girls updated Charlie on their day. They elaborated on Roman's backstory which was all new to Charlie.

'Well, I never. I knew he was a refugee from Europe after World War Two, but I had never heard the detail. He pretty much keeps to himself. So he must like you girls to entrust you with his story. I knew he and Mr Fraser were close and of course Joan trusts him completely.'

'Joan? Who's Joan?' piped up Bonnie.

'Joan is the boss. Mrs Fraser aka The Boss Lady.'

'Will I meet her?' asked Bonnie. 'And will she ask me into her house? I'd love to see inside. Maybe for tea and scones like ladies of such a grand house would do?'

Charlie snorted at that. 'I'm not sure Joan is the sort to do High Tea. More like beer and chips. But funny you mention going to the Big House.'

'Funny? What's funny about it?' asked Jodie, ever the literal one.

'I mean an odd coincidence. Joan mentioned today that it might be nice if we all came over for dinner on the weekend. Euan will be home on his uni break and she thought he might welcome some company. And of course she would like to meet you too Bonnie. How about that?'

'Yes please,' chimed Bonnie. Her excitement obvious by the way she bounced up and down in the seat. Then glancing across at her cousin it was clear Bonnie was morphing into planning mode.

'Then we have a lot to do. I was hoping to convince you to go on an outing tomorrow Jodie and forgo the pleasures of rose pruning. If we are to dine with the gentry on the weekend you will need a new look – and maybe a manicure,' she said giving Jodie's hand a doubtful look.

Then remembering her manners Bonnie gave Charlie a doubtful look. 'That is if it is alright with you, Charlie?'

He smiled. 'Of course. You girls go have fun. Jodie deserves a break. She has worked awfully hard since she came here. And not only that but Joan has put you on the payroll. I collected your wages today which you may wish to put to good use.'

'You can be sure we will spend them on creating a new look for Jodie. No more Miss Farmgirl' assured Bonnie.

'But I need new work boots,' said Jodie.

'Only if they look good,' responded her fashion stylist.

Chapter Thirteen

'Where are we off to?' asked Jodie as they headed down the dirt road away from the farm.

At Bonnie's urging they were early out of bed. Despite Jodie's grumbling there was no time for a cooked breakfast, Bonnie assured her there would be time for a lunchtime feast. Clearly they weren't heading to nearby Cressy if they had to get up so early. Jodie was intrigued.

'Never you mind Miss Bossy Boots. You will find out soon enough. Why don't you put a cassette on? The case is at your feet. You choose.'

Soon they were listening to music played by some group called Fleetwood Mac. Bonnie sang along in a vaguely tuneful voice. Jodie not being familiar with popular culture listened intently and decided she quite liked the song and would focus on memorising the words so she too could sing along.

The drive passed quickly and after a quick stop at Longford for fuel and a milkshake they approached the outskirts of Launceston. Jodie looked around intrigued.

'You know I've never been here before. Are we going into the centre of town?'

'Of course. That's where the good clothes shops are. To be honest I've only been here a few times with dad, but I think I can find my way around. I just need to follow this main road. You watch out for signs.'

Jodie was impressed by Bonnie's confidence. Imagine being sure you could find your way around even if you weren't sure where you were going. Maybe it had something to do being that much older. Jodie hoped that when she was 19 she would be just as confident as her cousin. Sure enough, as Bonnie had expected the way to the central business district was easily navigated. A car park was found in a side street and before she knew it Jodie was following in the wake of a very determined Bonnie.

'This way. Here's a very on-trend clothes shop and not too expensive. We need to find something respectable for you to wear to the Big House and I wouldn't mind a new top for me to wear with my black midi skirt.

'Don't forget I need new work boots.'

'As if I'd forget with all your nagging. Relax. Your dad gave me heaps of money. I think it must be your wages and a bit extra. He said something about us making sure we spoiled ourselves. I reckon we can do that,' smiled Bonnie confidently as she dragged Jodie into the shop.

Before long they were in the changeroom as Bonnie supervised her cousin's transformation. The young shop assistant was entering into the excitement, maybe because she could scent a number of guaranteed sales and brought in armfuls of outfits.

'What about this?' asked Bonnie holding up a slinky strappy dress with a drop handkerchief hem.

'Maybe if I lived in a tropical climate. But we're in Cressy and it's nearly always cold, if not freezing at night.'

Jodie contemplated the various outfits that had been displayed on a table in the changeroom. All were beautiful and far beyond anything that she had ever contemplated wearing. But there was one that stood out. Pretty but not too summery.

'I think this outfit will do,' she said holding up some black straight legged jeans and in the other hand a long-sleeved black knit threaded with lurex and enhanced with a sweetheart neckline.

'Well, it's very black, isn't it?' said Bonnie doubtfully.

'Possibly. But I thought I could jazz it up with a red belt and maybe with that shaped red jacket over there it might work. And I should still have enough left over to get another top – not black. I could wear with the jeans on other occasions. And some work boots.'

'Of course! How could I forget those work boots!' said Bonnie rolling her eyes.

But considering the outfit as Jodie held it up for inspection, Bonnie concluded it was rather nice. The lurex top was really quite sweet and if Jodie hadn't chosen it she might have been tempted. But as it was she felt rather happy with the satin strappy top and the fluffy mohair cropped cardigan she could drape around her shoulders. All in all a successful shopping expedition. And there was still time for lunch before hunting out some footwear.

After a filling lunch of fish and chips which Bonnie pronounced as superior to that eaten in Devonport they then went shoe shopping. Bonnie decreed that Jodie needed good shoes to go with her new jeans as well as work boots. Maybe some espadrilles which were so on trend. Or ankle boots? Shoes considered and tried on and the cutest little red ankle boots were purchased.

The day ended with the satisfactory purchase of a new pair of chocolate *Blundstone* boots. Perfect for farm work. The back seat of the car was crammed full of shopping bags – the sign of a successful day out. Both girls were happy with their purchases and spent the trip home chatting about their day and the expected outing to the Big House.

'Tell me, is Mrs Fraser very posh?' asked Bonnie, turning her head briefly towards Jodie then once more resuming her concentration on the road ahead.

'Not at all. First time I met her I couldn't believe how ordinary she was. Just like someone from our village back home. No fancy clothes – and her hands are even worse than mine. Ooops, we forgot the manicure.'

'No time. You'll just have to scrub up if you want to look respectable. But then again if her hands are equally bad then I'm the one who's going to stand out. And maybe the mysterious son. Euan isn't it? Tell me about him. And is there another son?'

'Well. I don't know much,' said Jodie as she settled into a gossip. 'They're twins, Euan and Rory. I think they're about 20 or 21. Euan is studying Agricultural Science somewhere on the Mainland. Not sure where, exactly. And Rory – well he's a bit of a mystery. No-one mentions him. He's not dead – or at least I don't think so. Maybe we should ask dad before we go over there for dinner, so we don't put our foot in it. Yeah, I think we should do that. I suppose seeing as Euan is studying something farm related he must plan on returning to the farm.'

'Yeah,' said Bonnie, her rising tone indicating a sudden interest in the possibilities of meeting the heir to the farm. 'An eligible young heir to a vast estate. Now there's a thought. Let's hope he's good looking.'

'And unattached,' laughed Jodie. 'I didn't realise you had plans to become a farmer's wife?'

'Probably not. Just a little fantasy. But the reality – all that hard work is a bit off putting – early starts and all that manure and smelly animals. More one for you. No. I have other plans. Although I might change my mind once I meet the mystery son and heir.'

'What plans?'

'Well. I'm not sure if anything will come of it but I've applied to the Hobart News to join them as a cadet reporter. I actually have an interview next week which is one of the reasons I was keen to stop in with you and Charlie on my way to Hobart. I can't think of anything more exciting than to be a sort of Lois Lane and be part of the news scene in Hobart. I know I would have to start small, but I can dream big, can't I? Maybe with my looks I could one day be one of those political reporters or a newsreader on tv. Wouldn't that be amazing?' Bonnie preened as she spoke, tilting her head as she glanced in the rear-view mirror as if to catch her complexion.

'Bonnie that's so exciting! I can just see you being famous. A big reporter with news scoops on some secret controversy. I'm sure you will impress them. Good luck. Fingers and toes crossed.'

***

It was dark by the time they arrived home, and both girls were exhausted. Bonnie more so having had to concentrate intently as she navigated the unfamiliar roads. Charlie, who had been trying not to feel too anxious, bounded out the front door as soon as he heard the sound of an engine. The front porch light shone a welcome which was confirmed by Buster's enthusiastic greeting.

'Girls. At last. I was starting to worry.' He caught sight of the shopping bags strewn across the back seat. 'Oh my, you have been busy. A successful expedition I assume?'

'Absolutely,' beamed Bonnie. 'We have shopped for Australia! Here Charlie would you please take an armful. Let's get inside out of this cold. Buster' she said bending over to respond to his enthusiastic welcome. 'Did you miss us? I don't think a shopping trip would be your idea of fun.'

Inside the fire was lit and the smell of some sort of casserole permeated the house.

'So sorry Jodie,' smiled Charlie. 'I know how much you like lamb, but tonight it's a chicken casserole the Boss sent over. She said she'd made too much and thought you might like something already prepared when you arrived home. Coq au Vin she called it – whatever that is.'

'Chicken in wine,' said the ever-cosmopolitan Bonnie. 'A French dish - obviously. Red wine I think, and maybe a bit of brandy. Should be mushrooms too. Yum. I'm starving.'

A long day, a delicious dinner and an early night for two girls exhausted from their excursion but contented with the outcome. They both knew they would shine at the dinner the next night.

***

Winter arrived with a vengeance on the next day. They woke to the sound of wind howling around the eaves and scuds of rain lashing the bedroom window. Charlie popped his head in to say goodbye. Already swathed in his long, wet weather coat and wearing gumboots he indicated he wouldn't be outside long. 'Just long enough to check a few animals and then I will be back. You girls stay in bed. No point getting up.'

Both girls agreed. Their beds were cosy and warm. The bedroom not so. Jodie still had her mattress on the floor in Bonnie's room as both agreed it was more fun that way.

Eventually the lure of breakfast and the thought of eating by the fire enticed them away from their nests of blankets and quilts. Bonnie in her usual manner bounced out of bed full of plans for a day spent inside.

'So much to do. First thing after breakfast Jodie, we will attack your hands. Well not literally attack your hands but give them a total makeover so they don't present as dirty brown peasant hands. I'm not sure I can do much with your nails but maybe a bit of a tidy up and some clear polish would be enough. Come on sleepyhead,' said Bonnie as she whisked the covers off her huddled cousin.

'Give over! That is so not fair,' grumbled Jodie as she tried, unsuccessfully, to retrieve her bedding. Eventually accepting defeat she scrambled off the mattress, found yesterday's discarded clothes and proceeded to get dressed.

Charlie had long gone by the time they arrived in the kitchen. The remnants of his breakfast remained. A mess of porridge congealing in a bowl.

'Now that's an idea,' said Jodie. 'Something warm for breakfast like porridge with lashings of brown sugar and milk. Work for you?'

'Too right but you'll have to make it as I never have.'

'Can't be too hard, can it?'

Two attempts later they sat down to steaming bowls of porridge and decided it was just what they needed for a dismal day.

'Pity we burnt the first batch,' said Jodie. 'I think I should tidy up before Charlie gets home as I would hate him to see the mess I've made of his kitchen. And he's forever telling anyone that's prepared to listen what a great cook I am. It's a good thing he wasn't here this morning.'

'You get started on the washing up and I'll set up for your manicure. Maybe using the coffee table by the fire. Getting your hands in the soapy water while you do the dishes will hopefully soften that ingrained dirt. So that means no dishwashing gloves. Agreed?'

'Yes ma'am!' said Jodie giving a salute.

The morning passed quickly. By the time a sodden Charlie returned the kitchen was spotless and a cake was baking in the oven sending a delicious aroma wafting around the house.

'My, you two have been busy. And cake – just the thing for a freezing me. Will it be ready soon?'

'Not long,' said Bonnie. 'And look,' she said, reaching for and holding up Jodie's hands. 'It was hard work but Jodie now has hands suitable for a lady and not a farm worker. Aren't I a genius?' Bonnie smiled at her own brilliance.

It truly was an indoors day. The wind and rain showed no sign of abating. Every so often Charlie would peer anxiously out the window, but he seemed reluctant to again venture outside.

'All the sheds are shut up and the animals can cope. Like us they will just have to sit it out. Thank goodness the start of lambing is a week or two away. Otherwise, I'd be out there rescuing orphan lambs. Much better to be here by the fire. Good thing I brought in heaps of wood yesterday.'

The open fire was a treat for Bonnie who was only used to electric heating. All day she kept it roaring, taking over the task of poking it with the fire iron to ensure the wood burned effectively. Charlie, ensconced in a dilapidated armchair watched on, every now and then turning a page of the local rural paper. From time to time he would head out to the front porch ostensibly to *check on the weather*. But the girls were not fooled. They knew he was heading outside for a furtive cigarette.

They were expected over at the Big House at 6 o'clock. Rather early for sophisticated Bonnie although she agreed with Charlie that because it was already dark it felt much later.

'And it's not even mid-winter,' grumbled Bonnie. 'Then it will feel like there is barely any afternoon before darkness descends. No wonder we all get so excited about the arrival of spring.'

Charlie was well aware that after all the time spent shopping for new outfits and preening the girls would be expecting his positive response to their transformed appearance. However there was no need to pretend to be other than amazed when the two young women presented themselves for his consideration. The transformation – mainly of Jodie - was amazing. Bonnie had always looked her age – a stylish 19 year old. But his little girl - well that was something else entirely. The sight of his little girl brought tears to his eyes as she pranced in circles showing off her new outfit, drawing his attention to her sparkling top, red ankle boots and clean hands.

'Look Dad,' she said fluttering her hands in front of his eyes. 'New hands and new me! Aren't I fantastic?'

'Amazing. And Bonnie you look pretty good too. Pity I'm not dressed up to your standard. But it will just have to do.'

The two girls critically considered his appearance.

'You're being too modest,' said Bonnie. 'Actually you scrub up ok – for an old fella.'

In his cream moleskins, dark grey fine wool sweater and checked jacket he looked more than ok. Charlie looked exactly like what he was – a farmer.

As it was still raining they agreed it was best that they squeeze into Bonnie's car and drive across to the Big House. But this time to the front door not the back gate.

'After all we are being invited to dinner and shouldn't sneak in via the back tradesman's entrance.'

'Oooh, the front door – too posh. I must remember to talk proper,' laughed Bonnie.

Her laughter faded as she walked up the steps under the portico and pressed the button by the immense multi-panelled timber door. Inside, far away she could hear the sound of the bell and then – nothing.

As if to ease her nerves Bonnie found herself asking questions about things she normally never considered important. Architecture.

'Tell me Charlie. How old is the house?'

'About 1830's I think. See the fanlight about the door. I suppose it is called a fanlight as the segments look like a fan spread out. And these glass side panels on either side of the main door – they're all features of Georgian architecture from about that time. Called Georgian after the king at that time. It was a very classical style – symmetry was important.'

Charlie tilted his head to one side considering 'You know. I bet they're out in the kitchen and won't have heard the bell. How about I give it one more try and then we'll go in. I'm sure they won't mind and the door is bound to be unlocked.'

There was no answer to the subsequent ring although they could again hear the sound of a bell echoing inside. Giving the door handle a twist Charlie pushed the door open and ushered the girls into a massive stone flagged entry hall. The girls took two steps inside then paused as they both took in the sight before them. And what a sight it was. Before them a substantial timber staircase beckoned them forward yet to the right and left were two rooms that equally demanded attention. Especially as in each room a crackling fire enticed them in. But which way to go?

'Oh my god,' sighed Bonnie. 'I thought it was grand outside but this tops it. I think I must have died and gone straight to heaven.'

'Changed your mind yet?' whispered Jodie. 'Fancy being lady of the manor after all?'

'It's kinda tempting.' And then as she caught sight of the young man striding towards them along the corridor beside the stairs she added. 'You know what? It's more than tempting.'

Jodie was in complete agreement. The apparition approaching them was enough to make anyone change their mind. She eyed him with interest. He really was rather gorgeous. Tall with shaggy dark hair and like his mother he had the most beautiful piercing eyes of sapphire blue. Overwhelming. Yet that impression was totally overtaken by the impact of his welcoming smile. A smile so wide and delighted that it was impossible not to smile back.

'Charlie!' this godlike man exclaimed as he reached out to shake Charlie's hand. 'So good to see you. It's been ages. And one of these beautiful people must be your daughter? And who else?'

'Good to see you too Euan. Welcome home. And do allow me to introduce my daughter Jodie,' said Charlie as he gestured towards Jodie. She stepped forward and shook hands with Euan, who smiled a welcome just at her. Or so it seemed. She registered the firmness of his hand and its warm comforting dryness.

'And this here is Bonnie, who is a relative – a distant cousin, sort of, I suppose.'

Bonnie stepped forward – all eagerness and bounce. Keen to attract his attention and of course she did. For that night Bonnie looked her best. Not that she ever looked bad. But with her titian curls cascading down her back, her artfully enhanced eyes sparkling at him and her full lips smiling a welcome she made an impressive image. Poor Euan didn't stand a chance. He was immediately smitten. But remembering his manners he gestured them towards the sitting room.

'Do come sit by the fire and warm up. You must be freezing. Jodie your hands certainly feel like ice. I'll run and get mum. She's in the kitchen setting out some food. Nothing fancy – just some dips and stuff. I'll fetch some drinks and will be back in a jiff.'

With a smile that encompassed them all he raced away. Jodie walked straight to the fire and with outstretched hands soaked up its warmth. Bonnie meanwhile stalked the room taking in its antique furnishings and decoration.

'Look at these paintings. They're fantastic. Maybe they're local scenes? Oh and here are some photos. Charlie who is who? Do tell.'

Charlie wandered over and contemplated the groups of photos displayed on a side table.

'Hmmm, let me see. I'm not sure I recognise all of the people but I know a fair few. Here,' he picked up what could only be a wedding photo. 'This must be Joan and Alastair on their wedding day. So young. And here are Euan and Rory as toddlers. Oh, and this one is Euan with Copper at a local horse show. Looks like they came first in a class as the blue ribbon would indicate. Not sure who these other people are – maybe relatives on Joan's side.'

At the mention of Copper Jodie wandered across to inspect the photo. It must have been taken several years ago as both Euan and Copper looked younger – and slimmer. Euan's victory smile directed at the camera was as wide as what he displayed just now. Jodie reached out and picked up this photo for further inspection. Just then Euan appeared in the doorway carrying a tray of glasses and several bottles. He looked across at Jodie.

'Ah, you've found my favourite photo. The day Copper and I won at Cressy Ag show. I was rapt, as you can probably tell from that photo. He's a champ. Have you met Copper yet?'

'Yes, Dad has taken me to meet him and Misty and the pony. He's gorgeous.'

'And I hear you're going to ride him?'

'Maybe.' Jodie's doubt obvious in the tone of her voice.

'I'm happy to give you a lesson. He really is a gentle giant. Perfect manners. Would you like me to help you while I'm here?'

'Maybe.' This time Jodie sounded a bit more confident. Being with Euan could be interesting. Bonnie certainly thought so.

'I for one have yet to meet this famous Copper. Maybe you can introduce me Euan? Tomorrow?'

Bonnie was never one to let an opportunity pass her by.

'Deal! So long as it's not raining.'

The arrival of Joan ended that conversation. Soon they were all sipping their drinks of choice – beer for Euan and Charlie, Gin and Tonic for Joan and Bonnie and lemon squash for Jodie. At 16 she was deemed too young for any alcoholic drink. And given her exposure to a mother with an aptitude for drunkenness Jodie was unsure that she would ever be tempted.

The evening passed in a rush. Jodie already knew how kind Joan was, but she was surprised how easy it was to talk to her – how with such skill she drew Bonnie and herself into the conversation. The dinner was relaxed. Euan and Charlie were both full of anecdotes and tall stories about eccentric members of the local community that surely must have been exaggerated.

The main course was no surprise. Lamb! But this time it was a tasty and fragrant lamb curry. Jodie made a mental note to request the recipe from Joan. It could be a useful addition to her growing repertoire of lamb recipes. She was learning that there were many ways of cooking lamb. Thank goodness!

And for dessert. Chocolate cake with chocolate ganache – of course. Jodie was discovering that the Boss Lady could bake a mean cake. She watched her father wolf down his piece and happily accept another. It was obvious to her that Charlie and Joan were good mates and she supposed that wasn't surprising given their past history – how they both had to work closely after Alastair's sudden death to ensure the farm's survival and how day to day life on the farm, when all had to pull their weight, meant they continued to work closely. Watching Joan chuckle at something Charlie said she wondered if the closeness could be something more. Surely not! She was the Boss Lady after all.

Jodie looked up to see Euan watching her watching Charlie and Joan. Did he suspect the same thing? If so it didn't appear to worry him. He still wore the same merry grin as he winked at her and said:

'Ten o'clock tomorrow. Up at the horse yards. You and Bonnie. Wear your boots and hopefully it won't be too muddy.'

***

Later that night in bed Bonnie and Jodie reviewed the evening's events.

'I feel like I stepped into a fairy tale when we walked through the door,' said Bonnie as she lay on her side hand under her head looking across to a sleepy Jodie who was tucked up lying on the mattress, cosy under blankets and quilt. If Bonnie would just shut up she would fall asleep in two ticks. But it was not to be. Bonnie was on a roll.

'I never knew people lived like that. Did you check out the cutlery and the dinner plates? Silver knives and forks and the cutest little cake forks. And that white china – edged with gold. Real gold, I think. Yes, it must be real gold. So posh. I was terrified of dropping my plate or my glass come to that. They were out of this world fancy. Maybe like what the Queen uses? And cloth serviettes – never ever have I had cloth serviettes. Truly posh.' Bonnie's voice trailed off as she contemplated how other people lived. Then just as sleep started to steal over Jodie, she piped up again.

'And that Euan. He was definitely like something out of a fairy tale. A real-life Prince Charming. Did you notice how he kept looking at me and wanting to talk to me. I hope he will still be as interested tomorrow. Mind you, I think it is not meant to be. The logistics of a long-distance romance would be way too complicated and I have my career to think about. But a girl can dream, can't she? Can't she Jodie?'

But there was no answer. Just the sound of quiet snoring. Jodie was fast asleep. Too tired to dream of anything. Although that evening's chocolate cake may have made its appearance.

Chapter Fourteen

From Daggy Sheep's Bottom

Dear Nanna and Pop

If I ever tell you I want to be a sheep farmer please commit me straight away! I've just spent the last two days helping Dad with the crutching. Gross! I never want to see a daggy sheep bottom again.

By now Bonnie should be with you. I wish I was there with her too. It would be such fun – just the four of us and I bet Nanna you have cooked up a storm. I so miss your cooking and I now appreciate all the hard work you have put in to feed us. Charlie likes what I make each night but I can tell you it's nothing compared to your creations and seems to take ages to prepare. That latest cookbook is pretty cool. I never knew there could be so many casserole recipes. Perfect for winter.

It was great having Bonnie to stay. Did she tell you she took me shopping to Launceston? My first trip to Launie and I hope Dad will take me again sometime. Great shops and a funny gorge we walked around after lunch. It was really dramatic like a big gash filled with rushing water and a cute tea shop.

And I finally got to see inside the Big House and got to meet one of the Boss Lady's twin sons. He was really friendly. Called Euan. There's another son somewhere. Of course there is – silly me! They wouldn't be called twins otherwise. Hah! Rory I think he's called. But no one talks of him and when I ask Dad he clams up. Nothing better than a mystery. Maybe I should get sleuthing.

Euan was here for his uni break and he helped me learn to catch, saddle and ride Copper. I will admit that I wasn't too keen on this as Copper is enormous, but Euan convinced me to be brave and to trust him and Copper. First time I was terrified but once I was on top – or mounted as we horse people say – it all felt right. Like I was on a warm slightly moving lounge chair. First ride Euan led me around the yard and then the horse paddock so I could learn how to move with the horse. Bonnie had a go too. She was a bit squealy, which I'm told you shouldn't do but somehow Copper didn't mind – although his ears did flicker to and fro every time she squealed. Bonnie decided horses weren't for her, so I got Euan's attention all to myself.

Since then we've been further out. Euan rides Dad's horse Misty and I'm now riding Copper off the lead rope. I sort of know how to steer him. To be honest he seems to know where we want to go. Still only walking. Yet to try a trot and I think a canter is way off. And I'm sure you're about to ask. No. I haven't fallen off. Although on the first day I did a sort of slide to one side but fortunately Euan was able to grab me and rebalance me. That was a bit scary and almost put me off horse riding.

I hope you two will come and visit soon. I know it's mid-winter, but we do a mean fire and the lambs are coming thick and fast. So cute. So far only a few orphan lambs or lambs the mother rejects. Mrs Fraser is managing them but Dad has warned me we will have to take some in if any more need hand rearing. I can't wait!

If you come and visit I will show off my cooking prowess and make you something out of the casserole book. And I'll introduce you to Copper – who really is rather beautiful. And smells nice. Unlike the sheep.

Lots of love

Your granddaughter. (Who still smells of lanolin even though I've washed my hands many times.)

P.S. Bonnie would approve. I've discovered lanolin from the sheep's wool works wonders on worker's hands.

Chapter Fifteen

No sooner had Charlie come through the front screen door than Jodie came barrelling out of the lounge room.

'Dad,' she yelled in excitement. 'Nanna just rang and she says Bonnie got the job. She will be starting her cadetship in about a month. Hurrah! And just as good – maybe even better as far as I'm concerned. Nanna says she and Pop are going to come and visit this weekend – maybe for a few days.'

A sudden thought. Maybe her father wasn't so keen on Nanna and Pop as she was.

'That is, if you don't mind?'

Charlie, whose thoughts had been focussed on rescuing a dying ewe and had barely registered what his over excited daughter was telling him, gave himself a mental shake. Something about Bonnie – that he could sort out later but also something about Nanna and Pop. What was that? Were they unwell?

'Say again? Nanna and Pop?'

'Yes Dad. Pay attention! Is it ok for Nanna and Pop to come and stay this weekend.'

The sense of relief. Thank goodness they were alright. Unlike that poor ewe.

'Of course. They're welcome to come and stay any time. Jodie will you be able to fix up the spare room and cook something. It may have to be lamb as I won't have time to take you into town to buy anything else. Unless you can convince Roman or Joan to do so.'

He observed his daughter atwitch with excitement. Sometimes she seemed so young, but he had to remind himself that she was just turned 17. Almost an adult. Now he thought about it she was old enough to sit for her driver's licence.

'Now that I think of it, it's time you learned to drive and went for your driver's licence. Then you could drive yourself to the shops.'

'Daaad,' Jodie spoke in the superior tone beloved by all teenagers. 'I already know how to drive. You've seen me drive around the paddocks. How much harder can it be on the roads?'

'Well, you see there are other cars for a start and something called the road rules.' Charlie smiled to soften the impact of his comment. 'Maybe if Pop is here for a while he can get you started. I'd do it but at the moment I'm just a bit busy...'

Jodie was guilt stricken. In her excitement she had forgotten how hard her father had been working now that lambing had started. Taking one look at his face – grey with exhaustion she realised that today had been a particularly bad day. Time to make amends.

'You poor thing. You look beat and here I am rabbiting on. Come on. Get those boots off and sit by the fire while I sort out dinner. Cup of tea?'

'Thanks Jodie dear. If you don't mind I think I will give the tea a miss and go for a beer instead. But the fire sure sounds tempting.'

Chapter Sixteen

Jodie was surprised at how much work was involved in getting the house prepared for guests. Usually housework would be unwelcome but for now it was a good distraction from braving the chill outside to help her father. He seemed to accept that there was a need to get everything as nice as possible for Nanna and Pop. Roman even helped. He said it was too miserable to garden and that taking Jodie into Cressy to buy food and obtain her Learner's Permit was a welcome distraction from looking through gardening books for inspiration.

On their journey into Cressy Jodie took the opportunity to grill her captive chauffer about the missing twin. It's not as if he could run away, she thought. So she prepared to cross examine him with barrister-like brutality. In the end there was no need to as Roman proffered all the information he had.

'There's not much I can tell you Miss Jodie. I've known the twins all their lives. For identical twins they have totally different personalities. You've met Euan obviously and would agree with me that he is kind and generous – just like his mother. Rory has always been a total contrast. Maybe it was because he was very sickly as a child. You know, very low birthweight, so he had to struggle to survive. Yes, maybe that was that. He was a whiny child. Nothing was good enough and he wanted anything Euan had. To his credit Euan was endlessly patient with him which I think may have added to Rory's resentment.'

'Were they friends?'

'Sort of. There weren't many other kids around here, so they had to play together. Once they were at school it was different. Euan was sporty and Rory was arty. One played football and the other sang in the choir but they muddled along OK, I suppose. But Rory had no interest in the farm, which was a shame as those days Joan needed all the help she could get. Even feeding the hens would have been a help. But no. If Rory didn't want to do anything he would just put on a scene so it was simpler to leave him alone.'

'He's not here now. What happened?'

'He just shot through as soon as he had finished school. One day he disappeared. He didn't even leave a note or tell anyone – not even his twin. Joan was beside herself. The Police were no help. I suppose they deal with disappearing teenagers every day and they figure they will turn up eventually – dead or alive. Some say they've spotted him in Hobart, but he had no interest in speaking to them. It's been awful for Joan. At least Euan has always been there for her. I don't know how she would manage otherwise. First Mr Fraser dying and leaving her in a financial mess and then the challenges with Rory.'

Jodie was dumbfounded. She sat still while she processed what Roman had told her. Even when her mother had been at her most unhinged it had never crossed her mind to run away. Maybe that was a sign she was such a wimp or it could be that what with the emotional support of Pepper, Nanna and Pop she had enough strength to cope with her mother. Jodie tried to imagine having a mother such as Joan and a brother such as Euan and failed to understand how that could be a problem. She would happily have traded places. To her mind growing up in such a location with such kindness gave Rory nothing to complain about. Now if he had experienced her mother then she would totally understand. Probably something she couldn't share with Roman, so she contented herself with showing sympathy.

'Poor Joan. And poor Euan. It must have been beyond unsettling. More like awfully tragic. Maybe one day he will come to his senses and come home.'

'Maybe.'

This conversation had clearly ended. Jodie focussed on her shopping list. Did she have everything? Chicken for dinner. Maybe one of those casseroles from the cookbook Nanna gave her. Apples for apple crumble for dessert. Bacon to go with the farm eggs for breakfast. And she must not forget the bread. Lots of it for toast and sandwiches. Bread rolls might be nice to go with dinner. That would make the meal fancy. Pity she had no linen serviettes like they had at the Big House. Paper napkins would have to do.

Jodie felt very grown up preparing to entertain her grandparents. It was going to be a treat and even more so after she answered the phone that morning.

'Did I tell you Roman? Not only are Nanna and Pop visiting, but Bonnie is also staying one night on her way back to Devonport. She has to go home and pack and then return to Hobart to start her cadetship. So exciting.'

Jodie almost purred with happiness. Three of her favourite people all together with her and Charlie.

'Yes, Miss Jodie. I do believe you mentioned it as soon as you hopped in the car. A great treat for you. Maybe you might like me to find you some flowers to decorate the house? There's not much around at the moment – being winter and all. But I can find you some camelias, and even some early jonquils. Will that do?'

'Yes please Roman. That would be perfect.'

***

By the time Nanna and Pop arrived on Friday afternoon Jodie was the proud mother of two orphaned lambs. More than proud, she was totally besotted. They had been installed in a fenced off area in an outside shed, safely out of the cold breezes that wormed their way into the shed and able to snuggle down in the masses of scattered bedding straw.

Pop, who had much experience in raising livestock, was dragged over to inspect the lambs as soon as he arrived.

'What do you think Pop. Will it do or should I bring them inside?'

Pop smiled at his granddaughter who by now was almost as tall as him. Almost as tall, but still a child in many ways. Maybe it had something to do with this isolated life that they had imposed on her. Maybe it was time to open Jodie's eyes to a bigger world, but would she be safe? For all the disadvantages brought about by its isolation this farm had one major benefit. It had kept Jodie safe and away from prying eyes for the last two years. But maybe it was time for this Sleeping Beauty awake. A matter to discuss with Charlie later tonight – maybe. But for now he needed to address his granddaughter who was looking at him with questioning eyes.

'I'm not sure your father would welcome these young ones inside. They do make quite a lot of poo you know. And this is rather cosy – especially if you close the doors at night. Now I think they're becoming rather agitated. Is there something you need to do?' He smiled and pointed at the two bottles warming in the bucket of water.

'Of course,' said Jodie. 'You do one and I'll do the other. Then we can give them another bottle before bedtime. They so love their food. The way they wiggle their little tails when I feed them is just the cutest. I think that black faced one is going to be my favourite.'

Joe Daley smiled at his granddaughter. Trust her to be a soft touch. He could almost predict that he would be asked further down the track to take this little one home with him to join his goat menagerie. Oh well he supposed he could manage another mouth to feed. Anything to see the smile on Jodie's face.

Lambs fed, and secure in their pen, garage doors firmly shut and off they headed inside. It was settling into another cold night with drizzling rain threatening to turn into sleet. A time to be inside by the fire. And a time for Charlie who was stomping up the front steps to leave his woes behind and defrost. But not before he opened his coat and handed another newborn lamb to his daughter.

'Take this mite Jodie while I go mix up some colostrum. The mother had triplets and rejected this one. Maybe because it had something wrong with it and is going to die. But we owe it to the poor thing to give it a chance. Please grab that old towel in the laundry and give it a good rub. Then we need a box with a hot water bottle under some blankets. Pop will help you. I'll go sort out the colostrum. This one will have to stay inside tonight. Maybe it will survive the night, maybe not. So don't get your hopes up Jodie.'

The lamb was certainly newborn. A collection of stick-thin bones covered with short haired fleece. It was cold and barely alive. Surely it would not survive. Jodie flew into rescuer mode. The towel located she gave the lamb a thorough rub over just like the lamb's mother would have done to get the circulation going. Then she wrapped the lamb up tight in a woolly blanket while Joe fussed over the lamb's bedding arrangements. A wooden crate had been located in the laundry and an old hot water bottle found on the laundry shelves. The kettle boiled, the hot water bottle filled and then placed in the crate and covered with further blankets.

'Keep the lamb close to your body warmth until such time as we see him – or her show some signs of life. Maybe come closer to the fire. Your dad will be back soon.'

Jodie sat cross legged in front of the fire, holding the swaddled bundle tight. She was still wearing her outside work coat. A padded coat with fake sheepskin lining. Slightly waterproof and totally windproof, it was her favourite item of attire for everyday farmwork. A bit too warm for inside leisure but she hoped it might help revive the lamb.

They all had their jobs. While Jodie focussed on the lamb, Nanna was tasked with heating the dinner and Pop brought in firewood from out the back porch. Before long Charlie returned.

'Sorry it took a while. The colostrum was over at the Big House and it's a stinker out there. I was skidding all over the road. I'll just mix this up and we'll see if the lamb will take any.'

Jodie suddenly thought of Bonnie. Surely she wouldn't be travelling in this weather. She mouthed *Bonnie* at her grandfather and looked at him questioningly.

'No. It's alright. She said she wouldn't drive up til tomorrow. Something about a party to attend in Hobart tonight,' reassured Joe. 'And I expect she won't turn up 'til late tomorrow morning if we're lucky so I suppose you'll be on lamb duty tomorrow. Not that I expect young Bonnie will be interested in smelly young lambs,' smiled Joe.

Dinner was delayed that night as they attended to the lamb. Saving a life always had priority. Or as Charlie said – giving it a chance and hoping for the best. As he dribbled a small amount of colostrum into the almost lifeless lamb's mouth he spoke: 'Nature is fairly resilient and if it's meant to be, then with a bit of food and warmth the young ones should come good. But if this one doesn't then maybe it was never meant to survive. We can only do our best. If it's still fragile in the morning – then we'll decide what to do then.'

With dawning horror Jodie realised what Charlie meant.

'No Dad. No.'

'It may not come to that. As I said let's see how it is in the morning and look- it's now swallowing. Not much but some. If we can keep getting something into its stomach, then maybe – just maybe we might turn the corner. And maybe by then it might suck on a teat. Mother nature may throw a lot at us but fortunately many animals are remarkably tough. Although to keep positive I often remind myself that the need to survive can override all else.'

He turned his head and sniffed: 'Is that dinner I smell? Terrific. Can I help Nanna?'

They all agreed that it wasn't a night for formal dinner around the dining table. Instead they sat by the fire next to the wooden box and ate their dinner from plates precariously perched on their knees. Somehow nothing was spilled.

'Just like a picnic,' said Nanna.

From time-to-time Jodie glanced anxiously at the small lump lying motionlessly in the box. Charlie noticed.

'Relax Jodie. We're doing all we can do,' he said. 'All we can do now is hope for the best. We must keep this little one as cosy and warm as are the others in the shed. Just think of the others roughing it outside in the paddocks in the freezing cold. Like I said – lucky they're tough.'

They fell silent as they all listened to the wind increasing in its ferocity. The rain continued its relentless splattering against the windows.

'At least we have no hail,' said Charlie. No sooner had the words come out of his mouth than the wet sound of rain against the windows became something harder. A crisper sound that indicated a transformation into hail.

'Oh, no, I spoke too soon.'

'Let's hope it won't last,' commiserated Joe. 'Looks like you will be up early to check the stock tomorrow. Will you need a hand Charlie?'

'Thanks, mate. That'd be grand.'

As if it wasn't noisy enough – what with the howling wind and the crashing of hail against glass then there was more. All jumped at the sound of the front door being thumped which overrode all else. Being hit with vigour and over it all a voice could be heard calling out to be let in.

'What the?' muttered Charlie as he rose and rushed to the door. All the others stood and looked towards the front door in apprehension. Charlie swung the door opened and was greeted by the sight of a tall water-soaked figure holding a dripping suitcase. And behind another shadowy figure.

'Bonnie?' queried Charlie. The shadowy figure might possibly be Bonnie, but he was uncertain why she should be here earlier than expected.

'Yeah, of course it's me. Can we come in? We're freezing.'

Charlie stood aside to let the pair in. With a grunt he pushed the door closed against the invading gale. Nanna meanwhile had morphed into mother hen mode. She rushed to Bonnie and removed her coat, clucking as she did so.

'Get yourself straight to the bathroom and into a hot shower. You'll find some towels there. No time to worry whose they are. Jodie will rustle up some clothes for you – won't you Jodie?'

Jodie nodded as she stared at the dripping stranger standing behind Bonnie. He looked strangely familiar. Her father's gasp made her turn to him and she saw him staring with amazement at this person. So he'd recognised him. Who was he?

'Rory. Is that you?'

Jodie nodded. Of course, that's why he looked familiar. The mystery twin had resurfaced. Jodie studied him intently as he removed a dripping coat and sodden beanie which he handed to her Pop. Just like a dog he gave himself a little shake which scattered droplets onto the rug.

'Looks like you also need a hot shower, me lad. But you'll have to wait for Bonnie to finish and knowing that girl she'll be there for ages' said Charlie.

Jodie realised that, of course Charlie would know Rory. After all he had started working on this farm when the twins were lads. They must go way back. Her dad must know Rory very well. Which made it even weirder that her father had refused to talk about him whenever she tried to find out more information. In fact Roman had been the most forthcoming and even he hadn't told her much. She eyed this stranger with interest.

'Nah, it's alright Charlie. If I can just grab a towel and some spare clothes if you can spare them - that would be great. I'll be sorted in no time. And then maybe a hot drink might help defrost me. What a night! If I'd known it was going to be this bad, I would have stayed put in Hobart.'

Sometime later the grouping around the fire had expanded to include two now dry and slightly warmer people. The others watched silently as they ate and drank. Then once it was clear they had finishing eating the questioning began. Nanna started first.

'Bonnie dear, we weren't expecting to see you until tomorrow. How come you're here tonight?'

'I dunno. I was missing you all and thinking how nice it would be to be here all together – around the fire. Just like this,' she beamed at her gathered family who stared back at her expressionlessly. 'Yes, yes. My fault I suppose. I didn't realise that the weather would be this bad and then to make things worse my car conked out just down the road and we had to walk the last bit in the pouring rain. Not the entry I had planned. I managed to steer the car to the side of the road as it was dying so it should be alright there tonight – I hope. Charlie, can you look at it tomorrow?'

'Sure and on a night like this your car should be safe. No-one is going to be going anywhere. Or' he corrected 'most sane people would be tucked up inside. Bonnie, what were you thinking? You could have been hurt. Let's hope you didn't leave your car too close to the creek. It can flood you know.'

Bonnie's agonised expression was all the answer he required.

'Oh well. Never mind. You're safe and that is all that matters.'

Charlie's gaze moved along to Rory who, dinner finished, and plate placed on the floor, was staring thoughtfully into the fire.

'Well, Rory, what brings you here? Does your mother know you were coming? And how do you know Bonnie?'

Rory stretched out his long legs and eased his neck and shoulders before answering. He was taking his time, almost as if he didn't know how to respond.

'What brings me here? Mmmm, not really sure. I'd met Bonnie at a night club – last weekend was it, Bonnie?'

He looked across at Bonnie who gave him a nod and a small encouraging smile. Even she could tell Charlie was not welcoming Rory with open arms. Maybe it had been a bad idea of hers to encourage Rory to accompany her.

'And – no. Mum doesn't know. I thought it might be a nice idea to surprise her.'

Give her a heart attack more like, thought Charlie. But he said nothing, just nodded as if to indicate Rory should continue.

'I suppose I wanted to see everyone – and to see the farm. I hadn't realised until I left how much everything here meant to me. But I thought I'd burned my bridges, so to speak, and could never return. But talking to Bonnie here gave me the courage to come back and face the consequences – whatever they will be' he said as he smiled across at Bonnie, who smiled back in return.

It was all too sickening, thought Jodie: that this Rory person thought he could waltz back and all would be forgiven. After all the hurt he had inflicted. And the way he was making puppy dog eyes at Bonnie was just plain nauseating. She so wanted to hurl but that would be the waste of a good dinner. Look at them – it was disgusting. How could Bonnie fall for his tricks. Mind you he wasn't too hard on the eye. To Jodie's not so sophisticated eye Rory presented as a rougher version of his brother – dark hair close cropped on the top and hanging loose at the back. Wearing one gold earring - a diamond stud maybe - and was that the hint of a tattoo poking out from under the cuff of the sweatshirt Charlie had lent him? Yes - definitely a tattoo. There was something about him – a rough edge that made him somehow attractive. A hint of danger and perhaps that was what had appealed to Bonnie who was still making goofy eyes at him.

'Your mother should be here any minute,' said Charlie in a serious tone. It was clear he was not impressed. 'I rang her while you were getting changed. As you can expect your arrival tonight has come as a complete surprise to her, so maybe you might try to be a bit sensitive about what you say. I expect you'll be very tired and happy to go home with your mother. You have so much catching up to do. We've all had a big day so ...' he broke off, 'Ah I hear her now. I've put your wet clothes in this bag, and you can return my stuff later on. No need to hang around. I'll show you to the front door. That way we won't keep your mum waiting.'

And before Rory could object Charlie had grabbed Rory by the elbow and escorted him to the front door. The others could hear the murmur of voices then the crash as the front door was once again shut against the wintery gale.

'Well, that was masterful,' said Joe as Charlie re-entered the room with a grim expression on his face.

'I don't like to dump Rory on Joan like that, but I hope he will be sufficiently remorseful to behave himself. Anyway, I'll check in with Joan tomorrow. I don't know about the rest of you, but I'm beat. Joe – can I leave it up to you and Jodie to feed all the lambs tonight? You know the gig don't you?'

'No worries,' assured Joe. He waved Charlie out of the room. 'We will all be fine.'

Bonnie who had been watching proceedings, open mouthed, spoke up - 'Lambs? Where?'

'Well there's one in that box right near your feet. He's newborn and needs to be kept warm but see if I pull this cover off slightly you can check him out. I'll have to give him a bottle shortly which he may or may not take. If he doesn't I'll dribble some more colostrum into his mouth. Joe says I have to feed him two to three hourly so I might as well sleep here by the fire. The ones out in the shed are a bit older. Once we feed them tonight they should last 'til early in the morning.'

At the mention of the demanding feeding routine Bonnie's interest evaporated. All of a sudden she started to talk about how exhausted she was – the long drive you know – and how she needed her beauty sleep so she would look her best to see Rory in the morning. Not that anyone else was interested in what she was saying. Joe, Nanna and Jodie were totally focussed on the lamb.

'Do you think he looks any better Pop?' asked Jodie.

'I really can't say, Jodie dear. But hey – he's still breathing, and we got a bit of colostrum down him a little while back. Let's warm some up and try him again. How about you focus on this poor wee mite and Nanna and I will do the others. Looks like it could be a very long night.'

And it was. When Charlie emerged first thing in the morning he found his girl fast asleep in the lounge chair before a roaring fire. He carefully checked the lamb and noted with relief that he was still breathing. Maybe he would survive after all. Charlie had been dreading consoling his daughter who he considered had been burdened with too many losses in her lifetime.

He was busy feeding the lamb when Jodie stirred.

'Good morning Jodie,' he said looking up and smiling at his daughter. 'You've done well. Looks like this little one is coming good. He looks more alert already and seems to be sucking much better. In a day or two with this sort of progress he should be able to join the others out in the shed. Did you get any sleep?'

'Not much.' Jodie yawned and stretched, dislodging the quilt that she had tucked around herself. 'Still it will be worth it if the lamb survives. He's so tiny - and so cute.'

An opinion that was echoed many hours later by Bonnie when she eventually emerged from her bedroom. The lamb was once again tucked up in the box although his little head was revealed for inspection.

There was considerable discussion as to what to do that day. The weather had eased but was still wintery with a cold wind blowing. No more rain though – thank goodness. Charlie and Joe agreed that once the shedded lambs were fed they would then investigate Bonnie's car to see if they could get it to start.

'And if we can get it to go, would you mind driving it up here Joe. I also need to check the sheep – if you can lend me a hand with that later it would be useful. And I suppose at some stage we should check in with Joan to see she is ok and hasn't murdered that wayward son of hers.'

'Fine with me' agreed Joe.

After they'd clothed themselves with beanies, coats and gloves – almost as if they were braving an Antarctic blizzard - they were gone, Charlie calling Buster from his kennel as he went.

'We won't see them for hours now,' grinned Nanna. 'Joe will be happy as Larry to spend time with Charlie. They always were good mates and it warms my heart to see them pick up just like they were years ago. Now,' said Nanna focussing on the business at hand, 'I need to do some baking. Jodie please show me what ingredients you have and I'll do what I can to make something tasty. I know the boys will be starving when they return. So my dear, you and I have a bit of menu planning to do.'

Nanna regarded Bonnie who was busy filing her nails.

'What are your plans Bonnie?'

'Oh, don't mind me. I will keep the lamb company. And maybe Rory will appear later. Isn't he a doll?' she asked, but not expecting an answer. For as far as Bonnie was concerned it was obvious there was no doubting Rory's sterling qualities. Jodie was not so sure. Judging from the way her Nanna rolled her eyes at this comment it was possible she also had her doubts.

Chapter Seventeen

Later on when she reviewed the events of that weekend Jodie concluded that so much of her life changed from then on. When people spoke of life changing events she thought first of the death of her mother which jolted Jodie out of her life as she had then known it. And then she remembered the events at the farm that weekend when Nanna, Pop and Bonnie came to stay. Who would have realised that Rory returning to his family would change so much.

The first thing Jodie noticed – a nice thing actually - was how happy Charlie was to be around Joe and Nanna. They clearly were dear friends. It made her feel regretful for what Charlie had given up and his sacrifice in leaving Bronte Rivulet. The impact of his marriage break up must have been so much more immense for Charlie than Jodie. After all she was a little girl who had no memories of her father. And the impact of Charlie's departure on her mother seemed minimal. Jodie could not recall her mother speaking of regret or even showing any lingering affection for her ex-husband.

Jodie tried not to think about how much nicer her childhood would have been if Charlie had remained on the scene. How they might have created memories of happier times spent together bonding as father and daughter. Her recent years with Charlie had revealed his kind and caring nature. He even liked spending time with her – unlike her mother. And he had never yelled at her. He didn't even yell at Buster.

The second thing Jodie noticed – and it was hard not to – was how obsessed Bonnie was about Rory. All she could talk about was how they met. At a nightclub of course. How he bought her a drink. At least one Tia Maria and Coke, possibly more and then how he asked her to dance. One thing had led to another and apart from her job interview they had spent the entire week together. Bonnie was full of Rory's praises. Yet when grilled she became vague about what he did for employment and who his friends were.

It was only when she told him that she was heading to a farm near Cressy for the weekend to see family that Rory revealed he came from that area. Imagine the excitement when they discovered that the farm she was to visit was his family's farm.

'It was like it was meant to be,' exclaimed Bonnie with glowing eyes.

Trying to look equally rapt Jodie smiled at her cousin. Of course, she was happy for her but Bonnie's constant description of this paragon of virtue was unrecognisable from the Rory that others had described to her. Someone had got it wrong, but she had no idea who. As far as Bonnie was concerned the remainder of the day passed in a bubble of bliss. Rory had turned up mid-way through the following day and took his newly beloved on a tour of the property, although as Bonnie assured him, 'I have been here before you know but I'm sure I've yet to see it through your eyes. I just know it will be even more special. Maybe you can show me your childhood bedroom.'

Rory with a suggestive leer assured her he would be happy to do so.

Jodie tried to remain expressionless and not show what she really felt. She almost lost it when she glanced over at Nanna who was sitting by the fire with her knitting. Nanna was once more rolling her eyes.

Then the third weird thing that happened that weekend was how often Nanna, Pop and Charlie would retreat away from the fire ostensibly to do something, like set the table or locate something Nanna needed in the pantry. Why didn't she ask her, Jodie wondered. Next thing she would notice was the three of them in a whispered huddle. And if they looked up and saw her watching one of them would speak in a louder, everyday voice and mention something that she knew was completely unrelated to the whispered conversation. Very suspicious.

And the final weird thing? Well, that was the strangest of all. Jodie knew she should have seen it coming. After all it had become obvious to her that her father and Joan were extremely close. No surprise there. They worked together most days, either on the farm or in the study wrestling with the accounts and now, given recent events she wondered what else they wrestled with.

It all came to a head on the Sunday night when Joan invited Jodie and her family over to the Big House for dinner. Euan was still away on the mainland with his studies, but Rory continued to be in residence.

Bonnie was in a tizz making sure she was as beautiful as possible for the outing. Nanna, Pop and Charlie less so. More like they were resigned to going. Jodie was reluctant to leave the lamb. Yet she also was curious as to why they were all being summonsed to dinner. Maybe if she fed the lamb just before they left, she could leave the dinner early with an excuse that the lamb needed feeding again. Yes, that would work so long as they took more than one car. She suggested it to Nanna who seemed surprisingly agreeable. Maybe she also was reluctant to go?

'Of course, my dear. I don't like to stay up late so maybe you and I at least and possibly your grandfather could sneak away. We can't abandon your precious lamb,' Nanna said with a smile.

The lamb was making tremendous progress and was now located in the laundry. Christened *Lambkin* Charlie assured Jodie that he would be ready to join the others the next day.

'Jodie, you really shouldn't spoil him so much. He will be a nuisance once he grows up. Being charged by a hand reared adult is no joy, trust me. I have the scars to prove it.'

But Jodie was not convinced her new baby was yet out of the woods. Even more reason to leave early.

The night was coming in cold when they left, promising frost by morning. All were bundled up in warm coats, beanies and scarves. The heaters in both cars were turned on full but had barely warmed up by the time they reached the Big House. Like the last time Jodie, Bonnie and Charlie had been for dinner they arrived at the front entrance. The garden was a glittering fairyland with trees lit by sparking lights. The curve of the circular drive marked out with staked lights and the two lights by the front door blazed a welcome.

Nanna and Pop who had never been there before were suitably impressed by the massive house lit up as if for a performance. And maybe given the subsequent performance it wasn't surprising that a scene had been set. Which was reinforced by the alacrity with which Rory threw open the enormous front door.

'Welcome everyone' he declaimed as he ushered them all into the entry and divested them of their coats and woolly accoutrements. The stone flagged entry was chillier than last time. But the sitting room was cosy warm. An open fire lent its flickering light to the room. Thankfully there was further heating in the room – a panel radiator on the wall which was warm to touch. Jodie hoped the dining room would also have such a feature or she would regret taking off her coat. Jodie had worn her now favourite black top with the lurex thread and her black jeans. Her long hair pulled back in a ponytail she thought made her look rather sophisticated. But it didn't really matter what she wore when she was in the same room as Bonnie. She knew there was no comparison. That night Bonnie shone in a rich velvet maxi dress of deepest blue, almost black – high necked and long sleeved it was made out of some sort of stretchy material that clung to every curve. Jodie felt like the young inexperienced country lass that she was.

The evening started well enough. Pre-dinner drinks by the fire in the sitting room. Champagne for everyone but Charlie, Pop and Jodie. Beer for Charlie and Pop and elderflower cordial for Jodie. This was a new taste for her but after she took a tentative sip Jodie decided she quite liked it.

'I'll give you the recipe if you like,' said Joan. 'It's fiddly but not too hard and is very refreshing in the summertime. Old houses like ours have lots of elderflower bushes and it is good to use them somehow. The elderberry cordial is darker and stronger and not exactly to my taste.'

Nanna nodded in agreement. Soon she and Joan were in earnest discussion about the merits of various pickling and preserving recipes. Jodie already knew her Nanna lived to cook, but she had no idea how Joan with a sheep property to run had the time to do anything else. This time her offer to help in the kitchen was accepted and she followed Joan down a corridor accompanied by her Nanna who assured them that 'many hands make light work.'

Jodie had never been in the kitchen before. It was down a long corridor and through a glass enclosed walkway. A long way from the dining room which explained why the curry last time had been lukewarm. Not that she had minded then. Lukewarm or not, it had still been delicious.

She followed the others into the biggest kitchen she had ever seen. Big, but cosy warm – heated she assumed by the range before which Joan's house dog luxuriated in its warmth.

'Don't mind the mess,' said Joan as she gestured around the room.

To Jodie's eyes the room had the cosiness of a lived-in home. Magazines pushed to one end of an enormous table, some unwashed dishes in the sink and a mass of papers on a small table by the wall that must be farm papers and accounts. Her eye was drawn to a big poster that proclaimed the benefits of visiting Cornwall by rail. The scenery depicted in the poster immediately made Jodie to also want to visit Cornwall.

Joan, upon seeing her admire the poster, mentioned it was a honeymoon purchase many years ago.

'We went to the United Kingdom for our honeymoon and just like the poster urged us to do we travelled by rail. We were away for quite a while and saw lots of the countryside, but I think Cornwall was my favourite place. Maybe because of all those Daphne du Maurier books that I had devoured as a young woman, visiting Cornwall was something I had to do. Fortunately, Alastair was agreeable and it didn't disappoint.'

Joan sighed. 'It was all so long ago. Like it was another life. So much has happened since then and I find it hard to remember the young woman I once was.'

Nanna reached out and put a gentling hand on Joan's arm.

'Never mind,' said Nanna.' I think that's something that happens to all of us. I hope seeing this poster every day brings back memories of happier times.'

The two women separated by decades in age but alike in so many ways smiled deep into each other's eyes until with a shake Joan spoke. 'Never mind me. I get a bit sentimental sometimes but that won't get dinner dished up. It's not much. Just lasagne and salad. Oh, and garlic bread, of course.'

'My favourite,' said Jodie.

'Just the garlic bread?' twinkled Joan.

'All of it. I'm starving!'

'Then we can't have that. Come on ladies, let's get dinner to the other starving hordes.'

A solemn procession ensued. Joan leading the way carrying an enormous tray in which the lasagne dish steamed. Nanna followed with a bowl of dressed green salad and Jodie brought up the rear with two hot loaves of garlic bread tightly wrapped in foil. She was so hungry she thought she could eat an entire loaf.

The lasagne was delicious as Jodie expected and somehow there was enough garlic bread for everyone. She noticed Bonnie picked mostly at the salad which didn't surprise her. Bonnie was always carrying on about her weight. Not a problem for Jodie. Farmwork, horse riding and gardening every day kept her slim and fit. The thought of gardening made her think of Roman. Why wasn't he here? She made a mental note to ask her father later that evening.

Dessert was cake – again. But this time an orange cake with cream cheese icing. Almost as good as chocolate cake – but not quite. She noticed her father demolishing a second slice under Joan's smiling gaze.

And then with a tap on the wine glass Charlie stood up and cleared his throat as he prepared to speak.

'Thank you, Joan, for a delicious dinner. I'm in awe of how you manage to find time to feed us all with such a meal after I know you've been out with the sheep all afternoon. However, you managed it somehow and we're all the appreciative beneficiaries. I think I speak for everyone to say we're all so very grateful.'

With much laughter they all raised their glasses to acknowledge their host's hard work. Then with further throat clearing Charlie continued, this time with a solemn expression on his face.

'I'm so pleased to share with you all some other good news. Today while we were freezing out in the paddocks delivering lambs, I had the bright idea to ask Joan to marry me. We've become very close in recent times and I hoped she might reciprocate my affections. To my great surprise and unending gratitude Joan accepted me. I hope you will also share in our happiness as we plan a life together.'

Joan and Charlie stared across the table at each other. Their love shining out for all to see as they quietly raised their glasses at each other in a silent and loving toast.

No one spoke.

Whilst this had not come as a total surprise to Jodie, having been aware of how close Joan and Charlie were in their everyday interactions, she had not realised they were THAT serious. Observing the others around the table she could see a range of different reactions. Her Nanna staring across the table to Pop and mouthing something like - *Did you know?* And his slight negative shake of the head in reply, given with a shrug as if to convey – *Well what would you do? They're adults.*

Bonnie meanwhile turned in amazement to Joan. 'A wedding? How marvellous. Will I be invited? Will it be formal or casual? And you must wait until the weather warms so I can wear something strappy.'

Joan smiled at her as if in agreement. Charlie raised his glass in a toast to his bride to be his loving smile reflected in the happy faces of Nanna, Joe and Jodie.

But Rory's reaction was the most astounding yet. With a shove he stood up and pointing his finger at Charlie he launched forth:

'How dare you think you can marry my mother? She is way too good for you. You! …. You're just a farmhand – old and definitely not one of us…' spittle flew out as he spoke and as he drew a breath to continue his mother interrupted.

'Rory! Stop it Right now. That is most unnecessary. I'm sure once you've calmed down and you've had a chance to reflect you'll regret what you've just said.'

A wave of red flushed across Rory's face. It was clear calming down and reflection were not on his agenda. Jodie was transfixed, as was Bonnie who gazed open mouthed at the performance. On the other hand Joan and Charlie appeared to be resigned. They had seen this all before. Any hope that an older and wiser Rory had left such behaviour behind was not to be.

'No, I will not calm down. This is so wrong. Mum you can't marry this second-rate man. How can you think of putting him in our father's place? Who knows what his long-term plans are? Do you really want to see your sons disinherited and this sad loser taking all? I see how it will play out. Euan banished to the mainland and me run off the property. How could you Mum?'

Even in a rage Rory was magnificent. Dark hair flying as he tossed his head, eyes flashing sparks of blue ice and his hands dramatically punctuating every word. Acting success was almost guaranteed Jodie decided. Women would swoon watching such a performance.

Charlie stood up. 'That's quite enough, Rory. You're upsetting your mother. I suggest you leave the room to calm down and return once you can speak to us politely.'

'Yes, that's quite enough,' sneered Rory. 'I'm outa here, but don't think this is the end. There's not going to be any wedding, if that's the last thing I do!'

He turned and strode out of the room slamming the door behind him. The people left behind remained silent. No-one knew what to say. Charlie slowly sat down. Heads swivelled towards Joan in expectation she would have something add. And she did.

'I'm sorry you had to witness that performance. Charlie and I have witnessed many of Rory's turns in the past so I suppose it comes as no surprise to us, but I suppose it can be a bit of a shock to anyone else. It's my fault in many ways. I should have given him some advance notice of what we were going to announce tonight. That may have calmed things but then again – maybe not. Rory might have just had longer to stew and prepare his diatribe. So sorry. It was meant to be a happy night and my son has taken the shine off.'

'Don't apologise, Joan dear,' reassured Nanna. 'Trust me. Our daughter could really turn it on when she didn't get her way. Sorry Jodie, but you know it was so with your mother.'

'I can confirm that,' said Charlie. 'We've all witnessed Donna's tantrums. Rory has potential, but he has yet to surpass Donna in the way of dramatic talent,' he said smiling at Joan. By now he had stood up and was moving to Joan. Once there he crouched down and with a comforting arm around his now fiancée Charlie continued: 'I think it might be best if I stay here tonight and you lot head home. Maybe we'll get a chance to talk some sense into Rory, but in any event I think I need to be here.'

Joan nodded. 'Mind you I think that's him heading off.'

The sound of a car revving and then speeding off could be heard.

'Well, that's that then,' said Charlie as he stood up and helped Joan to her feet.

'We'll clear up and the rest of you head off. It's late and Jodie – you have babies to feed.'

Jodie's hand flew to her mouth. In all the excitement she had completely forgotten about the lambs. What a night! And with this level of angst the wedding promised to be something else. Maybe they should elope. Yes, for the safety of everyone concerned maybe that would be for the best.

Chapter Eighteen

No-one seemed to be in a hurry to go to bed that night. Jodie was busy preparing the lambs' milk bottles helped by Joe, while Bonnie poked the fire into life and added wood to create a roaring blaze. Meanwhile Nanna fussed in the kitchen making hot chocolate for all.

Lambs fed the four relaxed by the fire sipping their steaming hot chocolate and gazing thoughtfully into the blaze.

'Well, that was some night!' said Joe at last.

'An understatement Pop,' said Jodie.

'Interesting, I would call it,' said Bonnie who always loved a bit of excitement.

'And the food was delicious,' said Nanna who as expected paid attention to other people's cooking.

'Did you check out the plates Nanna? That was gold on the edging, wasn't it?' asked Bonnie. 'And the serviettes? Proper linen they was. How posh is that?'

'Yes, Bonnie dear. Most impressive. You could see Joan had gone to a big effort for tonight. Pity Rory had to spoil it. Although I get the impression he has spoiled a lot of things in the past. I do hope he calms down and understands that his mother and Charlie deserve to be happy. After all they've both been on their own for way too long. Looking at them tonight it's clear they suit each other. I wonder why it didn't dawn on any of us before. What do you think, Jodie?'

'Well …' Jodie spoke slowly as she ordered her thoughts. She was still holding Lambkin, who tummy full was now dozing in her arms. She ran her hand down the length of his woolly body and continued: 'I knew they were good mates. Never cross with each other and often thinking alike about things that had to be done on the farm. I just thought that was because they'd known each other for ages and trusted each other – like a good team. Somehow it makes sense that their feelings have progressed from friendship to love. A bit of a shock, I guess, for the rest of us. But I think it's a happy shock. And good luck to them. I suppose Charlie will move in with Joan into the Big House. I'm not sure I want to. It's way too grand for me.' Jodie pulled a face as she contemplated how these changes might impact on her. Could she remain in this cottage on her own?

'Now that you mention it Jodie. Your dad, Nanna and I have been talking about what you might like to do in the future. I suspect Charlie hadn't raised the subject until his plans for a future with Joan were settled. But it's probably time someone mentioned it to you.'

Jodie stared at her Pop in shock. So that was what they were discussing in their whispered huddles in recent times. Why hadn't they asked her? It was her future after all. She felt herself becoming indignant, and a little bit hurt too.

'It's my future. Shouldn't you have asked me and not excluded me?'

'We owe you an apology Jodie dear. We should have spoken to you earlier,' said Nanna. 'You're right. It is your future and should be your decision. I suppose we are so used to treating you as a child, but you stopped being a child long ago.'

'You see,' Joe continued. 'It's probably our fault. We started the conversation with Charlie. We reminded him that you had agreed to spending three years up here on the farm so as to give time for things to settle back at Bronte Rivulet. Things have certainly moved on in the village. New people have moved in and new scandals have arisen – plenty of new scandals. You wouldn't believe what some people have got up to! You'd be amazed. There's one family…'

'Joe,' warned Nanna. She had that no nonsense voice on. Joe knew better than to mess with her when Nanna spoke so.

'Oh, never mind that. Just remind me sometime, Jodie to bring you up to speed with the local scandal,' he said casting a wary eye towards Nanna and grinning at Bonnie who was leaning forward with interest. She so loved a gossip. 'And you too Bonnie. I won't forget to share with you as well.'

'Joe,' Nanna's voice was even sterner.

'Alright then. So Jodie, you're almost 18. The three years is as good as up and you can now choose what you want to do. Of course you could choose to stay here and I think from what I've heard that might be tempting. You've become a proper farm girl and a bit of a gardener as well. Or so I hear. Although this proposed marriage might have thrown a bit of a spanner into the works?'

Jodie nodded. Life at the farm had turned out to be so much more fun than she'd anticipated. Hard on the hands and nails of course. But she had never intended to be a beauty queen even if she had the looks. And now there was the question of where to live if she stayed. She couldn't see herself living in the Big House. She'd get lost for sure.

'You're most welcome to return to the village and move in with us. Of course, you know that we'd love you to come live with us. But only if you want. Like I said the village has changed a lot in the last few years and those hateful people are either no longer there or are focussed on making other people's lives miserable. And I think you've grown up and become more resilient. Which is just as well as the police are no nearer to discovering who killed your mother. It may be that we will never know and not knowing may be something we will just have to live with. A sad fact of life. Do you have any plans for your future?'

Jodie grimaced: 'Let me sleep on it. After the events of this evening I don't think my brain can cope with anything else. I'll just put this one to bed and then I'm off. How about you Bonnie?'

'Sure thing, boss,' said Bonnie as she got up. 'I'm beat. See you Nanna and Pop. Not too early I hope.'

'You two sleep in,' said Pop. 'I'll do lamb duty. I don't sleep much anyway.'

'Too right,' grinned Jodie. 'You don't sleep much 'cause you're too busy snoring. We can hear you from our bedroom down the corridor.'

***

Later, after their teeth had been brushed, makeup removed, and warm pyjamas put on both girls snuggled into their beds. Jodie once more on the mattress on the floor in Bonnie's room. It was much more fun sharing a room with her cousin rather than being on her own. That thought made her wonder if she could live in this house on her own once her father moved out. Maybe not. Still there was much to discuss and analyse from that evening's events. Bonnie, ever the romantic, took a different view of Rory's performance.

'Wasn't he beautiful?' Bonnie extolled. Jodie had no doubt who she was referring to. Clearly she meant Rory and not Charlie nor Pop.

'Those eyes! That hair! Like a young Heathcliff,' spoke Bonnie dreamily as she once more visualised her hero when he was broadcasting his opinions. Although her recollection was possibly overlooking the spray of spittle.

'More like a spoiled brat' muttered Jodie, thankfully unheard by Bonnie who was lost in a fantasy of her and Rory walking down the aisle instead of Joan and Charlie and watched on by an adoring congregation.

'You know, I think I fancy him so much more. So much passion. He spoke from the heart. How could anyone not be moved. I do hope he returns to Hobart as I so want to see him again. Trouble is I don't know where he lives or his phone number or even who his friends are. What a tragedy it would be if we end up just like ships in the night. A passing romance with a tall, dark and handsome stranger never to be seen again. Such a tragedy.'

'Or a mercy,' muttered Jodie.

'No, there must be a happy ending. Of course, we will reunite at Charles and Joan's wedding. Like as in a movie so many misunderstandings resolved at the happiest of days – a wedding. I can see it now. Night, Jodie. I have some dreaming to do.'

And with that Bonnie rolled over and closed her eyes certain she would be dreaming about Rory – her soon to become sweetheart.

No sweet dreams for Jodie, however. She tossed and turned for what seemed to her to be most of the night. What to do? Should she stay here or return to Bronte Rivulet. Three years ago it would have been a no brainer. This was the last place she wanted to be. Stuck on a farm in the freezing cold middle of Tasmania with a total stranger who assured her he was her father. Three years ago, if she could, she would have run back home – back to the safety of Nanna and Pop. But now she wasn't so sure. It had snuck up on her, but in time Jodie had come to love the farm. Not only to love the sprawling surroundings but also to love being involved in the farm activities that changed with the seasons. She now enjoyed working with Charlie who had become a trusted friend, as well as a beloved father. That thought made her pause. Yes, that felt right. He was a decent man – and beloved. Pity her mother had not appreciated his good qualities. If she had then life would have been different. Jodie would have known her father so much earlier and her childhood memories would have been happy ones.

And there was Roman. Getting to know him and working with him in the garden most mornings had taught her so much. More importantly it had been fun. Roman with his funny anecdotes and interest in all living things had given her something to laugh at even when life had seemed so sad. Even learning about caring for bees, whilst initially terrifying had become a fascinating task. And the output was delicious – especially on Joan's scones.

And Joan. She didn't deserve to be treated the way she had been by Rory. Jodie would have given her all, sold her soul to the devil even, to have a mother like Joan. That thought made her pause. Hang on a minute! That may actually happen. The way things were going it looked like she might end up with a stepmother: the Joan she so fervently admired. Jodie crossed her fingers under the bedcovers and made a silent wish. But just because she fancied acquiring a stepmother didn't mean she wanted to live with them. Nor did she want to have anything to do with a stepbrother like Rory. It was only a small jump from thoughts of Euan. Euan as a stepbrother would be perfectly acceptable. She wondered where he was now and why he hadn't been here tonight for the special announcement. Did he even know about the engagement? And if he did know, would he react like Rory? She hoped not. Euan had always seemed so calm and not on edge like Rory. So many questions to which she didn't know the answers. And with a sigh Jodie accepted defeat and rolled over and somehow drifted away into a deep sleep.

Chapter Nineteen

There wasn't much to do next morning apart from feed the lambs, clean out their bedding and wait for Charlie to appear. Nanna of course had been busy in the kitchen and had already served them a delicious, cooked breakfast of bacon and farm eggs. And with breakfast out of the way Nanna had commenced fussing over lunch. Another one of her specialties was already in the oven: a salmon quiche made using ingredients she had brought up with her.

Pop was busy outside. Jodie could hear his tuneless whistle and the rhythmic snap of his clippers as he pruned the gnarled fruit trees by the back door. A whistle punctuated by the occasional curse. Bonnie and Jodie were once again by the fire. The chill of the winter's day, although sunny, did not tempt them outside. Today was the day Lambkin would join the other lambs out in the shed and Jodie was not looking forward to it. She was contenting herself with one last cuddle while she and Bonnie talked. Bonnie was focussed on Jodie and her future. Rory was either forgotten or resolved. Bonnie hadn't mentioned him all morning and for that Jodie was happy.

'So what are you going to do?' As usual Bonnie was direct and right to the point.

'I don't know. Hopefully, dad will be here soon and I can talk it over with him.'

'Go with your gut instinct. That's what I always do,' said Bonnie.

Jodie smiled. Of course, her cousin would prefer gut instinct over considered analysis every time. That's what made her so unpredictable and so interesting. But Jodie was not her cousin and had never had her sense of daring. Maybe it had something to do with being raised by her mother in her first fifteen years. She had learned early on that it was best to linger in the shadows and not be noticed. That was the only way to avoid her mother's stormy and erratic attention. Never knowing what would happen next had shaped her character. If she could dive into adventures like her cousin she would, but so many times she had held back. Even learning to ride Copper had taken more courage than she knew she possessed. And it was only by approaching the task in incremental steps urged on by Euan that Jodie overcame her fear and forged a bond with that big horse. Maybe this was a challenge that she should also approach in little steps and with some luck the final decision might reveal itself. Maybe a list of pro's and cons might help. But first she had to talk to Charlie. Talk to her dad. After all he was her father and must want what was best for her.

It wasn't until they were seated for lunch that Charlie appeared.

'Great. Time for lunch,' he said sniffing the air appreciatively. 'Nanna. You beaut! Your salmon quiche is the best. I hope you've left some for me. I'm starving.'

The others who by now had finished their quiche and salad sat and waited for Charlie to eat. Nanna who had refreshed the tea pot sat down again, poured tea into Charlie's mug and waited expectedly.

'Ah, I needed that. It's been a busy morning. I've been around all the sheep. Fed them and checked them. They've all coped with the bad weather surprisingly well. And I'll soon be able to turn those lambs out into the House Paddock. They will still need bottle feeding of course but the chance to run around in the sunshine will be good for them. And a bit of grass to practice on won't hurt.' He paused, looked around the table and continued: 'Why are you all staring? What's the matter?'

'Nothing,' said Nanna. 'We just think it's time we had a bit of a chat.'

'Yeah Dad,' added Jodie. 'When were you going to bring me into the conversation you were having with Nanna and Pop?'

'Ah, that' Charlie paused as he reached for his cigarettes.

'No, Charlie,' commanded Nanna. 'Now is not the time. Not inside.'

With a sigh Charlie put his cigarettes away. Even though he was master of his own house he knew Nanna's word was law. It was time to talk to Jodie and judging by the stern gaze she was directing at him she already had some inkling of what they had been discussing. Jodie's next comments confirmed this.

'Dad, when were you going to tell me that you had been discussing my future with Nanna and Pop? Don't I have a say in what happens to me? Or am I like the lambs shunted around regardless of my wishes?'

Charlie sighed: 'Jodie, it's not like that.' He rubbed his eyes before continuing: 'Of course you have the ultimate say in what happens. To be honest it took Carol and Joe reminding me that the three years you had agreed to stay here was almost up. It's gone so quickly and I hope you've had as much fun as I have had. Spending time with you and seeing you learn so much on the farm has been a real delight. I'm so glad you agreed to come up here. The Jodie who arrived those years ago is so different from the Jodie you've become. Believe me when I say I'd like nothing more than for you to stay. But I accept that there may be other things you might want to do. You might want to study or put your newfound skills to greater use. It's your choice – but I promise that I will always be beside you cheering you on whatever you choose to do.'

Jodie could feel herself tearing up. Looking at the others she could see they also had watery eyes.

'Oh, that was all so lovely,' sniffed Bonnie. 'Charlie could you be my father too? I don't think I've ever heard my father say such wonderful things about me!'

Even though they all laughed at that, Jodie was aware of others watching her expectantly. She had no idea how to respond. Somehow her father understood and suggested they all go for a walk.

'It's turned into a sunny afternoon and I think a walk might do us good. How about a walk to the Big House and we can show Nanna the garden in daylight. Jodie you could show Nanna around while I go check on Joan?'

Both Joe and Bonnie decided they had better things to do so it was only three people who headed across the House Paddock – of course with Buster bringing up the rear. He had no intention of letting the master go anywhere unsupervised. Jodie wondered how Buster got on with Joan's house dog.

'Trust me, Buster knows his place,' said Charlie when asked. 'He knows how to behave. Joan's dog is always boss.'

The side gate was reluctant to admit them and Charlie with much cursing struggled to push it open. Jodie helpfully suggested that maybe they needed the magic password for it to open.

'More like install a new gate,' grumbled Charlie. But for some reason the gate was treasured having been in the same place for many decades, yet like many other old things gravity had got to it.

I can relate to that,' laughed Nanna.

Once the gate surrendered to their efforts and they were inside Charlie headed towards the house telling them he would find them later and Jodie directed her Nanna along a garden path. Their process was slow. Nanna felt the need to examine every plant, even ones Jodie had never noticed before. The clumps of snowdrops under the trees were exclaimed over as were the yellow jonquils in full bloom. Something about them being surprisingly advanced for the season and over in the distance Nanna espied some very early daffodils.

'I suppose the shelter of the hedge perimeters protects the garden,' speculated Nanna. 'Yes, that must be it. How marvellous. What a delight it must be to work in this garden. I hope we can visit in spring when those cherry trees over there are in bloom. Somebody loved this garden many generations ago to plant such trees and just think you have continued the nurturing. You have left a bit of yourself here.'

Jodie could see Jean and Charlie heading their way. Once they grew near Nanna gushed her appreciation of the garden.

'Yes, it is rather lovely,' said Joan. 'But it is all thanks to Roman - and Jodie, too of course' she added. 'Roman has the artistic eye. Not me.' She smiled at Jodie. 'Remember that tulip bed out the front that first spring you were here?'

Jodie nodded. What a disaster it had turned out to be.

Joan turned to Nanna. 'I wanted something bright and cheery to greet visitors out the front, so I tasked Roman and Jodie to plant a bed of tulips. But not just any bed of tulips. I wanted the biggest and brightest of red, purple and orange tulips. They were an eyesore. On an overcast day they positively glowed. And of course they stayed in bloom seemingly for ever. I learned my lesson and the following year we reverted to pink, mauve and white. I have no idea what Roman did with those other bulbs. Maybe he threw them out?'

'Every gardener has their successes and failures,' commiserated Nanna. 'Gardens are always changing with the seasons. So the good thing is that the failures will never linger. But sadly, neither do the successes. Everything is fleeting. A reason to enjoy it when all our hard work pays off.'

Joan appeared to be her usual calm self. Although Jodie noticed one change. As they continued their perambulations around the garden, she noticed with approval that Joan and Charlie were holding hands. The engagement must still be on. The hand holding had also not escaped Nanna's notice.

'So how are things today, Joan?' she asked. 'Heard from Rory?'

'Actually, I have. He rang from Cressy this morning. Said he stayed the night in there. He has left my car with a friend who will return it. Rory seemed much calmer and said he was planning to return to Hobart. That's probably for the best at this stage. I would have preferred he hadn't cleaned out my wallet before he left. It doesn't surprise me and certainly disappoints me, so I guess that's another reason why I'm pleased he has left.'

Joan broke off as she realised she may have said too much. But Nanna with the sympathy of shared experience put an arm around her shoulder.

'Children!' she commiserated. Charlie has probably told you a bit about our Donna. Each time I thought she couldn't shock me anymore she went and did something worse. Sorry Jodie dear, but you will probably agree that your mother tested us all.'

Jodie shrugged. She'd heard it all before and really didn't want to hear any more. Maybe she could find Roman and leave these two mothers to their shared misery.

'Is Roman here?' she asked and was directed to the greenhouse. Sure enough Roman was inside potting up vegetable seedlings. It was balmy inside – the sunshine heating up the enclosed space.

Roman with his back to her, intent on his task, didn't register another's presence until Jodie's voice rang out. He turned with a welcoming smile and waved a dirt encrusted hand.

'Ah, Miss Jodie. Welcome. So lovely to see you. Look at these lettuces I'm potting up. Then once they're planted in separate pots they will thrive and I will plant them out soon enough. And look at these petunias I'm growing on for spring. They will go in that front bed. Now that I get to choose the colours the result is so much better,' he said complacently as his chocolate brown eyes twinkled with good humour.

'Yes. The Boss was just telling Nanna the tale of those tulips.'

'Ah yes such a disaster! And yet out of the disaster came victory. Victory for me that is,' said Roman.

'What did you do with the old bulbs?'

'Promise you won't tell The Boss but they're over in my garden. Split up and looking as good as ever. The purples are under the pink crab apples. The red I have planted with white tulips and the orange look amazing on their own in front of some green shrubs. See, there's a right place for everything. Sometimes it just takes a while to discover where that thing belongs.'

These words immediately reminded Jodie of her dilemma.

'Roman, I'm stuck. You see Nanna, Pop and Charlie have all reminded me that my three years I agreed to stay here are almost up and I have to choose what I want to do. You know, I have to decide whether I should stay here or return to Bronte Rivulet with Nanna

142

and Pop – or do something else. I so don't know what to do. And Joan and Charlie getting engaged just makes it even more complicated.'

Roman nodded as he listened. Clearly news of the engagement came as no surprise. But when she thought about it nothing seemed to surprise him. As she paused and looked at him questioningly Jodie already knew that Roman would not tell her what to do. She then thought of something else.

'Why weren't you at dinner last night? Shouldn't you have been there for the announcement?'

'Ahh,' Roman was seemingly lost for words. 'I um, was over at the Big House earlier and had the pleasure of hearing the happy news and sharing in a glass of champagne.' He peered closely at Jodie. 'It is happy news. Do you agree?'

'Yes. It was a surprise, but I can see they do suit each other. I'm not sure Rory agrees though.'

'Ah, Rory,' sighed Roman. 'There's not much that Rory agrees with. But we all encounter such people. They're best to be avoided.'

'Is that why you weren't there last night?'

'Possibly. But keep that to yourself. In any event you have more important matters to worry about. I will not advise you Miss Jodie. I will only make one comment. Maybe your future is not a matter of either/or. Maybe your future encompasses both this farm and the village in which you were born. After all your father and soon-to-be stepmother will continue to live here – and don't forget that horse you're now fond of – and me,' his eyes twinkled. 'But'. He paused, 'but you also have a past in that village, family ties and maybe also unfinished business. Maybe there is a reason you need to go back to settle the ghosts so to speak. Have you thought of that?'

Jodie nodded. As always Roman spoke sense.

'You're right. Three years ago when I left I was shattered. Maybe I need to go back and make my peace with that village. And you know what? Spending some time with Nanna and Pop - and Bonnie might be fun. Thanks Roman. You're a gem!'

Roman watched her run out of the greenhouse and down the path, long hair flowing behind her. The last three years had been a delight as he had watched the once traumatised young woman heal and develop hitherto unseen talents. He would miss her, but it was for the best. She needed to face her past and maybe - just maybe her future might be back here.

***

That evening after dinner Jodie announced her decision.

'All of you. Stop talking and listen to me! I've been thinking about what you said Nanna, Pop and dad. And I've made a decision. I'll come back with you both Nanna and Pop. For now. I don't know if I will want to stay for long or for ever. But I will give it a go. I'm not even sure what I will do there, whether there will be any work for me but at the very least Pop you can help me get my driver's licence.'

She looked around the four people who were her life. They all looked stunned.

'Well go on. Say something.'

Bonnie spoke first. 'Hurrah! We can continue to share a room. You know I'm staying with Nanna and Pop until I have saved enough wages to rent in Hobart. We'll be able to go clubbing and go to concerts – well, once you turn 18 or get a fake ID. We're going to have such fun.'

The disappointment was plain on Charlie's face. His pain was her pain, and she rushed to reassure him:

'Dad, it's not forever. I will be back. Discussing it with Roman made me realise that the decision is not an either/or. In fact I think it might be possible to choose to have both the farm and the village in my life. I'm not sure exactly how but I do know that I love both and I have to find a way in my life to include rural and semi-rural. Anyway, I think my going away and giving you some space will give you and Joan time to establish your own household.'

Charlie's emotions were clear as he gazed at his daughter. He was so proud of his little girl. How had she grown to be so wise and so clear in what she wanted? She certainly never got that from her mother and he felt he couldn't claim it was his doing. His eyes welled with happy tears.

'Dad,' said Jodie as she rushed to his side and enveloped him a tight bear hug. 'It's alright. I will come back. Trust me.'

Charlie smiled through his tears. 'It's not that. It's just that I'm so proud of you and the amazing young woman you've become. Of course, I – and Joan too, of course, would love you to make your home here. But equally we will support you in whatever you choose to do so long as you are happy.'

'Enough! That's way too enough emotion,' Bonnie interrupted the conversation, giving a wide yawn as she did so. 'If anyone should claim the glory for the incredible evolution of Jodie into an amazing human it should be me. I, her best and only cousin have been the number one influence – and need I say it? – the making of Jodie Wise. What a hero I am!'

Bonnie basked in what she saw as the appreciation of the others but in reality was a shared amusement – a shared loving amusement – of course.

Jodie pulled a face at her cousin then glanced across at her grandparents who appeared to be in silent communication. Nanna raising her eyebrows in a questioning glance directed at her husband. His replying shrug seemed to be an answer - *why not?* And then a nod from Nanna. Jodie was instantly suspicious. What was going on?

'Nanna?'

'Yes, dear?'

'Why are you and Pop behaving strangely? What's wrong?'

'Nothing, dear. We were just having a little conversation so to speak.'

'Conversation?' smiled Jodie. 'Hah! You weren't even speaking.'

'When you've been married as long as we have sometimes words are no longer necessary. We were just agreeing that it was time to share something with you all. It seems to us that these days, given you are all so close, what I'm about to reveal will have no impact at all.'

Now she had all of their attention. Jodie released her father and sat down at his feet. Even Bonnie was listening.

'Joe do you want to explain or should I?' asked Nanna.

'You go, Carol. You're better at explaining than me.'

'Alright then.' said Carol looking at each one in turn. 'It's really very simple and I'm surprised you haven't worked it out already. Joe and I were sworn to secrecy years ago, but I think it is now time to reveal all. Don't you agree Joe?'

Joe nodded at which time Bonnie blurted out 'Do tell. The tension is killing me.'

'And me, too,' smiled Charlie who was enjoying the drama. He had always had his suspicions but it looked like now they were to be confirmed. Funny how family secrets could be kept in plain sight.

'It's always been obvious. And I was expecting you two girls to work it out – that you two are related.'

'Of course we are,' said Jodie. 'We're cousins.'

Observing her grandmother's snort of laughter she continued: 'Aren't we?'

'A bit more than that. You two are half-sisters. Same mother – different father.'

'What? Mum had another baby – you?' said Jodie staring at Bonnie.

'Wow! That's so cool,' said Bonnie. 'I always hated being an only child and so wanted a sister – even a brother would have been alright, I suppose. But my father never seemed the clucky type and his marriage didn't last long enough to father another child. Hang on, Is he really my dad?' the cogs in Bonnie's brain were turning slowly but even she was starting to wonder what was the truth about her parentage.

'Probably not, I'm afraid,' said Nanna. 'You see Donna was very young when she became pregnant with you and she managed to keep her condition secret until she was about 7 months gone. Baggy clothes and all that can disguise so much. She had been quite secretive and to be honest – running wild. When we finally discovered she was pregnant to some extent it was a relief. In our village it's not unusual for there to be teenage mothers. At least she wasn't taking drugs. We hoped there was a nice young man in the background with whom she could settle down and raise a family. Someone a bit like you Charlie.'

'Ah, but it was way before my time,' said Charlie. 'Who was the father? Did you ever find out?'

'No idea,' piped up Joe. 'She refused to say even though we both asked her over and over. Saying the father deserved to know they had a child, but Donna wouldn't have a bar of it. Said it was her fault and she wasn't going to destroy his future. And no, Bonnie, it wasn't your dad.'

'By then Donna's pregnancy was so advanced that she needed to go to term but she didn't want to keep the baby. To be honest and sorry Bonnie dear that was a bit of a relief to us. Donna was too young to be a mother and could barely look after herself let alone a baby.'

She never could, thought Jodie.

'So what happened then?' asked an intrigued Bonnie. After all, this story was all about her. Just the way she liked it.

'So, we all knew your parents were not having much success starting a family Bonnie. I had the bright idea that they adopt Donna's baby which they were keen to do and we convinced Donna to hand you over after the birth. It was such a traumatic birth that I think she was happy to go along with our proposal. I never had the impression she regretted it. Do you Joe?'

'No. It was like after your birth she blocked out all memory of your existence and then about a year after that she met you Charlie. One thing led to another – a wedding and a pregnancy. She seemed so happy when she had you Jodie. Well, initially happy and even with a small baby in her arms she never mentioned her other baby. And even when you came to stay that time Bonnie, Donna gave no indication that she remembered you were her daughter. She had sworn us to secrecy so all we could do was treat you as best we could. It has been such a joy seeing you and Jodie form a close friendship – just like sisters should. And I'm so pleased that your lives continue to be intertwined.'

Bonnie gestured as if to wave all that lovey dovey stuff away: 'Never mind that Nanna. Lovely though it is. More importantly: who is my father?'

'Well, that's what I'm trying to tell you. We have no idea. It could be anyone. Donna was running wild in those days and yes,

I know Charlie' she said glancing at Charlie who was pulling a face. 'It was a pattern of behaviour that continued for many years afterwards. We've just had to accept that we will never know and to love you for who you are – our precious other granddaughter.'

'And my sister,' said Jodie, smiling across the table at Bonnie. 'Half-sister or full sister, who cares? You're still my sister and that means I'm entitled to borrow your clothes. We're similar sizes after all.'

'No way. Make up maybe, but clothes no!'

Nanna glanced at Joe and sighed with relief as if to say, *thank goodness that's over.* Jo nodded as if to agree.

The rest of the evening passed quietly. There were still chores to be done – lambs to be fed, wood to be chopped and brought in for the fire and washing up to be done. It was their last evening together. Next morning Bonnie was to head back home to Devonport to pack for her move down south. She had a week before she commenced her cadetship and needed to move and settle in with Nanna and Pop. Jodie planned to travel the next day with Nanna and Pop back to Bronte Rivulet. She didn't have much to pack – only a few books, her farm clothes and her one good outfit. In the three years on the farm she had needed very little by way of clothes. Maybe that would change when she moved back down south but with everything that had been going on her attire was of no concern.

After the lambs had been fed the girls retired to their room. Bonnie focused on folding and packing her clothes into her suitcase, chattering while she did so. It was a while before she noticed that her roommate was silent.

'Are you ok, sis?'

At that Jodie's head swung around and she softly smiled.

'Sis? I like that. Yep, I'm fine. Not sure about heading back to the Rivulet after all these years, although knowing I have a safety net and can come back here if I want kinda helps.'

'And knowing I'll be there as your support crew must help?' said Bonnie, secure in the knowledge that her involvement would always improve any situation.

'Yeah. Of course. And I'm really happy about what Nanna said. I must be a bit slow – or trusting. I just accepted what everyone said over all the years – that you were a sort of cousin and I never questioned it any further. Cousin or sister – it's all good. No, more than good. It's the best news I've had for ages.'

Jodie paused and looked thoughtfully across at Bonnie: 'Although I'm more than a bit cross with my mum. Why couldn't she have told me – or even better kept you. Growing up with a sister in that house would have made such a difference. Two of us against her. Imagine the difference that would have made.'

'Maybe, but what is equally possible is that she might have stopped with one and that would have been dire. I would have been in your situation on my own, dealing with our mother and you would never have existed and I would be sisterless. No – this has worked out for the best. I had the best childhood. My parents were pretty good. Until they broke up that is. Wait 'til I tell dad I know his dark secret! That should be good for some compensatory goodies,' she smiled and added, 'I know you had a shit childhood but somehow, you've come out of it tougher and hey, you now have me! It's time we went shopping in Hobart and did you a makeover. Trust me.'

***

The next morning went in a rush. Nanna insisted on cooking everyone a hearty breakfast of corn fritters and bacon. Charlie spoke of somehow enticing Nanna to stay – maybe by chaining her in the kitchen. He was going to miss her cooking he said. Although they all knew that as soon as they left he and Buster would be moving over to the Big House where he would continue to be well fed.

Bonnie was the first to leave, assuring Nanna and Pop that she would be with them in no time: 'But not before I've had a long chat with my father. He's got a bit of explaining to do!'

Nanna and Pop were buckled in the car with engine running yet still Jodie had yet to follow. She stood close to her father by the front gate unsure what to say. Buster, sensing change was in the air leaned in close. Jodie's hand trailed down and stoked his glossy fur. There was so much she would miss. Was she making the right decision? Was it too late to change her mind?

Her father sensing Jodie's growing reluctance took her hand as he opened the gate and directed her onwards.

'Off you go. Don't keep Nanna and Pop waiting. Remember if you don't like it there just ring and I'll be there in a flash to bring you home. Or,' Charlie reached into his jeans pocket and drew out a folded envelope. 'Here is an early 18th birthday present. It's for your first car. Joe will help you find a suitable one. And then whenever you like you will be able to drive up here and see us – and Copper too. Any time - once you have your licence, of course. Now that's motivation isn't it?'

'Thank you so much, dad!' Jodie flung her arms around her father, her anxiety now a thing of the past. Charlie was the best dad ever and had given her an unexpected gift that made all the difference: the freedom to come and go as she liked.

Jodie took one long glance across the valley as they drove along the dirt road still muddy from the recent rain. Three years ago she had gazed at these paddocks in horror. The windy vista and the wide-open spaces denuded of buildings and people had filled her with dread. At the time moving here with a stranger had seemed like a descent into hell. But she had promised her grandparents she would stay and now she was glad she had honoured that promise. For the Jodie of now was so different to the Jodie of three years ago. That Jodie would have been surprised to learn that she might be sad to leave these winter brown, closely cropped paddocks. Or to discover that the Jodie of now had come to love caring for sheep or had learnt to actually ride a horse – and maybe even enjoy it. Whatever lay ahead Jodie felt confident she could manage it. And if not she knew she was welcome to return to the farm.

Turning her head away from the unfolding vista she leaned forward and spoke to her grandparents: 'So, where are we stopping for lunch?'

Chapter Twenty

The three years she had been away seemed like a lifetime and yet as they approached the village Jodie could see that very little had changed. Still the same approach, driving past paddocks populated with various breeds of cattle – black, creamy and brown – the road bending then opening into the main street. Still lined with old buildings and deserted like it was the haunted street in some historical movie. She half expected the door to the general store to open and a woman in a long dress and bonnet emerge.

Yes. It all looked the same. They turned off the main street and headed along a short road before turning into another where at the end they turned into the driveway of Nanna and Pop's home. Memories flooded back. Memories of Pepper who she half expected to see running from around the back of the house – running to welcome her home. Her little dog who she hadn't thought of for ages and now the flooding memories hurt like a physical ache. So much pain it was almost impossible to draw a breath. Yet somehow she did and it gave her sufficient energy to carry her bag into the house.

Like everything else the house was unchanged. The kitchen - pristine as always and her bedroom as it always had been waiting for her to return. It all felt so bizarre. Jodie felt like she had travelled back in some sort of time machine. Nothing had changed. But she had.

Joe muttered something about checking the goats. A neighbour had been caring for them and his dog while they had been away, and he wasn't sure they would be alright. Carol spoke about preparing something for dinner and suggested Jodie stretch her legs and go for a walk and 'please bring back some milk and bread from the shop.'

Jodie shrugged. Maybe a walk would ease this sense of dislocation that was impacting on her. She walked past the tree she and Pop had planted on Pepper's grave. It was thriving and had almost doubled in size while she had been gone. Being deciduous all last summer's leaves had been shed but she could see the swelling of buds getting ready to shortly burst forth.

Jodie sent a small prayer Pepper's way: *You were the best dog. You made my miserable life tolerable. I still miss you. You would have liked Buster and the farm – and all that manure. I hope wherever you are in doggy heaven you are happy. You were the best.*

Giving a sigh she turned away and headed out the garden and up the street. The next thing she had to do, if only to banish the demons, was to visit her old home. Not that she wanted to do so but it was something Jodie felt she had to do. As she turned the corner she abruptly stopped. It had all changed. The windbreak of ancient pines was now completely gone and all trace of them removed. It was like they had never existed. She remembered the shushing sound of the wind in those trees at night that had soothed her to sleep. Now only a memory. Just like the house. Although that was definitely a bad memory. She stared in amazement at the bare dirt where once a house had stood. Then walked over to a sign announcing that a desirable residence would shortly be constructed on this site by a firm of local builders.

Jodie nodded. Now that was good progress. Sorry though she was to see that windbreak go, the demolition and removal of the house was something to celebrate. She had been dreading walking past her old home and had been worried seeing it would revive toxic memories. With the house gone and all trace removed maybe she could relax and put it all behind her. One day and hopefully very soon there will be another home in its place – inhabited by a family with maybe a tribe of children, a cat and a dog. And their laughter would help her to further banish any negative feelings that might linger. Or at least she hoped so.

Jodie's perambulations took her past her old school. It still looked the same. No surprise there. Not wishing to revisit memories of her miserable school days she sped up and followed the outer street of the village, noticing as she went a number of new infill homes constructed in paddocks where once ponies had grazed. Progress that would be approved by many Jodie supposed, but she kind of missed seeing the ponies. Eventually she arrived back at the main street and headed towards the general store. She noticed that the lady serving was a stranger who took her money without any indication of knowing her. Now that was a change that she liked.

As she went to open the door it opened and a person started to enter before seeing Jodie and standing back to allow her to exit. The person started, frowned and then exclaimed 'Jodie? It's you, isn't it? You're back!'

That was stating the obvious. Of course she was back. Otherwise, she wouldn't be standing in the doorway blocking traffic. He took her arm and pulled her outside away from the door. Jodie immediately recognised the person as Will, but she was still not sure she should acknowledge him. After all, in the three years she had been away he had not been in contact. Not a note. Not a phone call. Nothing from her so-called best friend. And she was not sure why.

'Yes, it's me. Hi Will.'

He beamed: 'It's so great to see you again. Have you got time for a chat? I'll buy you a coffee over there at the café. That is if you're not in too much of a rush.'

Might as well get it over with thought Jodie. And anyway, she could do with a coffee. So long as he paid, of course. And he owed her an explanation. At least if she never saw him again, she would then know why he had dropped her.

'Alright then. A coffee would be nice.'

They crossed the street and entered the old-time tea shop which was popular with the tourists. At this time of day, it was fairly empty and they found a table tucked away in the corner. While Will wandered across to the counter to order their coffee and some cake to share Jodie looked around.

To be honest she had never been inside before. Back then, in what she called the bad old days, she had never had any money to spare on treats like this. Come to think of it she still was cash poor. But no matter. She could see Will over at the counter paying for today's treats. Maybe he had a job. Or was he still at school? A question she immediately asked when he returned to the table.

'What are you doing now? Are you still at school? Or have you left?' she asked.

'Nah. I left last year. I'd had enough of the bus trip into town every morning. Can you believe it? The bus left at 7 in the morning and was not home 'til after 5. That was such a killer – especially in winter. So I decided I'd had enough and just left. Anyway, at the time I didn't want to study after school. I've been helping dad with the farm and that suits me. Fresh air and sunshine and I can choose my hours.' He smiled: 'or dad can. And you? You left and went somewhere, didn't you?'

'Yep. I've been away. And now I'm back, although I'm not sure for how long.'

Jodie studied him. His shaggy wheat coloured hair still looking messy in need of a cut. He had filled out. She supposed from all the farm work and there was a hint of gingery stubble on his chin. Not a lot. Just enough to give him a rugged outdoorsy look. He was the Will she remembered, just more so.

'I missed seeing you,' smiled Will as he stared intently into her eyes.

'Now, just hang on a minute.' Jodie could feel her temper rise. How dare he try that one on, all the while looking like he meant what he said.

'In all the time I've been away – almost three years – have I heard from you? Not once – not ever! And now you say you missed me! Really? Give me a break.'

Jodie rolled her eyes as she reached for her coffee. The sooner she finished it the sooner she could go. Pity about the cake. Looked like she would have to miss out on that. And it looked delicious. Still a girl must stand by her principles. Will clearly was a light weight. If he missed her so, then why didn't he make contact.

'Well then, Will. If you missed me then why didn't you make contact?'

Will spread his hands out wide as if seeking her forgiveness and he was: 'I'm sorry. That came out wrong. I was so glad to see you just now. Surprised too as I understood you'd left forever and didn't want to see me ever again. That hurt 'cause I thought we were best friends, but I had to accept your grandparents knew what was right for you.'

'My grandparents?'

'Yep. I think it was the day after you left. I went around to take you down to the river. I brought my dog Missy with me as she seemed to cheer you up and she always liked a swim in the river. Your grandpa told me you had gone away, and they weren't sure if you would ever return. I was gutted that you had left without telling me. Then when I asked for your address, they told me it would be for the best if I didn't write and let you be. That you needed to recover from the trauma. I suppose that made sense, so I backed off and got on with things. Three years is it?'

Jodie nodded.

'It seems like forever. But I can see that wherever you've been it's treated you good. You look great, by the way and your hair is amazing. So long. OK your turn now. Where have you been and why didn't you write?'

'I left in a hurry. My father turned up out of the blue and insisted I go with him. Nanna and Grandpa urged me to go and to be honest I wasn't really thinking straight. I didn't have the energy to work out what I wanted. So I just went along with what they urged me to do. I was simply going through the motions of living – sure I was breathing, but everything else seemed too much. Whatever they told me to do I did. A bit like I was sleepwalking through life. It took me a while to come out of that black hole and I guess when I eventually thought of you, I decided you were part of that old life and hadn't transferred across to my present.'

'But where were you?'

'Up around Cressy way. On a big sheep property that dad manages. Cold as. And the wind is ferocious. But the sheep seem to cope and it sure toughened me up. So much so I found it hard to leave today.'

'I can tell it's become a special place for you.'

Jodie nodded.

'If it's so special, why are you back here?'

Jodie shrugged. 'I'm not sure. I'd promised to go away for three years. My time away is almost up. Nanna and Grandpa thought I should come back and I think they worry I have no future up there. And Bonnie is moving this way. She's got a cadetship in Hobart. And she was keen for me return.'

'Bonnie, your cousin?'

'No Bonnie my sister. My half-sister.'

'No way! Tell me more.'

Will's enthusiasm made Jodie smile. His reaction reminded her of the Will long ago. A Will full of boundless enthusiasm – like some sort of energetic puppy. His explanation rang true but she would not forgive him until after she had a chance to speak to her grandparents. Still there was no reason why she could not be polite. If what he said was correct, and despite what had happened she was tempted to resume their friendship. With a sigh Jodie realised how much she had missed her friend.

An intuitive Will immediately noticed. 'Are you alright? Do you want to go?'

Jodie looked around and noticed the staff tidying up. It must be close to closing time and they'd yet to eat the cake. All of a sudden she was starving. Maybe that had something to do with the emotions swirling around in her body. Revving up the gastric juices so to speak.

'We'll go in a minute. But first we have a cake to finish.'

The cake – a very tasty lemon syrup cake was demolished in seconds. They stood to go and were out of the café before they were called back to collect Jodie's shopping.

'Oops,' said Jodie. 'Too much deep and meaningful conversation and I forget everything.'

'Can I walk you back home. Just like the old days?'

'Sure.'

And just like the old days they meandered back to Jodie's grandparents' house, down the hill to the river, along the riverbank, across the weir and up the road to the little cottage at the end. For a moment Jodie half expected to see Pepper charge out the gate and race towards them. But that was not to be. She almost teared up when Will spoke.

'Yeah, I miss him too, you know. He was a champ. Maybe if you aren't doing anything tomorrow, I'll pick you up and you can come and check out our farm. I've got something you might be interested in seeing.'

'What?'

'Never you mind. You'll find out tomorrow.'

By now they were at the front gate. With a wave and a promise to be there in the morning by ten, Will headed off, whistling as he went. Jodie turned and headed up the side path to the back door.

First thing she needed to do was talk to her grandparents. They definitely had some explaining to do.

'Is that you Jodie dear? You'd been away so long I was starting to worry about you. Would you mind calling Pop before you come inside. It's almost teatime.'

Still carrying the shopping bag Jodie headed down the back path, past the vegetable bed full of winter vegetables. Vegetables she now found easy to identify as she had become skilled in growing them with Roman: broccoli, cabbage and cauliflower. All ripe and ready to harvest. Through the back gate and into her grandfather's domain. She called out loud as he was nowhere to be seen. After a second yell she heard a shout and Pop appeared from out of the woodshed wheeling a barrow full of firewood and followed by his old dog.

'Looks like we're in for a cold one tonight. So I thought I should fill up the wood box. Were you looking for me?'

'Yep. Nanna said to call you in. Tea is almost ready.'

'Excellent. I don't know about you but I'm starving.'

157

Before they went inside, they first had to unload the wheelbarrow and fill up the wood box by the back door. Pop passed some kindling to Jodie with instructions to take it inside and that he would follow once he'd given the dog some kibble and settled him in his kennel. Somehow Jodie managed to juggle the load of kindling as well as the shopping bag which she gratefully passed to her Nanna.

'Thank you for getting the groceries. We needed the milk for our cuppa as I'm all out. And your Pop won't be milking the goats until the morning. Now, once you've got rid of that wood and washed up we can sit down to dinner. Assuming your Pop appears.'

'Yeah, yeah. I hear you woman,' Joe called from by the back door. 'Just have to get these boots off and I'll be in.'

Dinner was rissoles with gravy. Served with mashed potatoes and broccoli out of the garden.

'Not bad,' said Joe as he wiped the last of the gravy from his plate with a slice of bread. 'Now what's for dessert?'

'There's not much Joe Daley. You seem to have forgotten we have been away,' said Nanna with a stern look in her eye. And then she weakened. 'I suppose I could find you some tinned peaches and ice cream.'

'If that is all there is then I suppose I must make do with that.'

They'd almost finished and in a lull in the conversation Jodie spoke up:

'I saw Will at the shop today.'

'Will?' said Nanna in a strange tone of voice. 'That's nice. How is he?'

'He's fine. But he told me something rather odd.'

'What, Jodie dear?' asked Nanna as she looked across at Pop.

'He said that you two told him not to make contact with me. Is that so? When he told me this today I couldn't believe he was telling me the truth. Was he?'

Before there was any reply, Jodie could tell that Will had been telling the truth. She'd never seen her grandparents look so uncomfortable. So uncomfortable that they were almost squirming. Still no response.

'Well?'

Joe spoke slowly: 'Yes. He's telling the truth. We thought it would be for the best if you cut off contact with everyone in the village. We had intended for contact to cease for a short period – six or twelve months, and to then give him your address. But somehow time slipped away. We no longer saw Will around the village - and to be honest, we forgot. You seemed to have settled into your new life and there seemed no reason to change things.'

'Couldn't you have asked me what I wanted. Especially after I seemed to be more settled. I get it that you might have been extra sensitive at the start when I first left but once I started to enjoy life at the farm you could have asked. He was my friend.'

Jodie's anguish was made clear as her voice rose in pitch.

Her anguish was in turn reflected in her grandparents' faces.

'We're so sorry,' said Joe. 'We made a terrible mistake. Please try and understand those were dark days for all of us and we were trying to manage the best we could and to keep you safe. We had no idea if the murderer was still out there and could come back for you. Our fellow villagers were no help. Nor were the police for that matter. We only knew that we had to spirit you away to somewhere no-one could find you. Fortunately Charlie turned up with a solution. We owe you and Will an apology. Can you ever forgive us?'

Jodie sighed. So much hurt rippling out from her mother's murder. She thought she had put it behind her, yet the trauma continued. But was the decision to keep Will away from her unforgivable? Having lived through the aftermath of that event she could, if she was trying to be fair, understand her grandparents' motivation. Clearly they wanted to do whatever it took to keep their granddaughter safe, but did it have to be this? Cut off contact with her only friend. But then again maybe they weren't the only ones at fault. She could always have reached out to Will.

For a moment Jodie contemplated how life could have been if Will had been able to visit the farm. How much she could have shared with him and how that might have sped up her recovery.

Another opportunity missed. A bit like the way knowledge of the existence of her half-sister could have made her childhood so much better. Jodie paused as she considered the similarities. Opportunities for healing and happiness - both missed. Both missed because of decisions taken by her grandparents. Decisions possibly motivated with the best of intentions but decisions, that nevertheless had had a profound impact on her.

She realised it was important for her own future wellbeing to acknowledge past mistakes and move on. Especially as she contemplated the anxious faces of the two elderly people facing her. Jodie reminded herself that she had accepted and understood why they had not told her the truth about Bonnie until now. And now she was able to look forward to a shared relationship with her sister. Forget the half bit. She was her sister for keeps. So it shouldn't be that hard to apply the same reasoning to the failure to let Will know where she was. After all, the three years away ended up being amazing. She had a father who was kind of special, new friends in Roman, Euan and Copper and a soon to be, rather kind, stepmother. Rory didn't bear thinking about. And Will? Well, it looked like he still wanted to be a friend.

'Can I forgive you? Possibly. I love both of you after all. Can Will forgive you? I don't know. But could you apologise to him tomorrow morning when he comes to collect me?'

Chapter Twenty-One

Next morning Will turned up promptly at ten. Jodie was impressed. He hadn't changed at all. He was still someone you could set your clock by. So reassuring.

She ushered Will into the kitchen where Pop and Nanna were seated at the table waiting for his arrival.

'Cuppa tea Will? I've just brewed a pot and there's some cake if you want. Freshly baked date loaf. Fancy a slice?'

'Don't mind if I do, Mrs Daley.'

'Carol if you please. Now you're an adult there's to be no more Mrs Daley.'

'Of course … Carol.' He took an appreciative mouthful. 'Wow. This is amazing.'

'Another slice?'

'Yes please. I'd forgotten what a great cook you are … Carol.' It was clear Will would have problems adjusting to this change in nomenclature.

'Nanna, Pop – don't you have something to say to Will before we go?'

'Yes, yes,' said Joe. Turning to face Will he continued: 'Will, we both are very sorry about the distress we both caused you. In trying to protect Jodie in those terrible days after Donna's death we probably were way too protective. We tried to screen Jodie from everyone and that included you, too, Will. In hindsight that was the wrong decision. You should have been there for Jodie and we have no excuse. We're so sorry. I hope you can forgive us. We would dearly love you to be part of our lives again. You were such a part of this family when Jodie was little. I hope you can be again.'

Will smiled: 'No need to apologise. I wondered at the time why I was excluded but I somehow accepted it must be for the best.'

He turned to face Jodie: 'Running into Jodie yesterday really made my day. It's such a treat to see you again and to see you looking like the Jodie of old - except far better looking and so mature. Not old – just sophisticated.'

Jodie rolled her eyes. Then pushed her chair back.

'Come on, Will. You said you've something to show me?'

'That I do. Bye Joe and … Carol. Thanks for the cake.'

***

'So where are we off to?' asked Jodie. By now they were travelling out of the village in Will's battered farm utility.

'You'll see,' said Will turning his head to grin at her mysteriously. About ten minutes later he turned off the main road and headed up a long road that soon degenerated into a rutted dirt track. Ahead she could see a scrubby rise with stunted gum trees scattered around. They stopped at a farm gate. Like the true farm girl she was Jodie jumped out and struggled to open it. Maybe this gate was a relative of the gate back at *Gourock*. Or maybe it was just something common to all farms and reflected farmers' inability or lack of interest in undertaking repairs. Eventually she succeeded then waved a laughing Will through.

'You can leave it open if you want,' he yelled through the open car window.

'Thank goodness for that,' she smiled. 'I'll let you shut it on the way out.'

They followed the driveway which curved to reveal the cutest brick and stone building Jodie had ever seen. Long and low it made her think of something that had grown out of the landscape incorporating the materials that abounded thereabouts.

'What do you think?' asked Will. The pride evident in his voice.

'It's amazing. How did I never know about this place and did you always live here?'

'We used to live in the village and my grandparents used to live here. It was once an inn that catered for travellers following the track that headed over the hill to Hobart. I spent a lot of time here as a child. It's a special place for me. When my grandfather died mum and dad moved in and I moved into the converted stables out the back. That's where we are headed now. Uh oh,' he muttered. 'Here are mum and dad. I wasn't expecting to see them'.

Approaching them down the driveway was a smart silver Mercedes sedan which slowed when it drew close. The driver's window wound down and a head poked out. It was an older man, who looked similar to Will but so much better groomed. Dressed in a smart sportscoat complete with a tie he was clearly off to a special event. The passenger in the front seat was a woman, Will's mum she assumed. Through the tinted glass she appeared as a shadowy creature with something shining around her neck. A string of something white and glistening. Pearls Jodie assumed. And killer pearls at that.

'Is something the matter, Will? We weren't expecting to see you back so soon. Is everything alright?' He peered in more closely. 'And who's this?'

'Yeah, everything is fine, dad. This here is my friend Jodie Wise. Jodie, let me introduce you to my dad and that there is my mum.'

Jodie smiled and waved. Being on the other side of the car she didn't feel there was anything further she could do. Also she was feeling rather uncomfortable like they had been sprung doing something they shouldn't be doing or being somewhere they shouldn't be. Will's father peered intently at Jodie, almost as if he was trying to remember if he had met her before. As far as she could recall they hadn't. Although they had once lived in the same village Jodie and Will's parents had mixed in different circles and it was no surprise they looked unfamiliar.

'Josie. Lovely to meet you. I'm sorry we can't talk but we can't stay. We're late for an event at the Golf Club. I hope you shut the front gate son?'

'No dad, we didn't. But we won't be here long and we will shut it - and lock it when we leave.'

'You do that,' his father said in the voice of someone used to giving the orders and drove off in a cloud of dust.

'Well, that won't do wonders for his shiny car,' smirked Will. 'And I can just bet mum is right now going off at him for being late and messing her new car. Families! Aren't they a joy?' Despite these words it seemed to Jodie that Will seemed remarkably carefree.

'So Josie,' he smiled 'are you ready for your surprise?'

'Jodie might be, but I can't speak for Josie, whoever she might be.'

'Don't mind him. He's a bit up himself but at heart he's ok. Just a local boy who made good and married above himself. And boy, doesn't mum make sure he doesn't forget it!'

'That sounds awful. Will, I don't know how you manage.'

'I manage by keeping out of mum's way and only meeting dad when we are at work. He's a different person when he is mucking around out in the paddock with me and the staff. It's when he gets all Mr Landed Gentry that he gets insufferable or when he is out with mum pretending they're important. That's when he is to be avoided.'

'You know mum used to rent the cottage from him?'

'Yeah, he used to say it was a slum, but he wasn't going to tear it down as he was helping someone out – someone he used to know. That was your mum I suppose. They were pretty much the same age so probably went to school together – just like us.' Will slowed the car as they turned into a gravelled area behind the house.

'This is my home,' he said proudly as he gestured towards a brick and stone building. 'It was once the stables but has been converted to a rather nice place if I say so myself. I did the conversion,' he said modestly.

The stable was long with a steep pitched roof. Where the stable doors had been there were now large glass windows. In the middle where possibly there had been an opening to permit a cart to enter was a large glass door with glass side panels. An external row of stairs led up to what must have been the hay loft, the original opening was now a type of Juliet balcony.

'Come on inside and stop gawping.'

'Inside it was even more impressive. They entered through the glass door into a large living area with a kitchen at one end and a living area that opened through further glass doors onto a paved courtyard. Behind the kitchen she could see a corridor that she thought must lead to the bathroom and possibly a bedroom. A steep staircase led along the wall opposite the entry up to a mezzanine area off which she assumed the Juliet balcony opened.

'Will, this is amazing. And so much light. The sunshine coming in must make it so cosy during the day.'

'Yes, it is. But that's not what I wanted to show you. Come into the bathroom.'

'The bathroom?' This sounded a bit weird thought Jodie as she hung back. What had Will turned into? An axe murderer? Was he luring her to this isolated place as a form of payback for those lost years? Jodie tried not to look apprehensive, but her concerns must have been obvious.

'Trust me. I'm not an axe murderer. I just have something to show you. This way.' He gestured towards the bathroom.

She followed and there she saw Will's dog Missy in a whelping box with four little squirming bundles.

'Now I understand,' she said. 'I had wondered why Missy wasn't in the back of your ute this morning. She used to go everywhere with you. I was afraid to ask in case something horrible had happened to her. But she's been very busy. Can I get closer?'

'Of course. Missy is pretty relaxed. This isn't her first litter, so she knows the routine. They were born ten days ago and are doing fine. See, their eyes are now open. That happened yesterday. Missy here is a great mother. Aren't you girl?' he spoke gently to the dog who wagged her tail in reply.

'Now I'll just get some food for the old girl. You can stay and talk to them and I'll be back in two ticks. While she is eating, I'll see if the box needs cleaning and if you like you can have a cuddle. With the puppies that is,' Will added, his eyes a twinkle.

'Give over,' said Jodie giving Will a gentle shove. 'Of course I want a cuddle – of the puppies that is!'

The puppies, a squirming mass of blobby shapes, were not much to look at this stage, but Will assured her in no time at all they would be smaller versions of their mother with hopefully the shaggy black and white coat that Missy displayed. Although, he added they might also have a smokey grey in their coat – a sort of mottled effect, a bit like their sire.

Jodie crouched down by the whelping box and with a tentative hand gently stroked the puppy closest to her. It gave little squeaks as she did so.

'Oh, Will they're gorgeous. Well done Missy,' who by now had finished gulping her food and was leaning in on Jodie seeking a pat and an ear rub. 'What are you going to do with them all?'

'There's only four and I have a waiting list. *Smithfields* are fairly hard to come by you know. We Tasmanians lay claim to *Smithfields* as our Tasmanian breed although I think originally they came from England like so many other things. Not many people breed them these days and that's why Missy and I have been trying to do our bit to expand the breed. I've picked out this one for you. She's a sweet little one and I think you'd love her.'

'For me? Yes, she's awfully sweet, but Will I can't afford her. You must have lots of other people who can pay.'

'Of course I do, but that's not the point. I want you to have her and she is a gift. A way of saying sorry for not being there for you during the last few years. She will be a good buddy, just like Missy here. And with a bit of training - no make that a lot of training, she will become a good sheep dog. They're very smart but they do have a mind of their own and have to learn that you are the boss.' Will looked sternly at Jodie and continued: 'Jodie, now listen carefully. This is non-negotiable. The puppy is yours unless you have a life limiting condition or you have suddenly become allergic to dogs?'

'No. Never allergic to dogs. I love them. Alright then. Will McBride, if you're happy to entrust this precious puppy to me,

I will happily accept. But how long do I have to wait until I can take said young puppy home?'

'She has to be about eight weeks old before she can come live with you. But you can visit whenever you like and play with them. I'll move them shortly to the outhouse past the courtyard. By then they will be more active and need a bit more space. And hopefully give their mum a break. I'll start them on solids – in about three-ish weeks. It's not an accurate science. I need to be guided by how quickly they develop.'

Missy clambered into the whelping box, nuzzled at her babies then settled on her side into a feeding position. The puppies, with varying degrees of enthusiasm, squirmed across and started to suck.

'Well that's that then,' said Will as he stood and stretched. 'That's pretty much all they do now – feed, sleep and feed again. But give them a few weeks and they will be so much more livelier and so much more fun. They grow so quickly – which is just as well. After a few weeks Missy will be pretty much over it and desperate to get back to work. Come on. I'll show you around the farm. I'm sure it's not as grand as your precious sheep farm but it has its own charm. And dad has a new project which might be of interest.'

An intrigued Jodie followed him out the door. Hard though it was to leave those gorgeous puppies behind she was curious about what else Will could possibly have in store.

They headed across the gravel past the rear of the main house and then through a double farm gate. This time a gate that opened with ease. Following a well-worn track they walked along the side of the hill until it dipped down into a sheltering valley. There was a weathered shearing shed surrounded by a mass of sheep yards. No sheep in the yards today but she could see sheep further down the valley in a distant paddock.

'So yeah. Here's the business end of the farm. And tomorrow, if you have time, you could give me a hand with those sheep over there. They need yarding and drenching.'

'Sure. No problem.'

'There's something else I want to show you. Dad's new project is just over here. If we head up this rise you will see what I mean.'

They walked a little way further – following a track that rose out of the dip. Once they crested the rise, laid out before them was something clearly not sheep related. Jodie studied the ploughed dirt and the fence posts laid out in regular rows. It looked vaguely familiar, but she was not sure what it could signify. Will looked across at her to see her reaction. Clearly he expected Jodie to be impressed. But why? It was just an expanse of dirt.

'Well?' asked Will.

'Well, what? I mean I can see a lot of work is going into this project but what is it?'

'Ah you sheep farmers! There are other things to do with land than just farm sheep. And this is one of them,' he said. 'Or at least I hope it will be,' Will muttered under his breath before he continued: 'Behold! This here is my father's vision for a soon to be established vineyard. Maybe it's a vanity project. Maybe it's his way of cementing his legacy for the area. You know a vineyard producing quality wine that will be enjoyed long after he is gone. He's been talking about doing this for years, reading the books and consulting with the experts and finally he's made a start. He picked this site as the experts tell him it has the best location – sunny, sheltered and with the slope giving it excellent drainage. I've been infected by his excitement. So much so that I've started to do a wine making course by correspondence. I'm six months in and so far, so good. And if I stick to it I will end up with a Bachelor of Viticulture. Impressive, eh?'

'Very impressive,' agreed Jodie. 'So this then will be a vineyard one day?'

Will nodded and looked at her as if he expected her to say something else. Maybe something that indicated she shared his enthusiasm for his father's vision.

'That's amazing. And I'm seeing it at the vineyard's absolute start. At its birth so to speak. What's next?'

'Now the posts are in the next job is to next string up the supporting wires and then plant the vines. Dad has bought some

Reisling plants from the mainland and he has an order in for some Chardonnay but he's not sure if they will get here this season. It's a start and maybe next season we will have more land prepared for some red grapes – possibly Pinot Noir. Getting ready is a big job – you know the soil has to be improved and irrigation installed. We have a dam higher up the hill from which we've run a line which will drip feed water onto each vine. That took ages to sort out. We've got a few contractors helping but even so it's been a mammoth job. Planting has to happen soon. Maybe you can help?'

'Sure. There's nothing I like more than getting my hands dirty,' said Jodie, holding her work stained hands out for inspection.

Will chatted non-stop on the way back to the village. His family farm was really not that far away yet somehow it felt like it was in the deepest countryside. The wattles lining the road were a vision of gold and distracted Jodie from whatever Will was now saying.

'You're not listening to me, are you? I feel like you are somewhere else.'

'Mmm? Sort of listening but also admiring the wattle blossom. It's so much more advanced than up at Cressy. I suppose this is a softer climate.'

'Yep. But hopefully still a sufficiently cool climate for our wines. You know *Cool Climate Wines* seems to be the description everyone aspires to.'

'Wow, you're becoming quite the expert aren't you?'

'It's rubbing off on me' he said, not so modestly. 'If you're interested I'll take you to a wine tasting in Hobart some day.'

'Maybe,' said Jodie. The thought of wine made her think of her mother and they were not welcome thoughts. Growing grapevines was one thing but drinking wine was maybe a step too far. Or for now it was.

Will dropped her off with a promise to come and collect her first thing in the morning.

Chapter Twenty-Two

That evening over a dinner of roast lamb and baked vegetables they all took turns in sharing the news of each other's day. Joe had been kept busy pruning his fruit trees. Something he swore was the most tedious job ever.

'No,' said Nanna – cleaning the oven was which had kept her busy all morning and now it was dirty again with the splatter from the baked dinner.

'Better not to bother' said Joe. And received a laughing slap from Nanna for his pains.

Her grandparents listened with interest when Jodie recounted her day's experiences. They were familiar with the location of Will's parents farm but had never been there.

'*Bronte Park* it's called,' said Joe. I suppose it predates the village,' said Pop.

Nanna was interested in the house and Pop in the farm, which meant there was much to discuss.

'The house was the cutest place ever,' said Jodie. 'So different to the Big House at *Gourock* but just as old and very cute. I suppose it might have been built by convicts. Will tells me it was once a pub and certainly looks very welcoming with large double doors. Lots of windows and heaps of chimneys. I suppose each room must have had a fireplace. And Nanna, you should have seen Will's place out the back. He lives in the old stable block which he's converted himself.'

'And the garden?' Nanna asked.

Jodie frowned. Was there a garden? Not much that she could recall. A planting of Agapanthus around the edge of a circular drive out the front. Some sort of deciduous trees lining the drive that led to the stables out the back and maybe a walled garden. She had noticed a high red brick wall that enclosed the space behind the house.

'Not much garden, Nanna. Not like up at *Gourock*. Will had some big pots of red geraniums in front of the stables and I could see he had a little courtyard but I'm not sure what was in it.'

'Perhaps water is in short supply up there?' pondered Pop. 'After all they're too far out to be connected to the town water supply. Maybe that would explain the lack of garden.'

The talk of water reminded Jodie of the other news which she was sure would have been of interest to Pop.

'And Will showed me their work on a vineyard. Soon to be planted, he said. Planted with Reisling grapes I think he said. The preparations are almost complete – or so I'm told. It just looked like a big mass of ploughed up dirt with wooden posts plonked in.'

'Now that's exciting. I'll have to have a chat with young Will about that. I've often wondered if I should plant a few vines. Not many. Just enough to produce a dozen or so bottles of red for the Mrs and me.'

'Joe Daley! You romantic old fool you! Have you visions of us sitting outside at leisure quaffing wine on a summer's evening?'

'No, woman. I was thinking a glass of wine with our roast lamb dinners would be just the thing. The bee's knees so to speak.'

Jodie loved it when her grandparents spoke like this. Their mutual affection so obvious. She hoped one day there might be someone for her who would tease her in such a way. A bit like the way Will teased her today. That thought made her pause. Yes, she'd always considered Will to be her best friend, but could their friendship evolve into something more? Was this something she would want? Or would it destroy everything she treasured about their relationship? Just when it was returning to a close-knit friendship should she put that at risk by seeking something more? Jodie knew that if she consulted Bonnie she would advise her to go for it. That was so Bonnie. She dived into everything regardless of the consequences. But Jodie was not that sort of person. She held back. Not only that, with so little experience of relationships Jodie had no idea what to do or what to say. Perhaps the safest thing to do was to say nothing.

Nanna piped up, 'And I had a phone call from Bonnie this afternoon. She will be back sometime tomorrow. She had a bit of a chat with her dad about her parentage. Apparently that didn't go as well as she had hoped and we are to expect a call from him at some stage. Bonnie says he's not happy that we told you girls. I suppose that's to be expected. Ah well – maybe a conversation you can have with him, Joe?'

'Maybe I'll be out. Maybe it's better not to answer the phone.'

'Coward!' said his not so sympathetic wife as she flicked the tea towel at him.

***

Next morning Will had already arrived when Jodie finally surfaced. She wasn't much of a morning person and it was a bleary-eyed young woman with sleep mussed hair that wandered into the kitchen and slumped into a wooden chair.

'Good Morning! And don't you look well rested,' smiled Will, by contrast looking well awake and full of energy. 'We need to get going. That is if you are still up to it?'

Jodie, who was focussing on drinking her hot tea, considered how to respond to Will's comments. In the end she decided a withering look from over the rim of the mug would do.

'Here, get some toast into you,' said Nanna as she bustled around the kitchen, bringing steaming hot toast from the toaster, grabbing butter from the fridge and whatever condiments she thought her granddaughter would enjoy.

'And then get dressed. It looks like a cold one today and windy. Not great outdoors weather I'm afraid.'

'It will be fine … Carol,' said Will who was still struggling with the request to use her first name. For as long as he had known her she had always been Mrs Daley. Changing old habits didn't come easy.

'No rush Jodie dear,' said Joe. 'I need to chat with Will a bit about my plans for some grapevines. Will, me lad, I hear you are now a whiz on all things vineyard related. I have a few ideas of what I want to do out the back. While young Jodie gets ready come with me and I will show you the spot.'

Will laughed and spread his hands wide. 'Joe I don't know what tales Jodie has been telling you but trust me, I'm no expert. I'm very much a beginner in this space but I'm happy to share what I've learned so far if it would be of any assistance.'

The two men stood up and headed out the door leaving Jodie at the table contemplating the remaining toast. Could she manage another slice. Yes, she definitely could.

Later on a dressed and much brighter Jodie appeared out in the back paddock where she found the two men engaged in earnest conversation.

'You can see I really don't need all this space for my goats. I can spare that back paddock for something else and I thought I should give some grapes a go. What do you think? Do you think that's a good location?'

'Well it's sheltered and sunny and appears to be well drained. We'd have to test the soil of course but if the results are good or if it only needs a few additives to get it up to speed – you know possibly lime, then I can't see why not. I could help you if you want. Treat it like a project for one of my study assignments. Trouble is we've left it too late this season although we could at least make a start by testing the soil and planning what we need to do. I'm happy to help if you want me to?'

'Too right I do! You're on. When can we start?'

'You can start by organising the soil test. Once we get the results we can work out what to do next,' smiled Will. 'I'm a bit busy over the next few weeks so that will give you time to sort out the testing.'

'Come on Will,' said Jodie who was getting impatient. She wanted to get up to the farm and sort out sheep and check in on the puppies. All this talk of vineyards could keep.

The day went well. The sheep were clearly used to being rounded up and yarded. Just as well as they had no Missy to help. Fortunately the sheep were in the adjoining paddock and once the gate was opened and with a bit of urging they surged into the first of the sheep yards. Jodie was always amused at how it only took for one sheep, the boss sheep she supposed, to move forward to make all the sheep follow. Following the lead sheep and sensing the bit of green pick in the yard seemed to be all that was needed to get the sheep where they wanted them. Then it was a matter of running the sheep through the race as one by one they squirted the drench between their shoulder blades and along their back. It was a simple yet tedious process and took a while. Once they were all done Will opened another gate into a small adjoining paddock.

'They can stay in here overnight until whatever worms they have are excreted and then we'll move them elsewhere tomorrow. I've been spelling a good paddock down the hill that they'll enjoy.'

Jodie considered the sheep who were now moving as a mass into the small paddock. She was still learning about sheep. These didn't look like the Merinos Joan and Charlie farmed. Similar but different. Will explained they were cross breeds – a cross between the Merino and Border Leicester sheep breeds. Hybrid vigour and all that, he explained. And these particular sheep were the wethers- the neutered males that would be used for their fleece or meat - or both.

The highlight of the day, of course was when they returned to the stables and fed Missy and inspected the puppies. Jodie was convinced that in only 24 hours they had grown. Certainly they appeared to be more alert. Jodie was reluctant to pick up such small bundles even though she so wanted to. Maybe in a day or so when they were stronger. For now she contented herself with gently stroking each pup. Missy had been pleased to see them and even happier to be fed.

'She needs a lot of feeding so she can produce enough milk. They'll be drinking more and more and I have to be careful to ensure she doesn't lose condition. Sometimes with her shaggy coat it's hard to see how fat she really is. Shaggy coats can hide so much and they're great grass seed magnets. I always find summer a challenge. I'm constantly pulling out grass seeds from between her paws. If I didn't love *Smithfields* so much I would have bought a better adapted dog. A kelpie perhaps.'

'Have you always had *Smithfields?*' asked Jodie.

'Yep. Pretty much.' Will paused as he placed Missy's refilled water bowl on the floor then stood up stretching as he did so. Jodie could hear his neck cartilage crack as he moved his head from side to side.

'Ah that's better. Now where were we? Yes. *Smithfields.* My grandpa had them. About three of them who were amazing sheepdogs. He supplied the district with their progeny. Missy is one of his. Mum was unimpressed when grandpa gave her to me one Christmas. But she couldn't object as even then she had her eye on this house and wouldn't do or say anything to put that outcome at risk. I guess that was about 8 years ago – or maybe 7. Grandpa passed away while you were up at Cressy. You would have liked him. He was very happy up here on the farm and left the other stuff for dad to do. You know, running the pub and the rental properties. I miss him. Especially like today when we were busy with the sheep. That's the sort of stuff we used to do together. Never mind, that's life I guess. And we should focus on the here and now. Like how starving I am. Time for lunch. Pub or café?'

Jodie's eyes flared with alarm. Definitely not the pub! Her mother's workplace. No way!

Will could read the expressions racing across her face and understood.

'Too soon? Then the café it is. Good choice. They do a mean toasted sandwich. And then I must drop you home and go and collect these grapevines. Fancy helping me and the lads do some planting tomorrow? It could be a long day,' he said with a wicked grin.

Over lunch comprising hot crispy toasted ham, cheese and tomato sandwiches just oozing with melted cheese the conversation turned to Bonnie. Will remembered something that Jodie had said the day before. Something about Bonnie being her half-sister. He had always understood her to be a cousin. This was something he needed to clarify.

'You know how you said yesterday – or was it the day before? No matter but did you mention that Bonnie is your half-sister and not your cousin? I distinctly remember that. I think. What's that about? Is it true?'

Jodie, with a mouth full of sandwich nodded. She chewed and swallowed. 'Yep. It's true. A bit of a shock to Bonnie and me – but after the shock has passed we both quite like the idea of being sisters. Apparently it has long been a family secret only known by Nanna, Pop and Bonnie's dad.'

Jodie with her head to one side considered what she had just said: 'I suppose we should still refer to him as Bonnie's dad although Nanna and Pop are quite certain he is not Bonnie's biological father. But hey – he raised Bonnie so I guess we should think of him as her dad. Although Nanna said he is very cross that Bonnie and I now know. It was meant to be kept a secret, you see.'

'A secret? I wonder why and also I thought it was impossible to keep anything a secret in this small town. Keeping it quiet for so long – now that's an achievement.' Will, with a tilt of his head considered it further. 'But, hang on a minute. They kept the fact you two are sisters – or half-sisters, secret for years But did they also keep secret the identity of Bonnie's father?'

Jodie shook her head. 'No. Well it's a secret in the sense that the answer died with my mother. I'm pretty sure Nanna and Pop are telling the truth when they say they don't know.'

'Could it be your father?'

'Charlie? I don't think so and I don't think he was lying when he said he didn't meet mum until some time after Bonnie was born. Mum was awfully young when she fell pregnant with Bonnie. Nanna said she didn't know who mum was seeing as she was, as Nanna said, running wild. Well, didn't she always?'

Jodie sighed. 'Unless some bloke comes out of the woodwork claiming to be Bonnie's father, I guess we will never know. Another one of life's little mysteries and one Bonnie and I are quite happy with. You know, after the initial shock of having to share a bedroom with a stranger we've become good friends. We used to write letters and talk on the phone a lot when I first moved up to Cressy. In some ways she kept me sane. Bonnie might be a bit full on, but she always means well - and she can make me laugh. And I needed that – especially in those early days.'

Jodie glanced at Will and saw the guilty expression on his face. 'No, don't be like that. I wasn't having a dig at you. I was only explaining how close Bonnie and I have become after such a shaky start. And I couldn't be happier knowing we are going to be living together with Nanna and Pop. At least until Bonnie has saved enough to move out on her own. To be honest it was the thought of being with Bonnie that convinced me to move back here.'

Jodie looked up at the clock on the wall and registered the time.

'Wow! It's almost three already. I should get home. Bonnie might have arrived and don't you have grape vines to collect?'

This time Jodie insisted on paying for lunch. She'd managed to scrounge some money from Nanna who had promised to bank Charlie's cheque when she headed into Hobart that day. They'd both exclaimed when Jodie opened the envelope and saw the amount written on the cheque. More than enough to buy her a car and quite a bit left over to bank and maybe use some of it a bit later when she and Bonnie went clothes shopping. Although based on that day's activities it looked like her everyday attire would continue to be farm attire.

The note that Charlie had included in the envelope brought tears to both Jodie's and Carol's eyes. He had written about how proud he was of his daughter and the woman she had become. He wrote that her birth had been one of the best days of his life. Or so he had always thought, but now he had decided that getting to really know his daughter and spend time with her was even more rewarding. Charlie concluded his note by expressing a wish for her to return whenever she wanted. That she should consider his home, wherever it would be, to always be her home.

Jodie took those final words to be a reference to Charlie's upcoming residence in the Big House. She hoped Joan would be as welcoming to a stepdaughter.

***

There wasn't much of the afternoon left and Bonnie had yet to arrive. Jodie spent the time tidying the spare room. There were three bedrooms in Nanna and Pop's house. Her room was just as she left it all those years ago. It still had a Holly Hobbie doona cover and multiple soft toys randomly scattered on every flat surface. Her childhood reading materials carefully stacked on the bookshelves. Probably not books she would now want to read but would not want to throw them out either. Too many happy memories of reading Roald Dahl and the like. Maybe it was time to raid Nanna's bookshelves – or join the local library. The spare room was next door to Jodie's room and was pristine, like every other room in Nanna's house. She wasn't sure if Bonnie would be happy having a room to herself but thought she should have it looking perfect just in case. All she needed to do was pick some flowers to put on the bedside table. With secateurs in hand she wandered around Nanna's front flower garden. There wasn't much to choose from it still being winter. Eventually she decided on cutting a small bunch of daphne. As she carried it inside already the spicy fragrance wafted around her.

Bonnie didn't arrive until just before dark. Her arrival was not as dramatic as last time. This time there was no ferocious storm nor a roaring wind. Just a still, almost dark wintery evening that promised frost before dawn. The back porch light had been left on and as they were sitting down for dinner they heard the sound of a car pulling up in the driveway.

'At last,' smiled Nanna. 'What perfect timing! Jodie dear. Please bring over another plate and some extra cutlery.'

Tonight's meal was one of Jodie's favourites. Macaroni cheese. Something she had perfected cooking for Charlie. Yet somehow

Nanna's version, like so much of her cooking, always tasted better. An opinion confirmed by Bonnie who launched into her serve with gusto.

'Nanna. This is the best. I was hoping we might have pasta. I don't know how you do it but your version of macaroni cheese is superior to anything else I've ever had. You must have a secret ingredient. What is it? Do tell.'

Nanna shook her head and as she did so various grey curls dislodged from her bun. A mess that she ignored. 'The only secret ingredient my dear is love. I love cooking for you and more importantly I love seeing you eat it all. The biggest praise as far as I'm concerned is a plate licked clean and no leftovers.'

'Doesn't work for me,' complained Pop. 'What will I have for lunch tomorrow?'

'Joe Daley. Quit your grumbling! Isn't there always something for lunch? If you were to pay attention you would notice chicken stock simmering on the stove. It's possible – and I give no guarantees but that stock might be the base for soup for tomorrow. Or if you give too much cheek it might go to your dog.'

'No, woman. No! Have pity on a poor old man,' whined Joe even as he grinned at his wife.

Bonnie and Jodie exchanged smiles. Being with Nanna and Pop was such fun.

Somehow, they all decided they could squeeze in dessert. A decision that was confirmed once they saw the apple pie Nanna carried to the table. Apple pie served with ice cream or custard or, in Pop's case, served with both ice cream and custard. Then the three women shared in doing the washing and drying up while Pop went into the lounge room to stoke the fire and most likely snooze while pretending to watch the news on TV.

Nanna washed while Bonnie and Jodie wiped the dishes.

'So what happened with your father, Bonnie?' Nanna asked, while scouring a stubborn mark from the saucepan.

'Not much. He wasn't happy I knew about the adoption although I assured him I still thought of him as my dad. He seemed to think you guys had failed him by breaking your promise but as I said to him – Donna was dead. Jodie and I are both adults and if we can live with the truth so should he. That shut him up. Although you may hear from him, if only so he has a chance to whinge. He feels awfully hard done by. I think part of it is also that he feels he's been left alone up there in Devonport while we are all here. Like he's been abandoned. Poor dear,' Bonnie said with false sympathy. 'He knew I was always going to leave. I couldn't wait to get away.'

Later on Bonnie and Jodie were in Bonnie's room, Jodie lying on Bonnie's bed while Bonnie unpacked her two suitcases and hung her clothes in the wardrobe. Jodie was amazed at how many clothes Bonnie had and said as much.

'No way. I've just got a few things to tide me over. I'm not sure what a cadet reporter should wear but I've packed a suit, some smart trousers and this boring office type dress. The best stuff is in this case. This is stuff I will wear clubbing. Hurry up and turn 18 and then we can go out on the town and meet men. Maybe even Rory.'

She looked at Jodie questioningly who shook her head. No sign nor news of Rory. Once again he appeared to have disappeared.

'Never mind. Plenty more fish in the sea and all that … But,' she sighed. 'He was rather gorgeous. A real hunk.'

Jodie frowned. He was a real drop kick! But given he was out of Bonnie's life there was no need to say this. Better to focus on Bonnie's new career.

'So, when do you start?'

'Next week. But the HR person suggested I drop in tomorrow and do some paperwork and meet the team. Maybe even shadow one of the reporters if they are heading out on something interesting. I can't wait! But what should I wear?'

The next hour was occupied with trying many different outfits until Jodie couldn't care what her sister selected. She was tired and needed her sleep.

'You know what? I think any of those will be fine.' Knowing Bonnie's tendency to be contrary she randomly pointed to an outfit.

'Yes. I think that dress and jacket will be fine.'

And as expected Bonnie immediately pulled another outfit from the pile.

'No Jodie. Such a bad choice. This here is the one. Miss Professional Cadet Journalist here I come!'

And with a blown kiss and a smile Jodie slid off the bed and headed to her own room. She was beat and suspected any more listening to her sister would deprive her of much needed rest. Especially as the next day promised to be full on.

'What the? Where are you off to?' She heard coming from the adjoining bedroom.

'Good night, sister dear. Sweet dreams.'

Chapter Twenty-Three

The kitchen next morning was a hive of activity. Nanna was all a-bustle sorting out everyone's breakfast before she headed into Hobart to bank the cheque Charlie had presented to Jodie and to buy something for dinner. Bonnie had already said she would drop Nanna off in town. Nanna assured Pop she would take her little pull trolley and would catch the bus home. Pop was very keen to drive Jodie up to the McBride's farm so he could *check out the vineyard work.*

'Keen to have a sticky beak more like,' muttered Nanna. Fortunately Pop was out of earshot. Nanna turned to look at her girls. One looking immaculate, the other looking like the farm girl which she was.

'My, don't you look lovely, Bonnie dear,' Nanna said as she appraised the smart grey suit Bonnie was wearing.

'You don't think this spotted blouse is too much, Nanna?'

Nanna shook her head. 'No point asking me. I'm no expert on corporate wear.'

'And I'm not either,' piped up Jodie. 'But you look pretty good to me and the way you've twisted your hair into that scruffy bun suits you.'

Bonnie preened, 'Yes, I think this will do. Come on Nanna we've got to get going.'

It took a while for a flustered Nanna to locate her purse, her spectacles and her wallet but eventually they left. All that remained was for Jodie to pack some lunch and drag her Pop away from the back paddock where he was feeding his precious goats.

'Come on Pop,' she yelled. 'We'll be late and bring your boots! And your hat and your coat.'

As they drove Pop explained he had no intention of staying long. He just wanted to check out how the vineyard was being set up. And also to check out the farm Jodie speculated. This was confirmed when they drove up the driveway and he exclaimed in wonder: 'Well, I never. What an amazing place. Which way do we go now Jodie dear?'

'This way Pop, around the back. Will said he would wait 'til we arrive. We're a bit late, but I'm hoping he won't mind.'

'I'll take care of that,' said Pop and he did. Will must have been on the lookout, for as soon as they arrived he came outside. Pop stopped the vehicle and jumped out.

'Sorry Will. We're a bit late. My fault I'm afraid. You know how it is. I ducked out into the paddock and lost all track of time,' Pop smiled in such a way it was hard to be cross with him. Although it was clear Will was not convinced by the proffered excuse. He already knew how late Jodie could often be. As he started to put on his work boots Jodie came close and touched his arm as if to gain his attention. Will looked up.

'Umm Will. Do you mind if I just show dad the pups? We'll only be a minute.' She smiled winningly at him. How could he refuse.

'Of course. But quickly, We're already late. The others are waiting on us.'

Jodie dragged her suspicious grandfather inside. He barely had time to notice the comfort of the inside furnishings when he registered that Jodie was directing him to look into the bathroom.

'Oh, my,' he exhaled in delight when he saw the four puppies and their mother who was wiggling her own welcome. 'It's Missy. I wondered why you weren't with your master. Now I can see why. You certainly have been busy.' He turned to Jodie, 'They're beautiful but we'd better keep going. We don't want the boss to get cranky, do we?'

'So what do you think, Joe?' asked Will as they strode out the gate and along the track with Jodie struggling to keep up.

'The pups? Your Missy has done you proud. More *Smithfields* aren't they? It's good to see you keeping the line going.'

Jodie caught up and was able to add her bit: 'And Pop, even better, Will is giving one to me. One of the little girls.'

Joe nodded and exchanged a glance with Will. Yes, this would be a welcome gift. Maybe a little friend to fill the gap in Jodie's life left by Pepper. He had noticed how much his granddaughter had bonded with the lamb. Even giving him a name - Lambkin or something. For a moment he had even contemplated bringing it home until he thought better of it. What use would a male lamb be? It wasn't like Jodie would let them eat it. Yes, a puppy was definitely a more appropriate solution. He could tell from Jodie's anxious expression and the pointed glance from Will that a response from him was necessary.

'A puppy you say? What a wonderful gift. Now I'm not sure what my old dog will think. Maybe it will give her a new lease of life. Have you thought of a name?'

'Not yet. But Will says I can't bring her home for another six weeks so I guess that will give me lots of time to practice new names with her and to see which name suits her.'

By now they'd walked past the sheepyards and the wool shed which Jo eyed with interest. They were old although clearly had been well maintained and regularly used. Jodie looked down the hill for the sheep but they were no longer in the small paddock. When asked, Will said he'd moved them further down the hill into a sheltered paddock as bad weather was expected later on that day. All the more reason to get cracking.

'Well I won't slow you young ones down,' said Pop. 'I just wanted to see what you have done and then I'll leave. Will, would you please bring Jodie home when you're finished?'

'Of course,' said Will already looking ahead, his focus clearly on other things. Once they crested the rise the activity was obvious. A gang of people were already busy planting the vine stock. Some planting the young plants and others following behind securing some sort of vine protector. To protect against damage by hares,

Jodie supposed. Overseeing it all was a gentleman Jodie recognised as Will's father. Pop hung back and muttered something about having seen enough and backed away, before turning and heading back the way they had come. Jodie shrugged. Perhaps a glimpse was all he had wanted to see. Never mind. She had things to do. Soon she was part of the group planting the young grape vines. At present they were only sticks with attached roots, but she supposed given warm weather and rain they would flourish. So long as the hares could not get to them. She had seen the damage hares could do. Given half a chance they would strip a sapling down in one night. And the possums weren't much better. She stood back and tried to visualise a hill full of flourishing grapevines. Yes, it would be a thing of beauty and she hoped the vision shared by Will and his father would come to pass.

They were kept busy for most of the morning. And by mid-afternoon the vines were planted and protected in their grow tubes. Will explained that once they started growing in spring and the vines had got long enough they would need to train them onto the metal wire supports and where necessary tidy up excess shoots.

'It's quite labour intensive,' he explained. 'Planting, shaping, eventually picking the grapes and pruning. It all takes effort. But hey! Who wouldn't rather be outside than stuck inside in a sterile office?'

'Actually,' said Jodie as she warily eyed the gathering storm clouds. 'An office is starting to look rather attractive just now.'

Will followed her glance and then went into action. 'Quick, everyone. Time to get under cover. Jodie and I will gather the tools. You lot get going. We've almost finished. Just a bit of tidying up to do and that can keep until tomorrow. Thank you for your hard work. I'll be in touch.'

Jodie and Will scurried around collecting trowels which they hurled into large white tubs. Will's father had disappeared and they were left to trudge back to the stables struggling with the now full buckets. The rain which had been threatening started – initially falling gently as if to lure them into a false sense of security and then with a loud crack of thunder the heavens opened. By now they were near the woolshed and took shelter. There was a sense of safety and comfort to be felt while they sheltered inside this enormous structure as they gazed out at the teeming rain and watched the rivulets pour off the tin roof. The solid timber beams and the wooden floor, together with the imprinted aroma of lanolin from long dead sheep somehow reassured Jodie as she thought of the decades of use of this building. How it had stood solid and secure against the elements. And looked like it would continue to do so. The storm raged overhead. The thunder was deafening and the lightening lit up the surroundings like a fireworks display. A flash and a crack as the lightening connected with a tree then the thud of falling timber vibrated through them.

'I hope the sheep are ok,' fretted Will as he peered outside into the storm.' At least they can shelter in the trees out of the worst of the rain and hopefully be safely away from any lightning strike. Ah well, there's not much I can do for now. The rain should ease soon so we can make a run for it. No point us worrying about getting drenched. We already are,' he said with a grin.

Jodie looked down at herself and then across at Will. Both of them were dripping onto the worn floorboards. What she would give for a hot shower. A shiver passed through her which she found hard to stop.

Will looked outside: 'Yep, I think it's easing. Look the lightning is now over there striking across the valley. And look there by the crest of the hill – a rainbow. A sign! Definitely a sign!'

Jodie looked. Yes, it was the tail end of a rainbow. A faint one, but a rainbow nevertheless. Time to make a wish. But what should she wish for. At that moment Will's incredibly warm hand grabbed hers.

'Come on. Let's make a run for it. We'll leave the buckets here. I'll get them tomorrow. Quick, in case the storm comes back.'

It was just like the old days when they were children competing at the school athletics carnival. Even chilled and drenched Jodie could still experience the exhilaration of running against her best friend. Running and winning. She always was the faster one. Or was she?

'Come on, slow coach,' she yelled loud against the gusting wind. 'Race you!'

And they ran. Slipping and sliding along the muddy track but running nevertheless. It was a tie – two sets of hands grabbing the gate at the same time. Their lungs heaving with exertion and laughter.

'I'm sure I got here first,' protested Jodie, ever the sore loser.

'Accept it. You didn't win. Once you would be streets ahead but now it's a tie. And next time I will beat you.'

'I blame the conditions. A rematch is definitely on the cards. At the oval and not in the rain. You'll so eat my dust,' laughed Jodie.

'You're on,' smiled Will looking deeply into her eyes and liking what he saw.

The sound of a cough and a throat clearing interrupted their hilarity as they gazed forward and saw a woman staring at them. Dressed in a stylish leopard print raincoat and holding an unfurled umbrella. In gumboots of course – but matching leopard print gumboots. Altogether perfectly styled as if she was about to stride along a fashion parade runway and not along a muddy path towards two adolescents.

'Mum?' queried Will. 'What are you doing here?'

'I was looking for you of course,' came the crisp reply. 'I was worried about your safety. But it looks like I needn't have worried.' Her icy gaze turned to consider Jodie – 'And who might this be?'

'Mum, this is Jodie. Jodie Wise. You met her the other day.'

'Oh yes. Jodie. Well I think it is time you headed home,' said in the same unfriendly tone and with a grimace of a smile. Almost as if she was bringing to an end a playdate. Acting as if the two before her were not drenched but were two people who could wave each other goodbye and wander away into the night.

'Yes, mum. I'll take Jodie home as soon as she's had a hot shower and I find her some dry clothes. I don't want to return her to Carol and Joe suffering from hypothermia,' Will smiled across at Jodie happy with his joke. Jodie looked at him anxiously. How could he be so unaffected by this snooty woman?

'Shower? What, shower together?' Will's mother spoke as if they were committing a major crime or was it she thought they were doing something socially unacceptable – or an orgy? Jodie's thoughts galloped along as she tried to contemplate what exactly was so horrifying. She was cold - freezing even – and she needed a shower.

'Relax, mum,' Will opened the gate as he spoke and pushed past his mother. 'Jodie can go first and so long as she doesn't use up all the hot water I'll go second. Excuse us but I really need to get Jodie inside.'

They walked away, but not before Jodie glanced back and saw Will's mother glaring at her.

'Don't worry about her' said Will as he took her freezing cold hand in his very warm hand she noticed. What bliss. 'She'll calm down. She's always been a bit funny about my friends. Maybe she doesn't like sharing. Pity I'm an only child. Ah well it can't be helped. Let's get you into the shower. Luckily the bathroom is large so you should be able to avoid getting water onto the whelping box. But I will move it as far away as I can. Try not to drip water on them as you walk past.'

The hot shower was bliss. With each second Jodie could feel her limbs defrost. Will had some rather fancy shampoo and conditioner which she made good use of. Jodie could have stayed in there all night but mindful of the need to leave some hot water for Will she reluctantly turned the taps off. It was a bit disconcerting showering with an audience. Not Will, but Missy who watched her suspiciously, as if at any moment she would be forced to have a wash.

'No, Missy. You're safe with me. I think you have better things to do than have a wash. I'll get out of your way and leave you to the boss.'

Jodie yelled out she was finished and were there any clothes as it seemed too cold to run around starkers.

'I don't know. It might entertain mum – or give her an apoplexy. Anyway I've left some clothes by the door. Some tracky dacks and a sweatshirt. You'll have to go commando as I'm sure boy briefs won't work for you but this should do to get you home looking halfway decent. Oh, and I have some Ugg boots somewhere that you can borrow. Let me know when you are dressed, and I'll come out of the bedroom. And I've left you a hot drink on the kitchen bench.'

While Will showered, Jodie wandered down the corridor and found a steaming mug of coffee waiting for her. Milky and sweet – just as she liked it. As she sipped her coffee Jodie moved around the room and considered the many books crammed into the shelves that filled the empty space under the stairs. So many books, so many that she had yet to read and that she would quite like to read. Those books on viticulture she would give a miss. Although she suspected her Pop might be interested in those. But there were some others - crime fiction, biographies of famous people and even a few fantasy novels.

Will, coming out of the bathroom with towel draped around his hips and using another towel to rub his hair dry, said 'Like anything you see?'

Now how was she to answer that question? Clearly he meant his library, but looking across at him in all his glory, spotlit like a young god, her immediate thought was – all of it!

With a slight blush, and hoping he didn't notice, Jodie turned towards the bookshelves: 'There's heaps I haven't read and would like to. Can I borrow some?'

'Help yourself. Anytime.'

'Alright. I think I might take some of these old Agatha Christie novels. You know, I've never read any of these. They look like easy reads. Something to read just before sleep.'

She ran her hand along the shelf and selected three: *Murder on the Orient Express, The Mysterious Affair at Styles* and *Crooked House*.

'Here, let me see what you've chosen.'

Will wandered over – still wrapped in one towel with the other draped around his shoulders. As he drew close she could smell the warm just washed goodness of his skin. She found herself speaking as a way of distracting herself from these new to her feelings: 'Yes, I think these should do. The titles all sound exotic and mysterious. I'll return them as soon as I finish.'

'And please, help yourself to more. I'll just get dressed and then I'll get you home. Do you need to ring your folks so they don't worry?' As he spoke Will turned and headed down the corridor. Despite herself Jodie found her gaze following the progress of that broad back and giving a sigh she reached for the phone which was answered after three rings.

'Nanna. It's me. We got caught in the rain. I'm fine. Got a bit wet that's all. Anyway I've just had the best hot shower ever and will be home soon. Hope I haven't missed dinner? I'm starving.'

When they reached the house Jodie left the car, a plastic bag of wet clothes and books in hand.

'Thanks for bringing me home. Don't come in Will. It's late and you need to get home. I'll see you soon – I hope?'

'Sure and while I think of it. We're having a little celebration at the pub on Friday night. You know to celebrate the planting of the first vines. About 6 o'clock. You and your family are most welcome. Your Pop might enjoy grilling dad about the challenges in establishing a vineyard.'

A party! Jodie was sure Bonnie for one would be there. It was time she overcame her bad memories of the pub. She should go. Safety in numbers and all that. And at least at such an event Will would be fully clothed. Pity!

'Sure. We'll be there. See you then.' Jodie turned to leave then thought of something else. 'Thanks Will for the dry clothes. And by the way – bring on the next race. Just so I can prove once and for all that I'm faster than you.'

'You're on!'

Chapter Twenty-Four

The others had already eaten but Nanna, bless her, had saved Jodie an enormous plate of tuna mornay. Hot, salty and creamy – covered with a crunchy, cheesy crust and garnished with chopped parsley. Just the way she liked it. In any event she was so starving she would have eaten anything.

Eagle-eyed Bonnie observed Jodie's changed attire.

'It's all a bit big for you, Jodie. Is this your new look?'

'Hah! Funny. Not a new look at all. I got drenched when the storm hit and almost got hypothermia. I've never been so cold. Will lent me these clothes.' Jodie wiggled her toes in the fleecy Ugg boots. 'I have to return the clothes. Which is fine by me. But I might hang onto these Ugg boots. They're so warm. I wonder if they'll be missed?'

Jodie remembered Will's invitation. An invitation to them all.

'Before I forget, he's invited us all to a celebration at the pub this Friday evening. About 6 I think he said. To celebrate the planting of stage one of the vineyard. Fancy going Bonnie?'

'Absolutely!' said Bonnie. 'I'll be there. If only to catch sight of your precious Will who I haven't seen for years. Is he still as good looking?' she asked, not expecting a reply and then continued, focussed on her own adventures as often was the case: 'I may be a bit late as I'm going to be at work all Friday. But I'll be there. What about you two, Nanna and Pop?'

Nanna and Pop looked at each other. Nanna put her head to one side and Pop shrugged. That Jodie took to mean fine by me so long as you want to go.

'Yes I think we should go,' said Nanna. 'If only to give Pop a chance to find out more about this here viticulture. Looks like it is going to become his new passion.'

'And Pop, Will has lots of books on viticulture that I'm sure you can borrow if you like. He's lent me three Agatha Christie's to read so if you don't mind I'm heading off to bed to read. Good night all.'

Bonnie pouted: 'But you haven't asked me about my day?'

'Alright then. Come with me.' Jodie resigned herself to forgoing the pleasure of reading and focussed herself on sounding interested in whatever Bonnie thought fit to share. And there was a lot. Meeting the head editor, the assistant editor and learning what would be in store as a cadet reporter. At first she would be expected to shadow some of the more senior journalists and then once she had a feel for the process she might be assigned to court reporting or interviewing people regarding local interest stories or even covering events. Possibly also fashion or book launches or conferences. Bonnie's excitement at the potential variety of her work shone through. For someone like Bonnie, who thrived on endless change this could very well be her dream job. Or at least Jodie hoped so.

Finally Bonnie had run out of things to share and Jodie was able to shoo her out of her room, but not before promising to drag her mattress into Bonnie's room the next night.

'Not tonight I'm sorry, Bonnie. I'm too beat,' said Jodie, who even then was snuggling down under her quilt and surrendering to the pull of sleep. As she did so the image of that buffed body with the towel draped around his hips swam into her consciousness. What if that towel had slipped? With significant will power Jodie pushed that image away and let herself slip away.

Chapter Twenty-Five

Friday night was to be Jodie's first time back at the pub since her mother used to work there. There were times when her mother used to smuggle her into the kitchen so she could have something to eat – usually chips – which Jodie didn't mind and the kitchen staff in those days used to be kind. However the pub was still something she associated with her mother and by association brought about all those bad and sad feelings from long ago. For that reason she felt apprehensive about attending the function even though she thought she owed it to Will to attend his celebration.

Jodie tried to explain how she felt to Bonnie who told her not to be a goose. 'It's going to be fun and in any event nothing happened in the pub did it? Anyway, Nanna and Pop are looking forward to going. I don't think they get out much and you wouldn't want to spoil it for them, would you? And I'll be there too – at some stage. You'll be fine. You're a big girl now!' she said giving Jodie one of her impromptu hugs.

Friday night found Jodie walking up the road to the main street accompanied by Nanna and Pop.

'No need to drive. It's all so close,' said Pop. 'That way I don't have to watch my drinks. I wonder if Will and his father are paying? Then I certainly won't be watching my drinks!'

'Joe Daley,' warned Nanna. 'No such talk. What will your granddaughter think of you when you speak of getting drunk.'

'She won't be surprised. Will you, my pet?' he smiled as he put his arm around Jodie who was trying not to laugh. She knew that her grandfather very rarely drank. Something about it not agreeing with him after all the excesses of his youth. But if he liked to pretend to still be a wild young thing, well, who was she to disappoint him.

'You party on as much as you like, Pop. I'll look after you.'

'Hear that Carol? At least someone loves me.'

They arrived a bit after six and it was clear the party was already in full swing. Groups of people spilled out through the front door. Some smoking by the pot plants which no doubt filled a dual function as planters and ashtrays. Others huddled in small groups sharing gossip or confidences and others just drank. A number of them waved greetings at Carol and Joe. As long-term residents of the village they were known to many. Jodie hid behind them. She hoped no one remembered her. It was even more crowded and certainly noisier inside. Jodie glanced around apprehensively. There was no one there she knew. She found herself clutching Nanna's arm who glanced anxiously at her.

'Come on, dear. We'll go over to that side table out of the squash and Joe maybe you can go to the bar and get us some drinks. I think I'll have a glass of white wine and Jodie what would you like? A Coke?'

Jodie nodded. All the while searching the crowd. Where was Will? She could see his parents holding forth over by the bar and a few of the people she recognized from the vine planting day but that was it. And when she thought about it, why should she expect to know anyone? She hadn't lived in the village for years and even when she did she didn't know many people. Only Will.

And there he was – waving at her from across the room and somehow squeezing through the mass of people to get to her. She breathed a sigh of relief.

'You're here then. Thank goodness, I was beginning to worry. I thought you might change your mind as I know this isn't your favourite place, but I hoped you would turn up.'

'You're right. I almost didn't come but Nanna and Pop convinced me. Gave me strength, so to speak. They're here but I don't know where. Nanna was right behind me. Now she's gone.' Jodie looked around and then spied her grandmother happily seated at a small table, holding forth with some of her friends.

'I see her now. She's fine,' said Jodie.

'So how are you? Did you get everything tidied up back at the farm?' Jodie was very proud of herself making polite conversation when all she wanted to do was gaze at Will. He'd clearly made an effort that evening. He was so clean – and not scruffy at all – unlike the everyday Will. Hair slicked back and freshly shaved. Wearing new blue jeans, a black t shirt and a soft black leather coat. He looked amazing.

'You look amazing' Jodie blurted out, saying exactly what she had been thinking.

'Well, you look pretty amazing yourself,' he said.

Jodie looked down at herself. In her black jeans with her black lurex top she realised they matched.

'Look at us. A vision in black! A perfect match,' she laughed.

Will laughed and then looking serious he gazed into her eyes. 'You might be right. You've always said we're best friends but,' and there he paused as he drew her to him and whispered in her ear. 'Do you think we could be something more?'

Jodie felt the noise slip away and all that she could hear was the sound of her pulse thudding in her throat as she leaned in. Then glancing away as the emotions threatened to overwhelm her she noticed, across the room and staring intently at them was Will's mother. There was no doubt in Jodie's mind that Will's mother had just witnessed this interaction and was not impressed.

'Well Jodie?' whispered Will. And before she could respond the proceedings were interrupted by a piercing wolf whistle and the time-honoured way of calling people to pay attention – the tapping of a wine glass - could be heard. Will and Jodie turned towards the bar, still together but now holding hands.

'Listen up everyone!' called out Will's father. 'I know Will told me no speeches but hey we can't have a celebration without a speech and it will be a small one.' In the manner of a connoisseur, he sniffed and took a sip of what looked like a large glass of red wine, which he then held it up for inspection. 'It's not a bad drop but I'm hoping in years to come we will all be drinking and enjoying wine from my vineyard. I know we have only just completed the first planting and it will be some time until we are fully up and running, but I have big plans. A vineyard has always been a dream of mine. A vineyard that we will call *Bronte Park* just like the name of the farm and it will put this area on the map as the best wine producing area in Tasmania, if not the country. All big dreams start small. So please join me in toasting the success of this venture. To *Bronte Park Wines,* and to all of you who have helped me along the way. Cheers!'

The room erupted in cheers and laughter and many glasses were held aloft then pulled down and quaffed. A crowd of people huddled around the bar seeking refills. Jodie had yet to get a drink. She could only assume that Pop had forgotten. Just as she was deciding whether to brave the bar herself or send Will across Bonnie bounded into sight carrying two half full glasses.

'Here Jodie. One for you. Soft drink like you usually have. Is that alright?' She glanced down at Jodie and Will's intertwined hands and raised her eyebrows curiously and whispered: 'what have we here?'

Jodie shook her head then released her hand. At which point Will, who had been speaking to someone else, turned around.

'Will. Remember Bonnie? I know it's been a while. Quite a few years actually.'

'Bonnie! Of course I remember you. Even then you were awfully glamorous but now I hear you're a cadet reporter. How exciting. You'll be the queen of scoops.'

'I hope so. And congratulations on the start of the vineyard. I hope it works out.'

'So do I. But so much depends on the weather gods. But enough about me. Jodie tells me you are sisters. That has to have been the happiest news I've heard in ages. I just hope you will treat me with more respect than this one does! Oh no – here he comes,' muttered Will as he spied his father striding across.

'Good evening, young ladies. So kind of you to entertain my son. Have we been introduced?'

Will rolled his eyes but remembering his manners he spoke. 'Dad you've met Jodie before.'

'Of course. I remember Josie. Lovely. And this is?' he turned to Bonnie.

'This is Jodie's sister Bonnie who has recently moved here from Devonport.'

Taking her hand and pressing it tightly Will's father continued 'Such a pleasure to meet a beautiful friend of my son's. I'm Angus McBride and I'm sure I will enjoy catching up with you again. But if you will please excuse me I must drag my son away to meet some important business associates of mine. Come on, son. I will return him to you shortly,' and Angus, grabbing Will firmly by the elbow steered him away. Will allowed himself to be led away but not before he turned and mouthed 'sorry' at the girls.

'Poor Will,' said Bonnie. 'Imagine having such a sleazebag for a father. I thought my dad was bad enough, but he is so much worse. And what's with him calling you Josie?'

'No idea. He's done it before. It's possible that he could be deaf, but I think he might just be plain rude. And his wife is even worse. That's her over there simpering at those so-called important business associates.'

Bonnie looked across consideringly. 'Nice outfit, though. And get a load of those pearls. Must have cost a motza.' Then that thought was forgotten as Bonnie remembered her latest news that she was desperate to share with Jodie.

'You will never guess who I saw today?'

'Who?' Jodie searched her brain. 'Charlie, Joan or your dad?'

'No! It was Rory. And he was in court.'

'What?'

'You know how I've been trailing the others to learn the business. Well, today we were attending court so I could see how things went and what would be good matters to report. It can be pretty boring but I was paying attention, as next week I will be there on my own. So I was studying the court list when I saw his name – Rory Fraser – and I asked if I could stay on to hear what the problem was. Well,' she exhaled deeply. 'You'll never guess what! He was being prosecuted for Abalone poaching and apparently it wasn't the first time. The prosecutor was seeking the maximum sentence and he may still end up with that. The Magistrate will hand down her decision next week. What a bad egg. But you know he still looks gorgeous. He recognised me and winked. Down but not out apparently. I think I might like court work. The Associate also winked at me. And he looked just as nice and hopefully doesn't have a criminal record.'

Bonnie looked around the room. 'Anyone else to check out here? And what's with you and Will? Looking pretty cosy I see,' she smiled suggestively.

'It's nothing. We were just having a chat that's all. But you know what. I'm beat so I think I might walk home. You check out the talent and when you run into Nanna and Pop just let them know I've headed home for bed.'

As Jodie slipped through the crowd in the direction of the Exit she looked around for Will. He was no-where to be seen. All she could see was his father holding forth by the bar and his mother glaring at her from where she stood with a group of friends. What a strange person she was.

It was dark and cool outside. Jodie breathed in deeply. The clean air was a welcome change from the smoky fug inside. She walked slowly along the path glad to be heading home. It had been worth going she supposed if only to learn that Will was as keen on her as she now realised she was on him. Maybe there was a future for them and certainly now she had returned to the pub for the first time since her mother's death she could only assume that subsequent visits would get easier.

The evening was still. Jodie was so lost in her thoughts that at first she didn't notice the sound of a vehicle. And why should she. She was walking along the side of a road after all. It was some instinct, a sense of danger that somehow alerted her just before the sound of the car's engine changed as it suddenly accelerated. She turned and was blinded by the bright lights of a vehicle heading at speed directly towards her. Later on she couldn't explain the instinct that in the split second before impact made her veer to the right and with a sudden burst of speed leaped over the four-foot-high brick wall that marked the start of the front yard of a local shop. She jumped, landed and then jumped again. This time onto the top of the wall to the side of the shop. And then she scrambled over the wall and landed hard on the ground on the other side. These two walls were what saved Jodie's life. The existence of the first wall destabilized the progress of the car so it tilted to one side. Yet it was still moving with such momentum that it carried forward on its side and then slammed into the higher wall. This was a solid convict built stone wall, built to last and a speeding Mercedes was no match for it.

The crashing sound reverberated through the village and brought people running from nearby and out of the pub. They were greeted with the sight of a silver Mercedes lying on its side with engine revving and wheels still spinning. The people sprinted to the car. Will and his father in the lead. They had recognised the car.

Angus reached the car first and yanked the door open. His wife spilled out. Her head covered in blood. Of course she hadn't been wearing a seat belt.

'Rona, Rona can you hear me? What happened? What were you doing?'

Rona moaned as Angus turned and yelled at the crowd: 'Someone please call an ambulance.'

'Onto it, mate,' someone in the crowd replied.

'I don't think you should move her dad,' said Will. 'Let's wait until the ambulance arrives. Who knows what she might have broken. She certainly hit both walls at force. I wonder why the car crashed this way and why was mum out here?'

'Beats me,' said Angus. 'Maybe she forgot something at home and was headed back.'

'But dad, this is the wrong way home.' Will looked around, listened as he heard a faint sound and yelled out to the gathering crowd: 'Does anyone have a torch?'

'Yeah, mate. Here you go', and a torch was passed over. Will switched it on and swung the torch around. The car headlights had been illuminating part of the wall but not all of it. Will swung the torch to and fro all the time listening for what appeared to be a faint sound – a moaning that seemed to come from behind the wall. The wall was about six foot tall so he figured he should be able to leap over - maybe. Then again – maybe not, for with a swing of the torch he realised that the wall ended at the boundary of the block of land and abutted the driveway that ran down the adjoining land. All he needed was to step onto the driveway and look behind the wall. Which he did and as he shone the torch onto the other side, there he saw the source of the moaning. Jodie. He rushed to her side.

'Jodie? Are you alright? What happened?'

By the light of the torch he could see she was sprawled on her side – sprawled possibly in the same position as she landed. Sprawled and moaning. He rushed over and scooped her up, then carried Jodie back down the driveway where he gently deposited her on the footpath near the car. He needed to get her inside in the warmth as he could see when he shone the torch briefly on her face that her pupils were dilated. Concussion he assumed. But first he needed to get a rug before he would carry her anywhere.

'Can someone get me a rug? Quick!'

Will turned to look at his mother. His mind was racing. Surely the two injuries were not connected? His mother stirred. Her eyes opened and she looked across at Will and smiled. Then she looked past him, saw Jodie and screamed.

'No! No! You're supposed to be dead. I hit you with the car. How can you be alive? I was going so fast and you were right in front of me. I hit you. I know I did.'

'Rona. Calm yourself. The ambulance will be here any minute.'

Rona struggled as she tried to pull herself out of the car and crawl towards Jodie all the time screaming her anger: 'You have to die. You have to die. Just like your mother did. She died so quickly. Why won't you? You devil spawn.'

Will moved quickly to block his mother as he yelled: 'Dad come here and stop her. She's gone crazy.'

He looked at his father who stood frozen staring at his wife in horror. And then he stepped away like he couldn't bear to be near her.

The sound of an ambulance approaching shattered the silence. Still Rona struggled forward, her need to get to Jodie overriding the pain from her injuries.

'I will get you and I will kill you just like I did your mother. You two are evil, do you hear me? I won't let you have my son just like I stopped your mother in the past. I bashed her head, until the bitch was dead and I loved every moment of it.'

The paramedics arrived and assessed the situation in a heartbeat.

'Well, the good thing is that she's conscious and rambling and certainly capable of moving so she should be ok to be put on a stretcher. But she seems rather agitated. Perhaps sedate her? Is anyone coming with her?'

Will looked across at his father who was shaking his head and staring down at the ground as if he couldn't believe what he had just heard.

'Dad. Are you going in the ambulance?'

'No. Son. After what I just heard I don't think I can bear to be near her. I think maybe I will need to give a statement to the police though.'

'The police?' queried a paramedic.

'You see,' said Will, pointing at Jodie still lying on the ground. 'My mother just tried to run down this young woman.'

'So we will need another ambulance then?'

Will thought quickly. The situation with his mother had to be sorted out first and the Police had to be involved. Maybe they would guard his mother. For in her present state, she was a danger to them all. He struggled to decide what to do and glancing over at his stunned father he knew he would be no help.

'Look, can I suggest you take mum away? Dad why don't you follow using my car and I'll take Jodie into the Pub and we keep and eye on her to see how she feels.'

'Good idea but bad idea. I've been drinking. I can't drive.'

'Then you'll have to go in the ambulance. She shouldn't be a danger to anyone in her current state. Look the sedative is working. You'll be needed in there to do the paperwork and to talk to the cops. Stay in town at a hotel or your club and we'll sort out getting you home somehow tomorrow. Just go!'

By now someone appeared with a blanket which Will carefully wrapped around Jodie and carried her back to the Pub. He noticed how she winced with every step he took and how she closed her eyes tight when they reached the bright lights at the entry. This was so not a good idea. He needed to get her home and into a dark room. No, better still, perhaps take her out the back into one of the hotel rooms. Bonnie materialised by his side.

'Bonnie. Quick! Please ask at the bar if there is a spare room out the back in the hotel tonight.'

It didn't take long and soon Will was able to settle Jodie onto a Queen size bed in a warm room out the back. He kept the lights off. The only illumination coming from the bathroom. Will still wasn't sure if he should call an ambulance. Now that Jodie was lying down and warm he needed to find out how she was feeling.

'Jodie can you tell me where it hurts?'

'All over, I think. What happened?'

'We're not sure but we think my mum tried to run you over.'

'Yes, that would make sense. I think I was walking home. I was tired and I decided to leave early and go to bed. So I was walking along and next thing I know a car came up behind, revving loudly. I turned and there were bright lights right behind me. I ran but I knew I had to somehow get out of the way so I veered – yes that's what I did. I jumped over a wall. Then I jumped over another wall and the car crashed into the wall. Didn't it? But why? Was there a problem with the steering?'

'You could say that,' said Will grimly. 'Do you think you could rest now and we will see how you feel in the morning?'

'Yes. I just want to sleep. But promise me you will stay – all night?'

'I won't leave you. It's a promise.'

Chapter Twenty-Six

A nd it was a promise he kept. After reassuring Jodie's grandparents and Bonnie that he would keep an eye on her and sending them home, Will stayed in that hotel room all night. Initially he sat in the club chair in the corner as he mulled over the significance of his mother's diatribe. If what she had said was the truth, and he had no reason to think she might have made it up, it appeared his mother had murdered Jodie's mother. And Pepper too he assumed.

But why? There had to be a reason. His thoughts churned as he tried to understand what had just happened. So much so that he felt physically sick and found himself rushing to the bathroom.

He always knew his mother could be irrational and as he returned to sit beside Jodie, Will struggled to calm himself and try to make sense of what had occurred. Maybe the reason for his mother's actions had something to do with his father. Will had known for a long time that his parents were not happily married and from time to time his dad had been seeing others. His mother seemed to turn a blind eye to such behaviour but maybe that time it had been different. Will really needed to speak to his father to find out more.

It was obvious however, that last night Rona had intended to kill Jodie and almost got away with it. Thank goodness Jodie was still quick on her feet. He just hoped she hadn't done herself any serious injury by jumping that wall. And what an impressive jump that had been. He supposed running in fear of her life had given Jodie wings. Wait until he showed her she could have just ducked around the side of the wall instead of jumping. But then again it was dark and maybe Jodie might not appreciate being told there was another way to avoid being hit. On reflection it was most probably definitely something he could keep to himself.

Jodie seemed to be sleeping deeply so at some stage in the wee small hours he snuck into bed and lay as far away from Jodie as possible. He didn't think he would fall asleep because of the trauma of the night's events. Yet somehow he did and was still asleep when Jodie stirred and saw him asleep next to her.

To her the events of the previous night were a blur – a terrible nightmare that seemed too awful to be real.

Yet here she was waking up in a strange room, fully clothed with Will sound asleep next to her. She had a slight headache and there was an area on her leg that felt sore but other than that she felt pretty good. Just hungry.

'Will. Wake up,' said Jodie as she prodded him in the ribs.

'Huh?' It took Will a moment to realise where he was and then with a start he sat bolt upright.

'You're awake. Are you alright? How's your head? How's your leg?'

'OK I think, but I won't know until I stand up. Which I should do now as I really need to go to the loo. And I really need something to eat. Where are we? Can we get food?'

'I have no idea if they do food. We're at the pub. But if you can manage to walk how about I take you home and you can have breakfast there?'

Jodie eased herself out of the bed, wincing as she did so then gingerly walked towards the bathroom. Will heard the toilet flush and then a cry. With a rush he was out the bed and at the door.

'Jodie. What's wrong? Is something the matter? Do I need to get a doctor?'

'No. Nothing like that. My new top is ruined.'

Jodie opened the door and pointed to the rip that ran along the side of her top. It had been shredded when she landed on the ground.

'Not only that, but' Jodie pulled down her also ripped jeans to reveal a mammoth bruise that was developing down one side of her leg.'

'Oh no. Your looks are spoiled,' cried Will giving her a wicked grin and pulling Jodie into a hug, all the while being thankful that it looked like she had avoided serious injury.

'Ouch. Careful,' winced Jodie. Then she smiled: 'looks like we may have to postpone that running race for a while.'

He shook his head: 'You'll do anything to get out of a race that you know I'm going to win, won't you? Even go to extremes like ruining your best clothes. But it won't work. I will still win.' With a smile he added 'Have you thought about high jump? I can see you have form?'

Before they left the room Will first had to ring a very anxious Nanna to update her on Jodie's condition and to put in a breakfast order. He told her not to rush as it would take some time to get her to the car. Which it did. Slow but steady progress which also reassured Will that while Jodie had suffered some injury none of it was serious. As to her headache she assured him it would be much better after a cup – or two - of tea. Trying not to look too obvious he managed to look deeply into Jodie's eyes and was satisfied that her pupils were back to normal.

They had started to head home via the main road but were soon stopped by a policeman.

'You have to go some other way I'm afraid, sir.'

'No problem, officer' said Will as he put the car into reverse.

Jodie stared at the wrecked silver car still lying on its side and half blocking the road. Blue and white police tape marked the area as a crime scene – which she supposed it was. The nose of the car jammed into the tumbled down walls. So it had really happened and wasn't just a nightmare. But whose car was it? What had happened? Jodie considered the rear stone wall. Will had told her he found her collapsed on the other side of that wall. In her muddled state none of it made sense. How on earth had she managed to scale that wall? She could only suppose fear had given her wings.

She closed her eyes. She so didn't want to see that mess again. She was starting to remember what had happened and how she had jumped for her life. But she still couldn't understand why. It was so difficult to process her thoughts when her head ached so. A glance at Will's solemn features and furrowed brow confirmed that any explanations could keep. Anyway, her rumbling stomach reminded her that there were other more pressing priorities.

They took the long way home via the back roads past scattered houses. Even using the back roads it didn't take long. It was such a small village after all.

It was a slow process helping Jodie out of the car and into the house. Her grandparents and Bonnie had rushed out to greet her as soon as they heard the sound of the car pulling into the driveway. With care they each directed the limping girl inside. It made a funny sight thought Will, like a huddle of caterpillars moving as one. The sort of sight they regularly saw around the village gardens in spring.

Once settled at the table, contemplating the food before her and sipping at her steaming mug of tea, Jodie looked around at her family. Will had already slipped away saying he had to go feed Missy and let her out for a run but assuring Jodie he would be back as soon as possible.

Jodie felt dazed. Everything in the kitchen looked just like it always did yet something had changed. She supposed the change was in her and something she needed to process. But somehow she was not sure she had the energy to do so. Jodie knew she needed to eat something. Just a short while back all she had wanted was something to eat. Yet when she considered the plate of corn fritters and bacon – usually her favourite – she felt nauseous. Nanna immediately noticed.

'If you can't manage it dear just leave it for now. I'm sure Joe and Bonnie will be happy to finish them off.'

'Too right, we will,' grinned Bonnie. 'Or we can share if you only want a taste. No rush, I'll try not to watch every mouthful you take. Promise.'

Jodie continued to sip her tea. That definitely tasted good. The dull ache in her head remained. Maybe she needed a second cuppa to make a difference. She knew she needed to eat as it had been a long time since a meal. She should be hungry, but the sight of the glistening corn fritters just made her want to spew. She pushed her chair away from the table and slowly stood up.

'I'm sorry Nanna. They really look delicious, but I just can't eat at the moment. I'm so hungry but I can't bring myself to do it.'

Joe, with the wisdom born of much experience spoke 'It's alright, lass. Take your time. You've had a bump on your head and a shock. You need to rest and let nature do its bit. We'll keep an eye on you. But trust me if you can't keep that mug of tea down then it's straight to the hospital for you. Agree?'

Jodie nodded and allowed herself to be escorted to her bedroom. And tucked into bed. The mug of tea, or what remained of it, and a glass of water were left on the bedside table. The room was warm, silent and dark with its curtains shut tight. Before she knew it Jodie was sound asleep. Jodie slept for hours and was pleased to discover when she stirred that she felt so much better. Still sore, of course – but less woolly in her head. She pushed herself up to a sitting position and reached for the water.

A head poked through the door. It was Will.

'Good. You're awake. You've slept most of the day away. One of us has been checking you from time to time but you've really been out to it. How are you feeling?'

'Much better, I think. But I guess I won't be certain until I'm standing up.'

'Here. Let me help.'

Will rushed across to her side and gently helped her out of the bed. Jodie glanced down at her attire and pulled a face.

'Couldn't someone have helped me undress last night? Am I fated to never lose these clothes. I'm so sick of them and never want to see them again!'

'Good idea. The best place for them is the bin. You know what? How about you have a shower and put on some clean clothes. Bonnie can help you if you need a hand.'

He wasn't sure she would agree to this suggestion, but Will thought someone needed to be there in case she fell over in the shower. To his surprise Jodie agreed.

'Yeah. Good idea. I'm sure I'll feel better after a wash. Let's do it.'

Sometime later a refreshed Jodie appeared in the kitchen escorted by a solicitous Bonnie. Her hair freshly washed and combed back it hung neatly around her shoulders and down her back. With her face scrubbed clean and wearing a plain undecorated navy sweatshirt she reminded Will of the young Jodie from his schooldays. A more subdued woman to be sure but her vulnerability was visible for all to see.

Nanna was in full fussing mode. 'Have a seat, Jodie. And here, take this. I've poured you a cuppa in your favourite mug.'

Jodie sipped from the mug and eyed the scones on the plate in the centre of the table. Freshly baked with a crunchy crust they were exactly how she liked it. She knew if she broke one open it would reveal delicious steaming goodness. The thought made her mouth water. Without conscious thought she reached for a scone. The reassuring crusty warmth was exactly as she expected.

Nanna watched with satisfaction the sight of her granddaughter breaking the scone open and smothering its doughy surface with butter which immediately melted. Jodie took one bite, tentatively chewed, then as the creamy, salty cheesy flavours hit she took another bite and then another. The scone was devoured in seconds and Jodie reached for another.

'Hold up, Jodie dear. I do have some soup to go with it and you may want to sample some of it with the scones? Chicken broth with a few noodles and vegetables in it. I'll dish some up now. Any other takers?' She looked around at the other salivating people clustered around the table.

'Don't mind if I do, Carol,' said Will.

'Yes, please, Nanna,' said Bonnie.

'Can't let it go to waste. Count me in,' said Pop.

'And maybe I should have some, too,' said Nanna. 'Just to be sure I've got the seasoning right. Here you go, Bonnie,' said as she passed a bowl of steaming, beautifully scented broth to her granddaughter.

Dinner was enjoyed silently as all concentrated on the meal before them. Jodie without any other conscious thought simply enjoyed the here and now of eating delicious food. Yet Will and Pop were thinking of the conversation that must follow. A conversation best to be had in relaxed comfort before the open fire in the lounge room.

Pop pushed his chair back as a signal mealtime was over. Jodie, who had been busy scraping the last of the soup from her bowl, looked up.

'Knowing you Carol and in fact knowing you from decades of experience I'm sure you are now about to offer us some cake. But before we eat cake and maybe have another pot of tea I suggest we adjourn to the lounge room. It would be a shame to let that fire go to waste. Come on Jodie, I'll help you up.'

Nanna nodded: 'Good idea Joe. Of course I've made cake. Ginger cake with lemon icing. Bonnie can give me a hand. And you, too, if you want Will. We'll be in shortly with all the goodies.'

The loungeroom was cozy warm. The fire was leaping and crackling just the way all good fires should be. At Jodie's request Pop settled her into a club chair. She thought that might be easier to negotiate when it was time to stand up.

They were soon settled and focussed on the gooey ginger cake which was enhanced with chunks of glace ginger. The tangy lemon icing serving as the perfect contrast for the spicy flavour of the cake.

Pop stood and topped up everyone's tea and then cleared his throat. He had something to share and all in the room now focused on him and not on the cake.

'Now I have a few things to discuss before Angus, Will's father arrives. He has a bit to share with us and to be honest he owes you three an explanation,' said glancing at Will, Bonnie and Jodie one by one. 'He should be here shortly.'

Joe continued: 'And now for an update. I understand your mother Will is still in hospital and is under police guard. It looks like she might have a fractured arm and shoulder and possibly has some brain damage. They won't know how bad it is until the swelling on her brain goes down. But for now, she's been put into an induced coma. As she's currently in that state I'm not sure that a police guard is absolutely necessary. But rules are rules, I guess.'

'And dad?' asked Will.

'He's holding up,' said Pop. 'He's already talked to the police who will be wanting a statement from all of us. Angus told them Jodie was still recovering and put them off until tomorrow. But we're to expect them to be here first thing in the morning.'

Jodie could feel her exhaustion wafting over her.

'Do I need to be here, Pop? I could do with a lie down.'

'Sorry Jodie. I think you do need to be here. Trust me. This is important. It won't take long.'

Will contemplated Jodie's grandfather. Clearly he knew what was to be revealed. He must have had a long discussion with Angus that morning. But he was not one for sharing other people's tales. Will liked that about Joe. He was a good man. As to hearing any further news about his mother as far as he was concerned her actions were unforgiveable and he had no intention of ever seeing her again.

'Ah. There's a car now.'

They all listened to the sound of a car approaching. The engine stopped, a car door slammed and then the sounds of footsteps were heard approaching up the drive.

'I'll let him in.' Joe pushed himself out of the chair and heading for the back door.

Those remaining in the lounge room heard the sound of a door opening, the stomping of boots scraping on the back door mat accompanied by inarticulate conversation.

The Angus that appeared in the doorway was a different man to the one that had been on display the night before. Then he had been happy, energetic and full of his own importance – and need we say it? Rather drunk.

Now he was a lesser man. Shrunk in on himself and grey with worry and lack of sleep.

'Hello all,' he said as he waved at the people around the room. 'Good evening Carol. I'm so sorry to barge in on you all like this.

'No problem at all Angus. Especially in times like this. Cuppa?' she said gesturing at the teapot.

'Any chance of something stronger? No offence Carol, but it's been one of those days. Although I wouldn't say no to some of that cake.'

While Pop bustled around locating and then pouring some whisky – one for Angus and one for him, Angus greeted the others in the room one by one.

'Hello son. I thought you might be here. And Bonnie, isn't it? It was a pleasure to meet you last night. I haven't seen you for a long time. And Jodie I'm truly glad you are up and about. And yes, I do know your real name. I'm afraid I was just playing games to annoy my son. My apologies.'

Pop returned with the glasses of whisky. Angus took a sip then sighed with delight.

'Joe you old rascal. Why have you been hiding this away?'

'I figured tonight you need the best to give you courage.'

'Too right there, mate' smiled Angus as he took another sip and, drawing breath prepared to speak.

'Please bear with me. This is going to take a while.'

Chapter Twenty-Seven

'I don't need to state the obvious,' said Angus. 'It's clear that last night my wife, Rona, intended to kill Jodie by running her down. And Jodie,' Angus turned and gazed directly at her, 'I am so sorry for the distress she caused you.'

'It's not your fault Angus,' said Jodie.

'You're very kind, my dear. But I blame myself. I should have realised last night she was on edge and when she rushed outside, I should have gone to check on her. To be honest we had been fighting and I could see she had been drinking way too much so I assumed she was running outside to throw up. Then I heard the screams from the onlookers outside and I just knew something awful had happened. It's a miracle you survived. That car was way too powerful. At the time she insisted on buying it I told her it was too much, but Rona being Rona had to have it. When she's like that she's unstoppable.'

'But Angus,' Carol interrupted. 'What I don't understand is why she would want to hurt our little girl? Jodie has done nothing to her and in fact as far as I'm aware she didn't even know her.'

'That's where you're wrong Carol. Jodie's biggest offence was to exist. This all goes way back to long before I met Rona. So let's start at the beginning, shall we?'

Angus settled back into his chair as if he was about to tell them a story. A story so bizarre that it was hard to believe it was true.

A long time ago when he was in his mid-teens Angus attended the same village school that Will and Jodie attended many years later. He was in the same year as Donna. One thing led to another. They became close – very close. And before she knew what was happening 15-year-old Donna was pregnant. Not being terribly sophisticated it took her a while to realise what was happening to her body.

'We were so young and so naïve. I think her periods were irregular at the best of times, so it took her months to realise something was happening. I wanted to marry her, of course. Yes, we were underage and what we had been up to was a criminal offence but we weren't the only ones doing it. I urged her to tell you two, Carol and Joe, but she refused. Obviously, you eventually worked it out. She refused to marry me. Said she wouldn't ruin my future. She knew as well as I that my parents would disown me and turf me out. She told me whatever she chose to do it was her decision and she already thought she had a solution. You know what Donna was like. When she made up her mind that was it. There would be no other way but Donna's way.'

He looked across at Bonnie. 'I wasn't there for your birth Bonnie. I'm so sorry but that was how it was in those days. Things are changing now thank goodness. But a kind nurse smuggled me in the next day and I was able to hold you briefly. Even as a newborn you were a beauty – just like you are now. I had to hide in the adjoining room when you two arrived, Carol and Joe. That was a bit traumatic. Donna had already told me you had no idea who the father was.'

'That's right,' said Carol. 'We had no idea.'

'So, without telling me, Donna adopted you out to her cousin and his wife and I never saw you again until last night. I knew immediately who you were. My beautiful daughter, but it was clear you had no idea. I could see that I horrified you – another old drunk man way too full of himself. I slunk away, not sure if I ever would have the courage to speak to you again.'

Bonnie, ever the softy, spoke in a kind tone: 'Horrified? No. Slightly bemused? Yes. But now I'm starting to understand. Please go on.'

'The next few years were pretty awful. I finished my schooling at a private school in Hobart, then went to university. I started working for my father then I met Rona. She was so vivacious and glamorous – a bit like Donna now I think about it. We married, we had you, Will, and we muddled along – some good times and some awful times. And it was about – let me see,' he looked at the ceiling while he did the mental maths. 'Um … about 15 years ago that we then came across each other. Donna had moved back to the village after her marriage had ended. She had moved in with you two and when I ran into her she was complaining about how unhappy she was living back home. I had recently inherited a cottage from my granny, and I said she could live in it once I fixed it up and I also offered her a job at the pub. I still felt responsible for her you see. She inspected the cottage and said it would do but would only let me do the bare minimum. I guess she didn't want to accept charity from me. And that's how she came back into my life.' Angus paused and took another sip. His glass almost empty he made the universal gesture waving the glass at Joe indicating the need for a top up.

'And was that it?' asked Will.

'Not quite,' said Angus. 'The years passed and we all muddled along somehow. Donna never settled to village life as I think you all knew. Sometimes after her evening shift had ended we would sit at the bar and chat about this and that. I had always felt responsible for her and liked to check in with her to see how she was managing. That spark between us had never gone away and just like when we were teenagers one thing led to another. I was seriously thinking about asking Rona for a divorce. We had been miserable for years.'

'I'd noticed,' said Will.

'I'm really sorry, son. I can never make it up to you, but I will try.'

'And?' asked Bonnie, now on the edge of her seat.

'Donna and I started to make our plans. I was going to sell everything. I knew that for Rona to agree to a divorce I'd have to pay her a large whack of my fortune. But it would be worth it. Donna and I talked about moving up Devonport way. Now I realise she must have intended to renew her acquaintance with you Bonnie and hopefully bring us all together. So we made our plans. But somehow Rona must have found out I was seeing Donna. One night when I was in Hobart, Rona must have gone around to your home Jodie and confronted Donna. We all now know what happened next. At the time I thought Donna had been killed by one of the many low life's that she knew. I never knew I was living with her murderer. I was heartbroken and I suppose that in my sorrow I didn't realise Rona's behaviour had modified. She knew I had planned to divorce her. I suppose Donna had revealed that in their confrontation and I suppose in the months that followed Rona was doing her hardest to make me change my mind.'

Angus sighed and with both hands reached under his glasses and rubbed his eyes.

'What a disaster. I feel like it's all my fault. If I had been more assertive, I should have insisted on us marrying before you were born Bonnie. I'm sorry. So sorry everyone but that's all I seem to be able to say. Sorry. I know it doesn't change things, but I hope it helps somehow.'

'Dad you were only 15,' said Will. 'Your thinking then was as a 15-year-old. Donna found a solution, and it seems perfectly reasonable to me that you went with that. And anyway, if you had married Donna then I would not be here with you all. I wouldn't exist.'

'Nor would I,' piped up Jodie.

'And I,' added Bonnie, speaking slowly as she processed her scattered thoughts 'would not have a sister – or a brother,' she ended breaking into a smile.

'Your half-sister and your half-brother,' corrected Will with an apprehensive eye on Jodie. He so didn't want to be Jodie's brother.

'Yes that's correct,' said Angus. 'Seeing you two together last night and seeing you both looking so happy it made me think that life was working out for the best. And that maybe Donna was watching down manipulating our lives towards a happy outcome. But once again Rona had to intervene.'

'You know. I think Donna had the last laugh,' said Jodie. 'Last night I think she must have given me the wings to fly over that wall. Looking at it this morning I cannot believe that I cleared it. Thanks, mum.'

'You might be right, Jodie,' said Angus. 'She wasn't going to let Rona win this time.'

Chapter Twenty-Eight

The visit by the police took up most of the next day. Each were summonsed into the lounge room in turn and were interviewed and their words recorded. Because of Jodie's recent injuries and her grandparents' age they were excused from attending the local police station for their interviews. Bonnie insisted she couldn't leave as she was carer for Jodie. Not that Jodie needed caring any more. The headache had gone and only time would heal the technicolour bruise that had transformed her leg.

The police were methodical in their approach and took each person slowly through the events of the night. There was no need to give any explanation for Rona's behaviour as her damning words had been heard by all the onlookers and reported to the police.

Jodie, who had been dreading the interview, found the unemotional approach by the police – a man and a woman – strangely calming. Once it was over Will collected her and took her immediately up to the farm to be with Missy and the puppies. Puppy therapy he called it. The puppies were now old enough to be cuddled. Jodie took turns to hold the squirming bundles while Missy enjoyed some time outdoors with Will.

When Will returned, she complained: 'They're all lovely, of course. But I'm confused. Which of the girls is mine?'

'Well. I had in mind that one,' he pointed at one bundle who to Jodie's eyes looked the same as the others. 'But how about we put them down on the rug and we can watch them explore. They're still a bit wobbly, but they can move about a bit. We should be starting to see a bit of personality emerge and maybe there will be one that appeals.'

'The four puppies were plonked near each other on the rug and Will and Jodie crouched down nearby to watch. One immediately started to crawl towards Jodie. With wobbly pins he clambered onto her lap. Jodie immediately picked up the puppy and held it to her face.

'This one Will. Definitely this one!' she exclaimed.

'Hmm. Slight problem. That one is a boy! Maybe we should try this again when they're a bit older and steadier on their legs. Tell you what. I have some collars of different colours that we can put on them and that way you can start to tell them apart. Deal?'

Jodie nodded in agreement.

After Missy was fed and enticed back into the pen with the puppies they left and headed back to Nanna and Pop's house. Jodie could sense that Missy would soon be over motherhood. She and the puppies had been moved to a pen – a bit like a baby's playpen but puppy proof and it was clear that Missy was just about ready to wean them and have some peace.

No sooner had they walked through the back door than Nanna appeared.

'Charlie rang just now. He heard what happened on the news and he wants to know if he should come down. I think you should ring him back, Jodie. He sounded awfully worried. I did my best to calm him down, but you'll probably do a better job.'

But which number to ring. Jodie had both Charlie and Joan's phone numbers in her directory. Perhaps Joan's phone number? Of course he was there. Charlie answered on the second ring.

'Charlie Wise speaking.'

'Dad. It's me. Jodie. Nanna said you rang while I was out.'

'Jodie,' Charlie's relief was obvious in the sound of his voice. 'I heard the news. Are you alright? What a terrible thing to happen. I cannot believe someone would do this to you – or attempt to,' he amended.

'I'll be fine dad. Or I will be fine once the bruising goes.'

'Bruising. Where?'

And then Jodie was forced to describe her injuries to someone she knew was entitled to be told. However, she preferred not to elaborate. And this she said when Charlie urged her to come and stay.

'Maybe at some stage, dad. Thanks. But for now I'd prefer to stay here and take it quietly. I will be up at some stage though. There is someone I want you to meet. Actually, two someones. Will and a puppy who should be old enough shortly to come live with me. A *Smithfield.*

'A *Smithfield* you say? Excellent. I used to have one of those as a lad. You must bring the pup up so we can get it started on the sheep. They make good sheep dogs, you know.'

'So everyone keeps telling me!'

The conversation moved onto general chit chat and was largely focussed on wedding plans. The wedding to be held in December in the week before Christmas when hopefully the weather would be mild.

'Joan is hoping you will be bridesmaid. You'll have to wear a dress you know. I can't say I've ever seen you in one of those. And have your hair done fancy like. Do you think you can make the sacrifice?'

'For Joan, anything. After all, look at the sacrifice she is making taking my aged father off my hands.'

***

With much laughter Jodie recounted the gist of her conversation with her father when they all sat down to dinner.

'So it looks like the wedding is on. Just before Christmas. They're holding it in the garden with a marquee set up on the tennis court. I expect Roman will be frantic getting it perfect – not that it isn't always. I said to dad I'd head up there to help Roman once the puppy is ready to travel. And maybe Will you'd like to come with me and meet dad and Joan? I'm still struggling to remember who knows who in this disjointed family.'

'You're on. I want to see this amazing farm that everyone keeps telling me about. And the grand house that is even better than my home. I bet it doesn't have converted stables as fancy as mine.'

'Well actually Will, they do,' smiled Jodie. 'Including some that are in desperate need of a makeover. It must be something to do with old places but rather than renovate old sheds they've built metal sheds and stables further away.'

'That's so obvious, Jodes,' said Bonnie as she wrinkled her nose. 'It's so the house is not contaminated with the stink of manure.'

Once the laughter had died down she continued: 'Do you think they might let me cover the wedding for the social pages? I'm sure it's going to the event of the year. I could write something tasteful and they would have control of what photos get used. What do you think?'

'You can only ask,' said Jodie. Personally after all the controversy that had surrounded this family she thought it would be the last thing Joan and Charlie would want. But she also had experience of Bonnie's winning ways of persuasion. It was a gift. She could wear anyone and anything down.

Jodie shrugged: 'I've no idea. You'll have to ask them.'

'Excellent. I will. So when are you heading up to Cressy? I think I'll join you. So much better to have such a conversation face to face.'

Uh oh, thought Jodie. Already she pitied Joan and Charlie. Bonnie's victory was assured!

Chapter Twenty-Nine

The invitation arrived the following week. The envelope large, parchment-like and cream coloured. It was clearly quality paper, the addresses written in fancy flowing script. Actually there were three such envelopes that arrived on the same day. One addressed to Mr and Mrs Joe Daley. Another addressed to Ms Bonnie Jamison and the third envelope addressed to Miss Jodie Wise. Jodie who had collected the mail from the letterbox out the front ran inside calling excitedly:

'Nanna. They're here.'

She ripped the envelope apart and read out loud:

'Dear Jodie

You and a friend are cordially invited to the wedding of Joan Fraser to Charlie Wise to be held on Saturday 17 December at 3pm at Gourock, Estate Lane via Cressy.'

'And it has some other stuff about casual attire and bring a coat. Of course! Wouldn't everyone know to do that. Even in December it would be freezing! And something about no presents, just a donation to some animal charity. I like that idea but of course I'm going to give them a present … and a donation too of course.'

'Nanna how exciting. My first wedding! Who would have thought getting a stepmother would be such happy news! And, even better I get to wear a dress!'

www.ingramcontent.com/pod-product-compliance
Lightning Source LLC
Chambersburg PA
CBHW031100020726
47495CB00007B/1977